"You're supposed to kiss her, Peter," his groomsman said in a loud whisper.

The rector looked as though he was trying not to laugh.

Very carefully Darleston lifted the veil back from Penelope's face. He put a gentle hand under her chin and bent to kiss her lightly on the mouth.

Penelope was unprepared for this. Although she had known it would happen, it was the one thing that she had not rehearsed, and the strange feeling of yearning that swept over her at the touch of his lips was a complete surprise. She wondered if he had wanted to kiss her.

She felt the earl draw her hand through his arm to lead her from the church and realized that the hardest part was still to come.

She still had to tell him that he had been duped.

* * *

The Unexpected Bride
Harlequin Historical #729—November 2004

**Harlequin Historicals is delighted
to present Mills & Boon author
ELIZABETH ROLLS**

The Unexpected Bride

Elizabeth Rolls

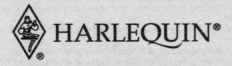

HARLEQUIN®

TORONTO • NEW YORK • LONDON
AMSTERDAM • PARIS • SYDNEY • HAMBURG
STOCKHOLM • ATHENS • TOKYO • MILAN • MADRID
PRAGUE • WARSAW • BUDAPEST • AUCKLAND

ISBN 0-373-29329-1

THE UNEXPECTED BRIDE

Copyright © 2000 by Elizabeth Rolls

First North American Publication 2004

www.eHarlequin.com

Printed in U.S.A.

Please address questions and book requests to:
Harlequin Reader Service
U.S.: 3010 Walden Ave., P.O. Box 1325, Buffalo, NY 14269
Canadian: P.O. Box 609, Fort Erie, Ont. L2A 5X3

Chapter One

An impartial observer might have been excused for stating that the crowd at Almack's Assembly Rooms on that fine spring night was entirely made up of members of the Ton who were intent upon enjoying themselves to the hilt. Young ladies dressed demurely in silken gowns of various pastel shades swirled past escorted by nattily attired beaux. Anxious mothers chatted together in groups, each certain that her daughter outshone every other girl in beauty and elegance. All in all it was a scene of great interest to the student of human nature.

One fair-haired young gentleman stood apart, however, looking the picture of gloom. Although dressed with great elegance and propriety he did not appear to be entirely at ease in his surroundings. He returned an occasional polite rejoinder to greetings from various acquaintances, all of whom registered surprise at finding him in such a place. Otherwise the Honourable George Carstares seemed to be very much in a brown study, with a frown of worry in his blue eyes.

He looked with ever-decreasing expectation and hope at the entrance doors of Almack's Assembly

Rooms. It wanted but ten minutes to eleven. If Peter doesn't arrive soon, he thought, they won't let him in at all. Lord! If those high-nosed ladies wouldn't relax their rules for England's hero, his Grace the Duke of Wellington, they'd certainly refuse admittance to Peter Augustus Frobisher, Seventh Earl of Darleston! Not for all his handsome looks and undeniable charm would they unbend!

It occurred to him on a wave of optimism that if Peter didn't arrive in time there was nothing to stop him leaving and seeking more convivial entertainment elsewhere. The Patronesses might insist arbitrarily that no one should enter after eleven, but there was nothing in the rules to stop a fellow leaving whenever he pleased. Mr Carstares devoutly hoped that such a thought would not occur to any one of the six great ladies who presided over Almack's. He had little doubt that they would be able to persuade the Ton to abide by such a decree, and then one would be in the basket!

A faintly surprised drawl brought an end to these depressing reflections. 'You here too, George! Whatever for? Don't tell me Darleston is sacrificing both of us this evening!'

Carstares swung around, the gloomy expression giving way to something more like his usual merry smile. 'Good God! Carrington! Did Peter ask you as well? What the devil is he up to?'

'Standing us up, by the look of things!' answered Viscount Carrington. 'Never mind, in less than ten minutes we can go and wait for him in the street! Give him another few minutes out there and then toddle off to more entertaining pastures!'

'Just what I was thinking!' said Carstares with a

grin. He ran a hand through his fair locks. 'D'you know *why* he asked us to meet him here?'

'Not the least notion. Do you?' asked Carrington curiously.

Carstares rubbed his nose thoughtfully. 'Got a slight suspicion. Was with him, you know, when he heard about the death of young Nicholas Frobisher in that hunting accident last winter.'

Carrington looked more than a little puzzled. 'Well, yes. I know Peter was cut up about it. He was fond of the lad, and he *was* Peter's heir after all, but there's nothing in that to make the fellow run mad!' Then, in very polite tones, 'Good evening, Lady Sefton. How delightful to see you!'

The kindly-looking peeress smiled gently at him and said, with not a trace of sarcasm, 'And so unusual to see you here, Lord Carrington and Mr Carstares! But you must come further in. The young ladies do not linger at the front doors in hope of dance partners, you know. I shall make it my especial concern to introduce you to the very prettiest!' Not a muscle in her face betrayed what George Carstares knew must be her considerable inward mirth at the expression of startled horror on the Viscount's face.

The Patroness delivered her final thrust with a dead straight face, 'And, of course, my lord and I shall look forward to your company at supper!' She departed to mingle with the crowd, not waiting to hear their response to what amounted to a royal command.

Carstares groaned. 'I knew one of them would think of it!'

'Think of what?' asked Carrington. 'Oh, never mind! We're done to a cow's thumb now! Get on with your theory, and later on we can toss for the honour of calling Peter out!'

After a moment to gather his wits Carstares continued, 'So Nicholas is dead. Don't suppose you know who the heir is now?'

'Can't say I do,' replied Carrington. 'I don't keep track of all my friends' distant relations!' Then, in tones of shock as a possibility struck him, 'My God! It couldn't be! Not Jack Frobisher?'

George nodded.

Carrington thought about it. 'Peter won't stand for that. He'll have to remarry. Unpleasant for him after his experience with Melissa, but he might choose better this time!'

'Hope so,' said George. 'Because I think that's what we're doing here. Helping Peter choose a wife! Or at least providing moral support while he chooses! And thank God—if he's here, he ain't contemplating marriage to Caroline Daventry!'

Whatever Lord Carrington might have said in response to his friend's suspicions was destined to remain unspoken. At that moment a startled hush came over the crowd and they realised that most people were staring in disbelief at the entrance. An even more startled murmur replaced the hush as the tall gentleman in the doorway moved into the room.

He seemed quite unconcerned by the collective gaze and whisper of the assembled throng, but stood and surveyed the scene carefully. His was a tall, athletic figure, dressed with unobtrusive elegance in the satin knee-breeches and swallow-tailed coat which were *de rigueur* for a ball. His cravat was tied with an artistry calculated to turn any aspirant to fashion pea-green with envy. The curly black hair was brushed into the fashionable Brutus and the dark brown eyes seemed to search the room.

After a moment this direct gaze fell upon Lord Carrington and Mr Carstares. A smile lightened the rather sombre countenance as the gentleman came towards them. This was Peter Augustus Frobisher, Earl of Darleston, veteran of the Peninsular War and hero of Waterloo.

He reached his friends and said with a faint twinkle, 'How kind of you not to depart! Had you quite despaired of me?'

'You'd have had two friends the less if you hadn't shown your front, my boy!' said Carrington trenchantly.

The Earl looked amused. 'How very extreme! You could have left, you know! In fact the thought occurred to me, while I was screwing up my courage in the carriage, that all I had to do was wait and the pair of you would shortly emerge. There's nothing in the rules to stop you leaving!'

His friends stared at him in speechless dudgeon. George was the first to recover the use of his tongue. 'Oh, yes, there is, when Lady Sefton has personally commanded your presence at supper!'

Darleston said soothingly, 'Never mind, there are worse fates!'

Before either of his indignant friends could draw breath to ask exactly what he had in mind, an attractive woman of about fifty came up behind them and tapped Darleston on the arm.

'Peter! You dreadful boy! What on earth are you doing here at the Marriage Mart?' Her voice held deep affection and Earl turned around with a smile of delight on his face.

'Aunt Louisa!' He bent to kiss her on the cheek. 'Simply for the joy of seeing you dressed like the Christmas beef! Can you doubt it?'

'Easily, you trifler! Oh, it is good to see you! And you too, George and Michael! How long it seems since you were all schoolboys racing around Darleston Court. Making the place hideous with your noise and muddy boots!' She smiled at the recollection.

The three gentlemen grinned, and Carstares said, laughing, 'Seems like yesterday for you, Lady Edenhope. You appear to remember our sins only too well!'

'I've cause enough!' she replied with a chuckle. 'I never did find out who put the frog in my bed!'

'All of us!' admitted Darleston. 'Carrington caught it with George's boot and I climbed up the ivy with it. A joint effort, in fact! And didn't we feel like sweeps when you simply gave it to Meadows the next morning and asked him to return it to the owner with thanks? He was furious with us!'

Lady Edenhope laughed up at them. She was not, in point of fact, related to Darleston, but had been his mother's dearest friend, and she cherished a deep affection for him. Knowing him as well as she did, she too had a very fair notion of the interpretation to put on his presence at Almack's after so many years. No doubt so did many of the Ton, she thought ruefully. The matchmaking mamas would be in full cry after the quarry in no time! Enough to make any man turn tail and bolt for cover!

At thirty-two, the widowed Earl was a matrimonial prize of the first stare. Extremely wealthy and possessed of an ancient and honourable name, he had charm and good looks that were the final seal upon his fate. Perfectly aware of this, for the past few years he had avoided the more respectable entertainments afforded by the Metropolis, preferring to spend his time in pursuits unlikely to bring him within the range of marriageable young girls and their mamas.

'Well, it is lovely to see you all here,' said Lady Edenhope. 'Now I must run along. I'm supposed to be chaperoning a friend's daughter and I mustn't neglect my duty. Not that it's very onerous. The dearest girl, and already snapped up!'

She departed into the throng and the three gentlemen looked at each other reminiscently. Darleston broke the silence, saying lightly, 'Well, ''Once more unto the breach, dear friends,'' as the Bard would have it! No doubt enough people know us that we shan't find ourselves utterly ignored.' This last was said in distinctly sarcastic tones.

They suited the action to the word and began to mingle with the crowd. One by one they found themselves being presented to various young ladies, all of whom seemed flatteringly anxious to please and entertain them. George Carstares and Lord Carrington took this in good part, and even found that they were quite enjoying themselves.

For Lord Darleston, however, it was quite another matter. Despite the fact that he had been introduced to the very attractive Miss Ffolliot, his mind persisted in wandering. Here at Almack's twelve years earlier he had met his first wife and fallen madly in love with her lovely face and charming ways. What a fool I must have been! he thought bitterly. Calf love! He had been *aux anges* at the thought that such a divine creature should favour him over so many suitors who had appeared to him far more eligible. A modest young man, he had been quite innocent of the lure of his prospective title and fortune. He had seen himself as a callow youth, miraculously favoured by the loveliest debutante of the season.

With an effort he jerked his mind out of the past and back to his companion. 'I beg your pardon, Miss Ffolliot, I was wool-gathering. What were you saying?'

Miss Ffolliot smiled up at him and said in a soft voice, 'It was of no consequence, my lord. Just a polite commonplace. Should we take our places now?'

'Most certainly we should,' he answered, and led her into a set. Really she was a very pretty girl, he thought to himself. Many spiteful matrons would have described her hair as red, but in fact it was a deep rich auburn and she had the delicately fair complexion which goes with such hair. Wide-set grey eyes gazed up at him in innocent enjoyment and her smile was quite delightful. Her figure was just what he liked too, slender but with a suggestion of womanly curves. All in all, thought Darleston, she was quite lovely!

As they danced he attempted to engage her in conversation, but she had very little to say for herself besides polite rejoinders to his comments. The only question to which she replied with any enthusiasm was his query as to whether she was enjoying her visit to Almack's.

'Oh, yes, my lord! Very much! It is nice to see so many new people and to dance all night!'

From all of which Lord Darleston came to the swift conclusion that this young lady would not do at all. While he did not wish to marry a chatterbox he preferred to seek a lady who had a little more to add to a conversation. Without wishing to be unkind, he found Miss Ffolliot a little dull for his taste. Very charming and sweet, but just not his sort!

At the end of the dance he returned Miss Ffolliot to her mother to find that she had been joined by her husband, a kindly-looking man of medium height, as well as Miss Ffolliot's next partner. He was introduced to Darleston as Mr Richard Winton, a gentleman of roughly the same age as the Earl, who recognised him as a fellow member of White's. The two of them chatted politely before Mr Winton excused himself and Miss Ffolliot to join a set.

Darleston noted without the least rancour that Miss Ffolliot was chatting merrily to her new partner without the slightest hint of shyness.

Mr Ffolliot watched the pair and said, 'Mr Winton is a neighbour of ours in the country. Phoebe always finds it easier to chat to old acquaintances!'

Darleston smiled and said, 'I tend to agree with her! And the dreadful thing is when someone who has been presented to you once should chance to recognise you and you simply cannot remember the right name!'

'Dear me, yes!' said Mrs Ffolliot with a chuckle. 'And they always seem so hurt if one admits one can't remember them! Mr Ffolliot has a truly terrible memory for names.'

'Nonsense, my dear! You do exaggerate!' protested the maligned gentleman.

'Not by very much!' she asserted with a twinkle. 'Still, no doubt Lord Darleston is not afflicted too badly. I'm sure people are only too glad to recall themselves to his mind!'

'Only too true, ma'am. You can have no notion of the number of people who claim long acquaintance on the basis of one meeting years before!'

'I can imagine!' laughed Mrs Ffolliot. 'Never mind, my lord! My husband and I shall remember to cut you the next time we meet, and Phoebe shall be given strict instructions to do the same.'

Laughing at this, Darleston made his farewells and departed to seek Carstares and Carrington. George was easy enough to spot. He was taking part in the same set as Miss Ffolliot and Mr Winton. And after a few moments' searching Darleston found Carrington listening very politely to Lady Jersey, another of the Patronesses, wickedly, if aptly, known as 'Silence'.

'Darleston, my goodness! I didn't believe Maria Sefton when she told me you were here! It must be years! Lord Carrington too! What a catch for us! Why, I declare there has not been so much excitement all season! Did I see you stand up with Miss Ffolliot? Such a sweet child, but a little shy. Parents charming, but the brother! Oh, my goodness! Oh, well! He's only her half-brother. The first Mrs Ffolliot died very young, I believe, and John Ffolliot remarried a few years later. It does happen, you see, Darleston! Now I must be off! Do come again! I'm sure it does us good to have such a shock!'

She fluttered away to inform all and sundry that it was just as she had suspected. Darleston was going to remarry. And about time too! After all, he owed it to his name! Oh, goodness me! Just think if one had to acknowledge that odious Jack Frobisher as Earl of Darleston! Besides, it was time and more that Darleston got over smarting about the way that baggage Melissa had treated him. Running off with Barton in that vulgar way! Just as well she did break her neck in that carriage accident! At least it spared Darleston the scandal of divorcing her!

Carrington and Darleston watched her go with a fairly accurate idea of what she must be saying. Half-annoyed and half-amused Darleston enquired, 'Did she stop to draw breath while she spoke to you?'

Carrington grinned. 'Not so that you'd notice! But she's as shrewd as she can hold together for all she rattles on so fast.'

'No need to tell me that!' answered Darleston with a grimace. 'I got the distinct impression that dear Silence knew everything about me! Right down to what brought me here this evening!'

In some amusement, Carrington said, 'Doing it far too brown, dear boy! I should imagine everyone who knows you worked that out the moment they laid eyes on you! Especially when they saw you stand up with that pretty little redhead!'

Darleston sighed, 'I suppose it must be glaringly obvious. But what choice do I have?'

'None, regarding your duty,' answered his friend seriously. 'But plenty as to the shape it must take. Let's face it, Peter, you are the most eligible of men. Wealthy, titled, and the ladies seem to find you tolerably pleasing to the eye. You could probably have your choice of brides.'

'How very dull!' complained Darleston. 'You make it all sound so respectable!'

'Well, that's what you want, isn't it?' asked Carrington bluntly.

Darleston sighed again. 'God knows why I bear with you, Michael! You have such an appalling habit of being disgustingly right! Ah! Here comes George. Did you enjoy yourself?'

'As a matter of fact I did,' answered Carstares. 'My partner, Miss Blackburn, was quite charming, and at least I won't have a head tomorrow morning from dancing with her! Or pockets to let, for that matter!'

'You'll find yourself with pockets to let all right and tight if you let your susceptibilities lead you astray and find yourself in Parson's Mousetrap!' observed Darleston caustically.

Carstares looked shocked. 'Me? Parson's Mouse-trap! Not likely. Younger son, you know! That's your fate, Peter, at least so I believe! We'll see you falling in love and waiting at the altar in no time!'

'Love!' ejaculated Darleston. 'You can't be serious! I tell you, I'm done with that rubbish! This is to be a marriage of convenience. As long as the girl is well brought up to know her duty and is not a positive antidote…' He left the sentence unfinished.

Carstares and Lord Carrington looked at each other in concern. This was even worse than they had thought! What hope had the poor chap of happiness in marriage if he was this bitter? Not to mention the poor girl who accepted his offer.

After a moment's silence Carstares said thought-fully, 'Then you'd better make damn sure the girl don't care a rush for you! After all, you don't want to treat some poor child to the same dirty trick you were served! Oh, Lord! Here comes Lady Sefton. Lay you handsome odds she's going to snabble Peter as well.'

The arrival of the amiable Lady Sefton effectively ended the conversation, but Carstares' observation had gone home deeply. The thought that he might hurt some unsuspecting innocent in the same way he had been hurt gave Peter furiously to think.

Although he bore his part at the ensuing supper party with charm and wit, his mind was frequently elsewhere. Until now his future bride had been a very hypothetical and unreal figure. Suddenly, even though her face and figure remained in the shadows, she became a person, with thoughts and feelings, perhaps a heart to be wounded. George was right, he thought. Better make sure she doesn't care too much, whoever she turns out to be!

Two days later the lovely Lady Caroline Daventry sat in her cushioned pink drawing room, glaring at the door as it closed after her fifth morning caller. Her normally languishing blue eyes were glittering with fury and every line of her lushly curved body was stiff with rage. Even the blonde curls piled so becomingly on top of her head seemed to quiver with emotion. She had been hard put to it to bite back a savage rejoinder as yet another sweetly smiling lady had told her in strictest confidence that it seemed 'Dear Peter' was considering a second marriage.

His appearance at Almack's and dance with Miss Ffolliot had lost nothing in the telling. The fact that he had remained chatting to her parents for several minutes gave weight to the wildest flights of fancy. It was even rumoured that Mr Richard Winton, hitherto the most likely candidate for her hand, was in a way to being cut out!

Caroline Daventry was no fool. She knew enough to discount the more fanciful accounts, but even so what was left alarmed her. It was a fairly open secret that she had been Darleston's mistress for the past year. Never had it occurred to her that he might consider remarrying. He had appeared to be perfectly satisfied with her favours, and she had been content to maintain her position as his mistress. But if he was to remarry then clearly the situation was altered.

Restlessly she rose to her feet and began to pace up and down. She must think! Obviously Darleston must dislike Jack even more than she had thought. That had to be the reason for this change of direction. So far so good! At least he wasn't fancying himself in love with some simpering little debutante! That made her task a little easier. Far less difficult to detach his thoughts from an abstract goal than from a specific person, but she must work fast. If Darleston *was* going to marry again then she fully intended to be the new Countess!

That same morning Lord Darleston had decided to try the paces of a new mare. He had bought her at Tattersall's the previous week, and every time he'd thought of taking her out something had cropped up to distract him. This morning he was determined that nothing should be allowed to deflect him from his purpose.

Therefore the unfashionable hour of eight o'clock had seen him swinging into the saddle of a mettlesome bay mare who appeared to be under the erroneous impression that her new master would be disconcerted by her habit of plunging a little as he mounted. Amused by these fidgets, Darleston had settled himself in the saddle and spoken to her soothingly.

The groom who had brought her around from the mews said apologetically, 'Very lively she is, my lord! She needs a good gallop!'

'Not to mention a firm hand!' said his master as he brought the mare's head up. 'Steady there you silly creature! It's early enough that we can probably get away with a bit of a gallop in the park. Thank you, Fred. I'll bring her around when I get back.'

The groom touched his cap respectfully and stepped

back as his master gave the mare the office to move. Having revised her opinion of the man on her back, the mare moved off at a decorous pace and tried to convey the impression that this was the way she always behaved. Fred watched the pair of them depart and then went back to the mews to tell his cohorts that the master could handle anything that ever looked through a bridle, even that flighty piece of blood and bone Griselda!

Upon reaching the park, Darleston was relieved to discover that it was practically deserted. Several horses were being exercised by grooms and a very few people were strolling along the paths. No carriages and no sign of anyone who might recognise him. Hardly a surprise at this ungodly hour, he thought. Most members of society would still be abed after the entertainments of the previous evening.

The mare, Griselda, was dancing impatiently, itching to go. For the good of her education Darleston held her to a steady trot for a hundred yards before pressing her to a canter. After another hundred yards and a quick glance around he gave Griselda her head and touched his heels lightly to her flanks. No further encouragement was necessary. The mare took off down the path with a delighted snort. For over a week she had been cooped up in a stable or led out in a string and she had had quite enough of such boredom. This was much more to her taste.

Darleston sat firm in the saddle and kept a light hand on the mare's mouth. Her paces, he concluded, were excellent. Smooth and effortless, with an impressive turn of speed. Her mouth, too, was good; she was extremely responsive to his hand on the rein. Her only fault, if fault it could be called, was her flightiness. Ah, well, we're all young once! he thought tolerantly.

On the thought he sat back and steadied the mare. A phaeton was being driven towards him at a smart trot and an incredibly large grey hound was running alongside. Good heavens, he thought. Who on earth would be out at this hour? He reined Griselda in to a trot so as not to startle the pair harnessed to the phaeton.

As the carriage drew nearer he realised that he knew the occupants. The gentleman driving nodded politely, but obviously would have continued had not Darleston reined in and said in tones of mock indignation, 'I didn't think you were serious when you threatened to cut me, sir! How do you do, Mr Ffolliot? And Miss Ffolliot! No need to ask how you are! You are looking charmingly!'

'Lord Darleston! This is very pleasant,' replied Mr Ffolliot. 'I don't believe you have met my—' He stopped suddenly.

Darleston, a trifle puzzled, said, 'But of course I have met Miss Ffolliot! She granted me the honour of a dance at Almack's the other night!'

'Oh, of course…er…quite so!' said Mr Ffolliot in some confusion. 'I beg your pardon, Lord Darleston!'

'Think nothing of it, sir. Mrs Ffolliot warned me of your lamentable memory!' said Darleston with a chuckle. He liked this unpretentious man with the kind eyes.

He turned to Miss Ffolliot and said, 'I do hope our dance holds a stronger place in *your* memory, Miss Ffolliot! Or do you have so many dancing partners that neither you nor your parents can disentangle us all?'

Miss Ffolliot gave vent to a delightful choke of

laughter and said, 'Oh, no, Lord Darleston. That dance is firmly fixed in my mind! It was most enjoyable!'

Darleston blinked a little. This merry creature was a far cry from the shy girl he had danced with at Almack's! And there was something different about her this morning. Something about her eyes. Although she smiled at him delightfully, he had the odd feeling that those wide grey eyes were looking right through him. Trying to gather his thoughts, he asked, 'And may one enquire what brings you out at this unfashionable hour, Miss Ffolliot? Surely you should be recruiting your strength after whatever party you graced last night.'

She laughed and said, 'Oh, but the park is so much more pleasant when there is nobody about! And much better than a stuffy ballroom! Besides—' she indicated the dog who sat panting next to the phaeton '—poor Gelert needs a great deal more exercise than he'd get if we came out at a fashionable hour and had to stop continually to be polite!'

'I do sympathise, Miss Ffolliot!' answered Darleston. 'I brought this lunatic mare out early for much the same reason.'

'She's a pretty thing,' said Mr Ffolliot. 'Quite a youngster too. How is she called?'

'Yes, she is young. Just over three. I bought her last week. Her name is Griselda. Steady you idiot!' This last to the mare as she fidgeted nervously. 'She is a little impatient as yet!'

'Surely she is ill-named then, my lord!' said Miss Ffolliot with a smile. 'Wasn't Griselda supposed to be very patient?'

'Do you mean that mawkish creature in Chaucer?' asked Darleston in some surprise. Most young ladies were well read in Byron, but he had yet to meet one with a knowledge of medieval literature!

'That's the female. She comes in *The Decameron* too you know,' answered Miss Ffolliot. 'How nice to find someone else who thinks she was a fool for putting up with that odious husband. She should have simply told him he was being an idiot!'

'Quite so, Miss Ffolliot,' he agreed with a twinkle. 'I can easily believe that you'd do just that!'

'I'd probably let Gelert bite him!' was the answer.

'That would certainly bring him to his senses in a hurry!' said Darleston, grinning.

He looked at the dog curiously. Never before had he seen quite such an enormous hound. Tremendously long legs and a deep barrelled chest gave the impression of immense power. He must stand at least three feet at the shoulder, thought Darleston in awe. The breed was nevertheless familiar to him from a horse-buying trip to Ireland years before. 'An Irish wolf-hound, isn't he? I've never seen such a magnificent specimen of the breed.'

Miss Ffolliot smiled at him and said, 'That's right! Most people enquire about his breeding in the most patronising tones and it makes me simply wild!'

Darleston chuckled. 'I can just imagine!' But all the while an odd voice in his mind was nagging at him. Surely Miss Ffolliot had been an entirely different girl in the ballroom! If asked, he would have sworn she wouldn't say boo to a goose! And hadn't she said the other night that she enjoyed dancing and meeting new people? And now she preferred the park at an early hour because it was empty and better than 'a stuffy ballroom'!

He quizzed her gently. 'I think you were not telling

the truth the other night, Miss Ffolliot. I distinctly re-call you saying how much you enjoyed meeting new people and dancing!'

Again he heard that appealing choke of laughter. 'Good heavens! Surely you don't expect a girl to in-form a gentleman to whom she has just been intro-duced that she hates meeting new people! Let alone that she dislikes balls when the poor man is dancing with her! How very rude that would have been in me! Besides, that dance was, as I said, very enjoyable.'

'Mere flattery, Miss Ffolliot!'

'Not at all, my lord. You dance very well!' she added in tones of great kindness.

He roared with laughter and said, 'That amounts to toad-eating, Miss Ffolliot! You are a baggage, I take leave to tell you!'

Then, as Griselda sidled restlessly in the cool breeze, 'I must not keep my "Impatient Griselda" standing any longer. Sir! Your most obedient servant! Miss Ffolliot, your most humble!' They bade him fare-well and, raising his hat to Miss Ffolliot, he pushed the mare into a trot and continued on his way. It oc-curred to him that he would enjoy meeting Miss Ffolliot again. She was a most refreshing, if contra-dictory young lady!

Chapter Two

Lord Darleston had been a trifle over optimistic in thinking that the park would be bereft of all the Ton that morning. At least two other people had seen him exercising the mare, and had also observed his conversation with the Ffolliots. The murmurs of interest which followed this episode came inevitably to the ears of Lady Caroline, who began to be seriously worried. Worried enough to be betrayed into making some rather snide remarks to Miss Ffolliot at a ball. Miss Ffolliot did not attempt to reply but simply looked extremely puzzled.

Quite apart from all the gossip, Lady Caroline had noticed an even greater degree of detachment in her lover than was normal. Never one to indulge in displays of demonstrative emotion, Darleston seemed to her to be more aloof and untouchable than ever. It was as though his mind was far away, even when he made love to her with all his usual skill and expertise. Lady Caroline turned various schemes over in her mind and finally decided on a course of definite action, for which she prepared by ensuring that Darleston did not see her privately for over a week.

The first direct step in her campaign was a discreetly worded invitation bidding his lordship to supper one evening. She knew that she would have to step warily. Darleston was neither to lead or drive. If he once suspected what she was up to then she might as well give up. Hence the supper invitation. A delightfully romantic evening *à deux* with his favourite wines and food would serve her turn. Afterwards, when he was in a relaxed mood, she could begin her task of distracting him from immediate thoughts of matrimony. Convincing him that she would be a suitable wife was much further on in her plans!

Accordingly Lord Darleston presented himself for a late supper on the designated evening, in a mood of agreeable anticipation. Lady Caroline kept a talented chef, and knew his taste in wine to a nicety, besides which her personal attractions were definitely alluring. He had seen little of Caroline recently, except at parties where perforce discretion was necessary. It did not occur to him that the lady had deliberately made quite sure he had had no opportunity to see her alone for some time. Better for her plans if he was eager to see her and enjoy her favours, she reasoned.

Darleston entered the drawing room to find Lady Caroline attended by her companion, Miss Jameson, a depressed-looking creature of about sixty. She was a cousin of the late Sir Neville Daventry and was supposed to lend an air of respectability to her relation's ménage. In reality Lady Caroline did very much as she pleased, dispensing with Miss Jameson's chaperonage whenever it suited her convenience.

Darleston greeted both ladies politely, and was especially kind to the older lady. 'Miss Jameson! What a pleasure to see you. I hope you are keeping well?'

It was part of his charm that he was always kind to
those less well off than himself. Kind, but never patronising, and Miss Jameson, as always, responded to
his friendly greeting with a smile that very few ever
saw.

'I am very well, Lord Darleston. And you? We have
not seen you for an age!' she said.

Lady Caroline cut in at this point, 'Yes, I am sure
Lord Darleston is well, Cousin Lucy, or he would not
be here! Now, we wouldn't want to keep you from
your bed at this late hour, so we will bid you goodnight!'

This abrupt dismissal brought a slight frown to
Darleston's brow, not because he was eager for Miss
Jameson's company, but because he found the ruthless
manner of it faintly distasteful. Lady Caroline did not
notice the frown. Like many self-centred people, she
was unable to comprehend that anyone would put up
with an inconvenient companion from a combination
of good manners and kindness.

Miss Jameson appeared unsurprised by the curtail-
ing of her evening. She had known perfectly well from
the outset that Caroline would get rid of her as quickly
as possible. The two years since Sir Neville's death
had left her few illusions about her charge's character,
and she had no doubts at all about the nature of Lady
Caroline's relationship with Lord Darleston. It was
certainly not her place to remonstrate with Lady
Caroline, she reflected, but it seemed a dreadful thing
to see such a fine man as Lord Darleston in her coils.

'I shall bid you goodnight, then, dear Caroline, and
you, my lord,' she responded in a dignified manner,
which afforded no hint of the sense of hurt she felt. It
would give her great pleasure, she thought, to put a

spoke in Lady Caroline's wheel. She was not quite sure what Caroline was up to, but she knew her charge well enough to know that something was afoot.

Darleston went immediately to the door and opened it for her, saying, 'Goodnight, Miss Jameson. It is most unkind of you to deprive us of your company. Perhaps I shall be luckier on another occasion!'

She looked up at him in wry amusement as she exited the room and her soft reply reached only him. 'Most unlikely, my lord! Goodnight, and God bless you!'

After shutting the door behind her, Darleston turned back to his hostess, who looked a little miffed. 'Really, Peter dear, I cannot imagine why you bother with Cousin Lucy! I only keep her here to silence all the tabbies!'

Darleston was silent for a moment, and then said with an assumption of lightness, 'Kindness costs nothing, Caroline, and I think her situation as a dependant cannot be a happy one.'

Although she could not understand his attitude, Lady Caroline was quick enough to realise that she had erred in some way. She glided across to him and twined her arms around his neck, 'Oh, Peter! 'Tis not that I meant to be unkind to poor Lucy! But I have seen so little of you recently that I longed to have you all to myself!' The blue eyes gazed up at him meltingly from under long curling lashes. A provocative smile was on her lips, deepening as she felt his arms slide about her waist.

Darleston looked down at her with a faint smile. Perhaps it was as well to let Miss Jameson have an early night, he thought as he kissed Lady Caroline. Her response was immediate and demanding. Nothing loath, Darleston tightened his arms about her and set about the enjoyable task of satisfying her obvious desire. His own physical desire was easily a match for hers, but as always some small part of him remained detached and indifferent.

After a few moments he released himself carefully and said, 'Perhaps we should have supper first, Caroline! Otherwise I fear your chef's talents will be quite unappreciated in comparison with your own charms!'

Satisfied that she had well and truly aroused him, Lady Caroline agreed. 'Whatever you wish, my lord. Just as long as the supper does not spoil your appetite!' She cast a meaning glance over her shoulder as she led the way to the small table set for two. A side-table nearby held a small but choice supper and several decanters.

As they sat down Lady Caroline said languidly, 'Do you know, Peter—except, of course, for your presence—London is so dreadfully dull at the moment? One gets so tired of seeing the same faces and hearing the same gossip! I declare it is beyond anything!'

Darleston was amused. 'My dear, are you contemplating a repairing lease in the country? I fear you will find that even more dull!'

A shudder of horror greeted this suggestion. 'The country! At this season! What an insupportable idea! Of course not! I am thinking of going to Paris. I have friends there, you know. And it seems such a long time since I visited France! And Paris is always so gay! Will you have a little duckling, Peter?' She judged that she had said enough for the time being.

Having accepted the duckling, and some asparagus, Darleston returned to the subject of Lady Caroline's projected sojourn in Paris. 'And what will be so different about Paris, my sweet? New clothes, admirers? New gossip?'

She gave a tinkling laugh. 'But of course, my dear! All those things! Now, enough of me! Tell me what you have been doing to keep you away from me all these days!'

Darleston hesitated for a moment. The last thing he wanted to do was confide in Caroline! 'Oh, just catching up with old friends and seeing to some business,' he said easily. 'Carstares and Carrington are in town at the moment. I've seen a lot of them.'

'Do you know, I even heard that the three of you had been seen at Almack's?' she said daringly. 'Surely a most unlikely place to find any of you! Let alone all three together! You must have raised such hopes in the hearts of all the young ladies and their fond mamas!' This last was followed with another tinkling laugh.

Sipping her wine, she watched his reaction carefully. She was perfectly aware that practically every woman in town with a marriageable daughter would be in full cry after such a prize as Darleston. She was also tolerably certain that this would be irking her lover almost unbearably.

His quick scowl confirmed her suspicions, and again she changed the subject. 'Do tell me. How does Mr Carstares, and Lord Carrington, of course?'

'Oh, they are well enough. Carrington has gone down to Bath to visit his young sister for a few days. She is at school there and has been unwell.'

'Poor child,' said Lady Caroline, thinking it was as well that one of Darleston's close friends was out of town. Carstares and Carrington together might manage to spike her guns!

She kept the conversation to neutral topics until the end of the meal.

When Darleston reached for the brandy decanter she rose to her feet and said with a smile, 'Perhaps you would excuse me briefly, Peter.'

He stood up and said, 'Only very briefly, Caroline! I'm sure you would not wish to keep me waiting!' After escorting Lady Caroline to the door and closing it behind her Darleston returned to the table and poured himself a glass of the late Sir Neville's very fine old brandy. Sipping it reverently, he sat down to give some thought to Caroline's scheme to visit Paris. He suspected that her main reason for finding London dull was simply that she had been subtly but effectively ostracised by quite a number of influential society hostesses.

Caroline had not been quite discreet enough with one or two of her lovers. It was even said that she had entertained a number of gentlemen at her Scottish home during her period of strict mourning. The Patronesses of Almack's had let it be quietly understood that for her to apply for vouchers would be useless. Nothing was said openly, of course, but Lady Caroline did not make the attempt. To be publicly denied would be insupportable.

Although she vowed that such entertainments were insipid and not at all to her taste, Darleston was perfectly aware that she wanted that entrée, even if only for the pleasure of spurning it. Obviously if she were in Paris there was no question of Almack's, and her reputation would not be such a barrier where she was not so well known.

The excellence of the brandy gave rise to more thought, and to a great degree mitigated against his lordship's rising impatience at the inordinate length of time Lady Caroline was taking. It did not occur to him that she wanted him to be extremely eager or that she wanted to give him time to think over her plans.

It suddenly struck Darleston that if Caroline decamped for Paris it would be deucedly inconvenient for him. He enjoyed her favours very much and was loath to go to all the effort of finding and setting up a new mistress. His own married experience led him to eschew all married women. Something in his nature revolted at the thought of offending another man as he had been offended. Unfortunately his preference was for women of his own order, which therefore meant a widow, and he was damned if he could think of another likely candidate to fill the position which would be left vacant by Lady Caroline's departure.

He had no illusions about the quality of Caroline's affection for him. She might go to Paris alone but she would certainly not return so. Not that she needed a protector in financial terms for she was quite well off! In fact that was one of the things that Darleston found agreeable about the relationship. It was conducted on equal terms with none of the necessity to buy expensive presents to keep his mistress happy.

He was just beginning to toy with the notion of following Lady Caroline to Paris when she returned. Her elegant gown of deep blue satin had been replaced by a dressing gown which consisted of floating layers of pink gauze. It was quite evident to Darleston that her ladyship was not wearing a stitch beneath it. He said nothing, but tossed back the last of his brandy with scant respect for so noble a vintage and stood up.

Lady Caroline glided to the sofa and seated herself with an inviting smile. The dressing gown fell open, exposing one elegant white leg which Caroline did not bother to cover. Darleston shrugged himself out of his coat and removed his cravat without taking his eyes from her face. He walked over to the sofa unhurriedly, but Lady Caroline could see the tension in every line of his athletic body. He stood before her, looking down at her voluptuous curves with increasing lust.

'Do you like my dressing gown?' she asked provocatively. 'It's a new one.'

He answered lightly enough, 'Very elegant my sweet, but I'll appreciate it more when I've torn it off you!'

The following morning Darleston slept late, not having returned home until four in the morning. His lordship's valet, Mr Fordham, was finally summoned from the servants' hall by his master's bell at midday.

Fordham found his lordship fully dressed except for the finishing touches to his cravat. He waited quietly, not wishing to disturb so delicate and important an operation.

Darleston caught his eye in the mirror, 'Ah, there you are Fordham. Good morning, or rather, since I perceive the day to be advanced, good afternoon!'

'Good afternoon, my lord. I trust your lordship enjoyed an agreeable evening?' replied Fordham very politely.

The long, powerful fingers on the cravat stilled in the act of setting a crease and the brown eyes glanced into the mirror again. 'Very agreeable, Fordham,' answered the Earl gravely.

'I am glad to hear it my lord. May I remind your

lordship that you had promised to wait on Lady Edenhope this morning?' asked Fordham.

'You may remind me, and you may also tell me why the devil you didn't awaken me over an hour ago to this purpose!' said Darleston, carefully examining the results of his labours.

'Your lordship may remember that upon the last occasion I ventured to do such a thing you hurled a boot at my head with great accuracy and consigned me to a place of extreme heat!' was the unperturbed reply.

Darleston, satisfied that his cravat would pass muster, swung around with a distinct twinkle in his eye and asked curiously, 'Why do you bear with me Fordham?'

The valet answered simply, 'I like you, my lord, and even if you did hit me with the boot you apologised later and informed me that you would prefer I remained in your employ rather than seeking the post you had recommended in the heat of the moment.'

Darleston chuckled and said, 'Very well, Fordham! Did you by any chance send a note round to Lady Edenhope?'

'Certainly, my lord. She sent this note back for you.' He handed Darleston a sealed billet.

'Thank you, Fordham.' He broke the seal and read the enclosed missive.

   My Dear Darleston
I shall forbear to ask exactly how you amused yourself last night if only you will have the goodness to be my escort tonight! My little protégée is unwell and my lord has gone into the country so I am bereft of a companion for the concert at the Hanover Square Rooms this evening. I know

you love music and the programme this evening
is rather lovely: all Mozart. So if you feel you
can bear my company I shall look forward to seeing you this evening.

All my love, Louisa Edenhope.

Darleston grinned. He wouldn't put it past Lady
Edenhope to know perfectly well where he had been
last night. He glanced at Fordham and said, 'You may
send a footman round to tell Lady Edenhope that I
shall be delighted to be her escort this evening.'

'Very good, my lord. I will go myself, if your lordship has no further need for me this afternoon.'

'Yourself, Fordham?' said Darleston in surprise.
'You are welcome to do so if you wish, but why?'

'Some exercise will do me good, my lord. Mr
Meadows has informed me that I am getting fat!'
There was a slight hint of indignation in Fordham's
tone of voice.

'I see,' said Darleston, somehow preserving a
straight face. 'You have my permission to take a walk
every day if you deem it necessary. You know my
routine. No doubt you can pick a time which will be
mutually acceptable to us both. That will be all for
now. You will lay out my clothes later, of course.'

'Naturally, my lord.' Fordham left on his message
and Darleston gave himself up to laughter. No doubt
Meadows, the old butler, was enjoying himself at
Fordham's expense, but there was no denying that
Fordham was starting to look a little tubby!

Darleston did enjoy the concert that evening. He
found Lady Edenhope's company restful, and it was
pleasant to sit back and listen to the music. One of the
things he missed most about his mother was her music.

She had been a fine singer and had played the piano-forte with great talent. There had always been music in his home and he missed it greatly. He thought idly to himself that he must try and choose a musical wife.

During the interval he remained with Lady Edenhope, chatting about the performance. Two of Mozart's string quartets had been played, and Lady Edenhope felt that a better balance of the parts had been needed.

They returned to their seats for the second half. 'That cellist was by far too loud in places, Peter. Particularly in the slow movements!' she asserted, and then realised that Darleston was not listening. He was staring at a lady she had already noted as being most oddly dressed.

All in severe black and heavily veiled, the lady sat two rows ahead of them and slightly to the right. She was escorted by a young person who was obviously a maidservant and had made no effort to speak to any-one during the interval. Looking at her more closely, Lady Edenhope came to the conclusion that she was quite young. The severe black was extremely flattering to an already slender figure.

Darleston continued to stare until his companion gave him a gentle nudge and asked, 'Do you know that girl, Peter?'

'What...? Oh, I'm sorry, Aunt Louisa! I wasn't re-ally attending,' he apologised.

'I noticed,' she said dryly. 'Is the young lady an acquaintance of yours?'

'I'm not quite sure,' said Darleston slowly. 'I *think* I know who it is, but I can't for the life of me imagine what she is doing dressed like that!'

'Most odd!' agreed Lady Edenhope. 'Oh, here is the orchestra. We had better stop chattering.'

They sat back to enjoy the two symphonies which followed. The last one was Mozart's final essay in this genre. Darleston had never heard the work before and was taken aback by the power of the music, particularly in the final movement. Here the closely knit interweaving of the melodies was utterly exhilarating, and when the end came Darleston felt that he wanted to leap up and yell like a boy. He contented himself with clapping vigorously.

The slender lady in black appeared to be similarly affected. She was leaning forward, applauding enthusiastically, and Darleston became more and more certain that he knew her.

Turning to Lady Edenhope as the audience began to make its way to the doors, Darleston said, 'Would you excuse me for a moment, Aunt Louisa? I should like to speak to that lady.'

'Of course, Peter,' she replied. 'I shall wait here.'

Darleston made his way forward against the crowd, nodding to acquaintances as he went. The girl in black had not moved from her seat, but seemed to be waiting for the crush to disperse. No one spoke to her, although many curious glances were cast in her direction.

She did not notice Darleston until he sat down beside her and said, 'Good evening, Miss Ffolliot! Did you enjoy the concert?' Several heads turned at once as he identified the mysterious lady.

There came a startled gasp and she swung around towards him. What he could see of the lovely face behind the veil suggested shock and consternation.

Rather surprised, he said, 'I'm sorry. I did not mean to startle you.'

For a split second she hesitated, and then said, 'It is Lord Darleston, is it not?'

He smiled and said, 'Quite correct! Although I am surprised you can see a thing through that veil!'

'But I...' She stopped, appeared to recollect herself, and said with an assumption of lightness, 'Well, my lord, you have lost me my wager!'

'Miss Ffolliot, I most humbly beg your pardon! What wager was that?' he asked in amusement.

'Why, that no one would recognise me like this! I did not think it possible. And indeed I do not think anyone else did know me!' she said, laughing.

Darleston chuckled and said, 'I'm sure they didn't. Certainly my companion Lady Edenhope did not. But I'm afraid that I gave the game away by speaking your name so loudly.'

She shrugged her shoulders and said surprisingly, 'Oh, well, I dare say it does not matter too much now. Did you enjoy the concert?'

'Yes, very much indeed. Especially the last symphony. I had not heard it before.'

'Had you not?' she asked. 'I have once. I think it is my favourite of his works. The last movement—I wish it could go on for ever!'

'That movement is particularly splendid,' he agreed. 'What is it that *you* like about it?'

She thought carefully for a moment and then said, 'It's all the melodies, I think. You know, how he fits them all together, especially at the end in the coda, where they seem to be tumbling over one another. It makes me want to run and jump. It makes me forget...' Again she stopped herself in mid sentence.

'Forget?' he asked curiously. 'What can a child your age wish to forget?'

'Oh, nothing really, my lord,' she answered awkwardly. 'I really should be going now.' She turned to the maid. 'Anna?'

'The crowd is gone, miss. Just his lordship, and a lady seems to be waiting for him,' was the reply.

Darleston was very puzzled by now. Wishing to prolong the encounter, he asked, 'May Lady Edenhope and I escort you home, Miss Ffolliot? I assure you it would be no trouble.'

She shook her head firmly. 'Thank you, my lord, but the carriage will be waiting for me.'

Sensing that she would really prefer to be alone, Darleston did not press her, but said, 'Then I had better return to Lady Edenhope! Goodnight, Miss Ffolliot, it was delightful to run across you again so unexpectedly. Please convey my regards to your parents, and of course to your dog!'

'Oh, Gelert!' She choked on a giggle. 'Not even I would dare try to bring him to a concert! Goodnight, my lord! If I had to lose my wager, I'm glad it was to you!'

'You are very gallant, Miss Ffolliot! Goodnight!' Darleston returned to Lady Edenhope, who was looking distinctly amused.

'Well, you have stirred up the gossips! Was it really Miss Ffolliot?' she asked as they went out into Hanover Square.

Before Darleston could answer, a bluff, hearty voice was heard from a carriage. 'Hello Darleston. Was that Miss Ffolliot? Charming lass! Good for you, boy!'

Darleston blinked into the amiable countenance of old Lord Warboys, who tipped him a knowing wink and continued to his coachman, 'Well, drive on, man! Drive on! Catch me death of cold!' The carriage clattered off, leaving Lord Darleston staring.

Several more encounters of a similar nature served to finish the job begun by Lord Warboys' example of well-meant but tactless jocularity. By the time Darleston had escorted Lady Edenhope back to Half Moon Street he had quite made up his mind to end all the gossip and speculation at least temporarily.

Five days later Lady Caroline Daventry left London for Paris. Three days after that Lord Darleston was reliably reported to be on his way to Dover to catch the next packet. Society shrugged its collective shoulders and forgot all about the momentary excitement raised by Darleston's supposed pursuit of the lovely Miss Ffolliot and invented other gossip for its amusement.

Lord Carrington, returning to town, shook his head at George Carstares and said, 'It will be the same next season! If only the silly fool doesn't take it into his head to marry Caroline Daventry!'

George looked up, shocked, from his copy of the *Gazette*. 'Don't think he's that taken with her, do you?'

Carrington looked cynical and said, 'I'd be prepared to lay odds that's what *she's* after! As for Peter, he seems to think that all women are much the same as each other. In that mood, there's no saying what he might do!'

'Good God!' said George, staring in disbelief at the *Gazette*.

'What's that?' asked Carrington, momentarily diverted.

'Says here that Mr John Ffolliot has been killed in a driving accident!' answered George.

'Lord, that's bad. Young Geoffrey isn't up to much. Doubt he'll make the grade. He'll be running through his inheritance in no time! Hard on Mrs Ffolliot. I believe they were devoted to each other.'

George nodded, 'Sad. Oh, well. Just have to wait and see what happens when Peter comes back. No good us taking a trip to Paris. He'd be furious if he thought we were checking up on him!'

'Can't say I'd blame him,' said Carrington. 'He's two and thirty and ought to be capable of looking after himself, even if he is an ass at times!'

Chapter Three

To the intense concern of Carstares and Carrington, Darleston spent the entire summer and most of the autumn in France. After a lengthy sojourn in Paris, during which he was reported to have danced scandalous attendance on Lady Caroline, he proceeded to attend a series of house parties in various *châteaux*, all of which were notable for the presence of *la belle veuve anglaise*, Lady Caroline Daventry.

At last, towards the end of October, George received a brief note from Darleston Court informing him that its noble owner had returned and would be perfectly happy to entertain the recipient as soon as might be convenient for him. The note ended: 'I have invited Carrington as well and hope you will both make a long stay. Christmas if you like! Sorry to have been such a rotten correspondent. Darleston.'

George breathed a sigh of relief. It seemed his lordship had no immediate plans involving Lady Caroline. He resolved to inform his married sister, with whom he had promised to spend Christmas and New Year, that he would be bringing Darleston. Not for anything would he willingly leave his friend alone at that season. He had as a boy spent a couple of Christmases with Darleston's family and knew that Peter would be more lonely than ever at that time.

Accordingly, he and Carrington drove down to Darleston Court hatching plans to keep Peter out of trouble. All went well, and when Carrington departed six weeks later, to join his mother and sister in Bath, Carstares bore Peter off to spend the holiday with Lord and Lady Fairford and their young family.

It seemed to George that when Peter returned to Darleston Court in late January he had lost much of his bitterness and was far closer to being his old self than would have seemed possible the previous spring.

In early April Darleston House in Grosvenor Square became a hive of activity as it was readied for the arrival of his lordship. Every room was turned out and cleaned as though it were not always kept in readiness for any unexpected visit my lord might choose to make.

Lord Darleston flung himself into the festivities of the season with no hint at all that he was an unwilling participant. The Marriage Mart was honoured with his frequent presence, and he danced assiduously with all the prettiest debutantes, but no one could detect the slightest sign that he was more attracted by one than another. To be honest, he appeared no closer to fixing his interest than last year!

It takes very little, however, to nudge a man into precipitate action. The hand of fate, once dealt, takes no account of rank or wealth but plays its cards with ruthless efficiency. Thus Darleston was sitting idly reading an estate report in his study one afternoon in late May when he was interrupted by his butler.

He looked up. 'Yes, Meadows? What is it?'

The butler coughed apologetically, 'I'm sure I'm sorry to disturb your lordship, but there is An Individual to see your lordship. Quite determined, he is. Says he'll wait in the hall as long as it takes to see you. I hope I know my duty, and I would have had him removed, but he seems terribly worried about something that concerns your lordship and wouldn't trust any of us to give a message! Wouldn't even give his name!'

Darleston looked startled. 'Good heavens! This sounds most melodramatic! Is he a Respectable Individual, Meadows?'

'I should say he was in one of the Trades, my lord. He was, I *will* say, very respectful,' replied Meadows.

'Very well, Meadows. Send this mysterious person in,' instructed Darleston.

He sat back to await his visitor, agog with curiosity.

He had not long to wait before a respectably dressed man of about forty stood before him. 'Good afternoon, Mr...er?'

The man said slowly, 'If your lordship will not be offended I'd be better pleased to leave names out of it for now. I will only say that I am employed by the *Gazette* as an editor. A couple of hours ago one of my boys brought this to me.' He held up a note with a broken seal.

'Go on, then,' said Darleston encouragingly. 'I assure you I am listening.'

'Well, my lord, the lad is very sharp, and he said the lady who delivered it seemed very upset and kept on asking odd questions about how we verified the accuracy of notices and suchlike. Almost as if she wanted to warn the boy! He took the money and gave her a receipt, but then he got worried and brought it in and told me the whole story. So when I read the notice I thought I'd just come along and check with you. Read it for yourself my lord.' He held out the note across the desk.

Darleston opened it and was at once aware of a very familiar scent which clung to it. He read the note and his brows contracted sharply. His visitor blenched as he looked up and asked in freezing accents, 'Did the lad describe the lady?'

'He did, my lord. He said she was quite old, maybe fifty or even sixty. Dressed very plain. Gave him a shilling, which he didn't want to take on account of he didn't think she looked as if she'd have too many shillings, despite being a lady, which he reckoned she was.'

Darleston was silent for a moment, then he said, 'I am much obliged to you and the lad. This notice has not my authority, and I will be further obliged if you will keep it to yourselves that it ever crossed your desk.'

'Begging your pardon, my lord, but there's no question of the lad or myself saying a word to anyone about this!' said the man.

'Good! I am more grateful than ever, and while I realise that you are a man of integrity and did not come with the idea of a reward, I beg that you will accept something. If not for yourself then for the lad.' So saying, Darleston reached into a drawer in his desk and drew out a roll of soft. He peeled off several notes and held them out. 'As I said, you are a fellow of honour. You will divide this fairly between yourself and the lad.'

His visitor flushed as he accepted the money and

said, 'I'll take it for the boy, my lord. Not for myself, thanking you kindly. Well, I'll be going, then. I take it you'll know how best to deal with the matter. I...I wish you luck! No, don't ring that bell. Your butler makes me nervous!'

He departed quickly, leaving the angriest man in London behind him.

Darleston strode over to the fire which was burning in the grate and cast the note into its flames. He watched it burn for a moment and then went back to his desk. 'Thank God for Lucy Jameson!' he said to himself.

He penned a brief note and then rang the bell. When Meadows came in response he handed him the note and spoke abruptly. 'Be so good as to have that delivered to Lady Caroline Daventry immediately. That will be all.'

Meadows took the note and left the room without a word.

Darleston left his mansion in Grosvenor Square shortly after ten o'clock that evening, clad in the satin knee-breeches and swallow-tailed coat which proclaimed his destination was a ball.

A footman, springing to open the door of the waiting town carriage, and being rewarded with a curt nod, wondered what had happened to put the master in such a temper. Generally he was pleasant enough, if rather aloof. This evening, however, the expression on his face was positively forbidding. Roger shut the door carefully. Whatever had put that look on the master's face, he preferred not to be involved.

'Brook Street. We are picking up Mr Carstares at his lodgings,' was the terse order. The carriage rolled away, clattering over the cobbles. Its occupant leaned back against the squabs, prey to bitter thoughts, all of which were directed at the fairer sex. To Lord Darleston, at that moment, the goddess Aphrodite held no charms whatsoever.

He shuddered at the thought of the ball he had promised to attend. Hordes of gauche young girls, all in hopes of catching a husband, all with ambitious mamas eager to make sure they danced with the most eligible bachelors or, as in his case, widowers. Blast them all, he thought furiously. He would stay in the card room drinking brandy!

The carriage drew to a halt in Brook Street unnoticed by him. Then George's cheerful voice said, 'Anyone home? Wake up, Peter, you're away with the clouds!'

He looked up in surprise into the open countenance. 'Oh. Here, am I? Sorry, George. I was thinking.'

'Bad habit that,' said George, getting into the carriage. 'People might notice and then where would you be?' Observing the frown as he looked closely at his friend, George asked, 'What's happened, Peter? Your face is enough to turn the milk!'

Peter was silent for a moment before replying savagely, 'Caroline!'

Momentarily puzzled, George enquired, 'Is she ill?'

'Not in the least! She sent a notice of our engagement to the *Gazette*!' was the sufficiently startling reply.

Speechless with amazed horror, George could only stare at his friend with a dropped jaw. His brain whirled as he contemplated the uproar which would greet the Seventh Earl of Darleston's betrothal to his mistress.

Finally he managed to say, 'Er…do I congratulate you?'

'You do! Fortunately the editor had the good sense to check with me before printing! I was able to stop it being published, thank God.'

'Anyone else know about this?' asked George.

'I hope not! Except for old Miss Jameson, who delivered the notice. From what the editor said she deliberately went out of her way to put them on their guard.'

After some thought, George said, 'Seems to me that if Lady Caroline has told people the notice is going to appear, and it doesn't, she'll look like a fool.'

'Good!'

'Won't like that, Peter.'

'She's not supposed to like it! I sent a discreet note to her house informing her that after a most interesting conversation with an editor of the *Gazette* I would be returning to Darleston Court tomorrow and did not expect to see her again!'

'Oh!' George digested the news that Peter had broken irrevocably with his mistress, then said cautiously, 'Probably a good thing.'

'I'm damned sure it is! Tonight I'm celebrating. Cards, dice and brandy are the order of the evening. Curse all women! The problem is that I have to marry! Caroline knows that, but if she thinks I want a child of hers to succeed me any more than my revolting cousin Jack…!'

George was fully in agreement with this sentiment. So Carrington had been right after all! No doubt she had subtly manoeuvred Peter into spending all those months in France. His retreat to Darleston Court and the Fairfords' for the entire winter, though, must have made her desperate. No doubt she had decided to risk all on this last throw when Darleston had returned to town and begun attending the sort of parties where one met eligible young ladies.

The problem, to George's way of thinking, was Peter's ridiculously low opinion of women generally. Much of this could, of course, be attributed to Melissa's behaviour. Lovely, faithless Melissa, who had run off with another man just as her husband returned, wounded, from Waterloo. Her defection had been no surprise to anyone, least of all Darleston, who had rejoined Wellington's forces as a volunteer in full knowledge of his wife's character. It struck George that Peter had an absolute genius for choosing the wrong woman. First Melissa and now Caroline. Expecting women to be like that, he could pick them unerringly!

Hoping to change the subject, he said casually, 'Had a letter from my sister this morning. In the family way again. Hoping for a girl this time. Says three boys in row is quite enough. She and Fairford want me to visit. Probably wouldn't mind if you came along again. Do you good to get out of London for a while.' He knew that Peter liked and respected Lady Fairford very much. In fact, on reflection, there were plenty of women whom Peter liked and respected but all of them were happily married!

Peter hesitated before answering, 'Thanks, George, I'll hold you to that later. But first I think I'll go to Darleston alone. I need to do some thinking. A terrible habit, as you say, but necessary. I must marry, but I don't want to find myself saddled with a second Melissa!'

'Certainly not,' said George. Then, 'Don't any of

the debutantes interest you? You certainly interest them!'

Peter laughed cynically. 'Not really. They all admire my wealth and my title and most of 'em are absolutely tongue-tied when I dance with them. That or disgustingly arch!'

George thought about that for a moment. 'Well, if you take my advice you'll marry the first eligible girl you meet with whom you can hold a rational conversation!'

Peter chuckled. 'I did meet one, now I come to think of it. Last year it was. Young Ffolliot's sister. Can't think of the girl's name now. Something beginning with a P anyway. But I haven't seen her this year.'

'Believe their father died suddenly last year. Driving accident. Carrington and I saw it in the paper,' said George thoughtfully. 'They'd still be in mourning.'

'But young Ffolliot has been on the town just as usual!' said Peter, very much surprised. 'He's not in mourning, surely!'

'Ffolliot wouldn't!' said George in disgust. 'Young waster! Carrington said something about it at the time. He'll be running through his fortune before long if he doesn't settle down.'

Their arrival at Lady Bellingham's ball put an end to the conversation as they stepped out of the carriage to join the crush of people flocking up the steps.

Lord Darleston's behaviour that evening was described by some as disgraceful and by others as exemplary. The first camp was almost entirely composed of young ladies and their ambitious mamas, all of whom were disappointed that such an eligible *parti* should elect to spend the entire evening in the card room, dicing while consuming untold quantities of brandy. The gentlemen in the card room, however, were of the opinion that under the circumstances Darleston's forbearance was remarkable. Admittedly he was badly foxed, not vulgarly drunk, as young Ffolliot was, for example, but on the whole he carried his drink very well.

The evening was a successful one for Darleston. He had begun with piquet, playing with George Carstares for chicken stakes. His lordship made it a rule never to play for high stakes with relatives, and had extended this taboo to include his best friend. After a couple of rubbers, in which the run of cards was fairly evenly divided, Darleston suggested they should give up trying to fleece each other.

'Had enough, George? Maybe we should try our luck with the rest of the world?'

'Not on my account, Peter. I can afford losing to you!' answered George cheerfully, hoping he would be able to check his friend.

'My dear George, may I recommend that you go to the devil?' asked Peter in amusement. 'Do you imagine I am so drunk I can't see through your appallingly clumsy efforts to keep me out of mischief. Believe me, I have no intention of adding to my problems by dissipating my fortune! Only myself!' He had been drinking steadily, but his speech was in no way impaired. Only the odd glitter in his eye betrayed the state of his temper. To any not intimately acquainted with him he appeared amiability itself.

George, having tried to hold him in as tactfully as possible, bowed to the inevitable and grinned at his friend's recommendation, merely saying, 'You'll have the devil of a head in the morning! I'm going back to the ballroom. You never know. I might meet the girl of my dreams on the dance floor!'

'More likely meet a sticky end!' said his lordship sardonically, raising his glass in salute.

He watched George depart and then turned back to the room in search of amusement. Someone tapped his shoulder. 'Hello, Manders,' he said, recognising a comrade from Peninsular days. 'Rubber of piquet?'

His friend demurred without hesitation. 'Not with you, Darleston! Even when you're foxed, you play out of my league. Wouldn't even be entertaining for you! But I don't mind taking you on at dice.'

'Whatever you please, old boy, but first I think I'll find some more brandy!' said his lordship agreeably. He caught at a passing footman. 'Do you think you could find me a bottle of brandy? You could? Splendid!'

He turned back to his companion. 'There we are! What more could we ask for?'

Manders grinned. 'Well, a couple more people to liven up our game, do you think? Here's your cousin Frobisher with a friend. Shall we ask them?'

In point of fact the last person in the world that Darleston would have chosen to dice with was his cousin Jack Frobisher, but he responded politely.

'Dear boy, whatever you wish.' He beckoned to Frobisher, saying, 'Good evening, Cousin. Manders and I are going to have a little game of dice. Do you and your friend care to join us?' He looked closely at the young man accompanying Frobisher. The youth was vaguely familiar, lank sandy hair, a chin which the charitable might have described as weak but was in reality non-existent. Darleston searched his memory. Young Ffolliot, that was it.

Unable to detect any hint that the young man was in mourning, he asked curiously, 'Heard you'd lost your father a while back, Ffolliot, but I suppose it's only a rumour?'

'Oh, Lord, no. It's true enough. Couldn't see much point in going into all that business of mourning when the whole world knows we didn't get on!' was the unconcerned answer.

Darleston was taken aback. Such casual disregard for a parent's death was nothing less than shocking. He cast his mind back. He had been only slightly acquainted with John Ffolliot, but his memory was of a kindly man with a well-developed sense of humour. Hardly the man to engender dislike in his offspring! In fact he recalled that the last time he'd seen the elder Mr Ffolliot he had been driving his daughter in Hyde Park.

That was right! It all came back now! He'd danced with the chit at Almack's and then spoken to her in the park. Met her at a concert too. Red hair, well, auburn anyway, and dreamy grey eyes. That was the girl! It occurred to him that there had appeared to be no lack of affection between father and daughter.

In a tone that was little less than a rebuke he said, 'Then perhaps you would be so good as to convey my condolences to your sister, Mr Ffolliot? I am sure from what I have seen of her that she held her father in considerable affection *and* respect. Now, shall we play dice? I have my own set here.'

Ffolliot turned red with anger, but a nudge from Frobisher recalled him to his senses, so he sat down at the table with the other three. Darleston raised his eyebrows slightly, but held his tongue. He produced his dice and the game began.

At first the luck all went Frobisher's way. A pile of guineas grew steadily in front of him, to the annoyance of his friend Ffolliot, who grumbled continuously. Eventually, tired of the incessant whining, Darleston said lazily, 'Mr Ffolliot would appear to resent your luck, Cousin. Surely not the part of a good friend!'

'Perhaps not,' was the unconcerned reply. 'However, the game does begin to lose savour. Might I be excused, gentlemen?' Frobisher rose to his feet, bowed gracefully and departed with his winnings.

As the game continued between the three remaining players Lady Luck chose to turn her face to Mr Ffolliot. Emboldened by this, and the amount of champagne he had consumed, he recklessly raised the stakes.

'Double each throw, gentlemen?' he challenged.

Darleston nodded imperturbably, but Manders said bluntly, 'Too high, Ffolliot. Don't be a fool! Luck won't stay with you all night. Especially if you can't afford it! I'm out!' He rose to his feet. 'Excuse me, Darleston, I'll see you later.'

Darleston smiled up at him, saying amiably, 'Thanks for the game, Manders. You must dine with me soon. I feel sure our tastes have much in common!'

He tossed back his glass of brandy, refilled it, and said to Mr Ffolliot, 'Fifty a throw, wasn't it?' The game proceeded, but Lady Luck, possibly affronted by Mr Ffolliot's behaviour, began to favour Darleston. That pile of guineas slowly made its way across the table. Finally they were all in front of Darleston.

'Do you wish to continue, Mr Ffolliot?' he asked politely.

'Yes! Damn you! Double the stakes!' slurred Ffolliot. The luck had to change! He glared at his opponent defiantly.

Darleston looked at him carefully. It was not in his nature to refuse a challenge, but it went against the grain to win money from a drunken youth who most certainly could not afford it. Wryly he admitted to himself that he had certainly provoked Ffolliot earlier. His code of honour dictated that it was time to call a halt.

The words were on the tip of his tongue when Ffolliot said loudly, 'I don't like your dice, Darleston!' A dead silence came over the room. People turned to stare in disbelief. To accuse Darleston of cheating was unthinkable! His courage, honour and pride were a matter of public record. George Carstares, who had just come back into the room with Lord Carrington, stopped dead in his tracks, fully expecting Darleston to call Ffolliot out.

Darleston, however, managed to hold his temper in check. His eyes blazed, but he leaned back in his chair and asked softly, 'Do you not, indeed, Mr Ffolliot? And what would you like to do about it? We can of course break the dice. But then of course you will owe me a new set.' Almost as an afterthought he added, 'And…er…satisfaction as well. Your choice, Mr Ffolliot! Or perhaps you have a set of dice we can use, and break at the end of the game, of course!'

Ffolliot's eyes fell. 'I…don't have a set with me… I…I must have been mistaken!' he stammered.

'Then shall we continue?' asked Darleston sweetly. The other occupants of the room lost interest, but George Carstares, watching closely with Lord Carrington, breathed a huge sigh of relief. He had no fears for Darleston's safety in a duel with Ffolliot, however, the law was strict about these little affairs.

'Damn it, George,' muttered Carrington. 'Can't this be stopped somehow? Ffolliot can't afford to lose. He's a blasted little squirt, I agree, but his sisters and stepmother have enough problems without Peter ruining him and calling him out!'

George shook his head. 'He'd tell us to go to the devil! Already done that once this evening! At least he accepted the boy's apology. No one can do anything with Peter in this mood!'

The game continued and Ffolliot's losses mounted steadily. His face became sickly as his vowels grew in number. From time to time he made a little headway, but this was always short-lived. Darleston threw a ten, those mocking eyes daring his opponent to call a halt to the game. Ffolliot's hand trembled so that his throw was clumsy and the dice fell to the floor. He bent to retrieve them, fumbling a little. Slightly flushed, he straightened up. 'I beg your pardon, Lord Darleston!'

Darleston nodded for him to throw again. He threw a twelve and shot a triumphant glare at the Earl.

Carstares and Carrington exchanged startled glances. 'Did you see what…?' began George.

'Let's wait and be sure,' murmured Carrington, placing a restraining hand on his companion's arm. They continued to watch the game carefully.

Now the game began to run in Ffolliot's direction. Lady Luck, it would seem, had relented towards Mr Ffolliot. Carstares and Lord Carrington drifted over to the table. Laying his hand on Ffolliot's arm, the latter said coldly, 'Mr Ffolliot, did I not hear you inform

Lord Darleston that you had no dice with you when he offered to let you change the dice?'

'That's right,' said Ffolliot, shrugging off the hand. 'What of it Carrington? I'm happy enough with the dice now! All a misunderstanding, eh, Darleston?'

Darleston looked in annoyance at George and Carrington, but what he saw in their faces made him hold his tongue. Again the whole room was focused on that small table.

Carrington was speaking again, 'I have little doubt that you are only too happy with these dice, since they came out of your pocket! Strange how the luck turned so quickly after you retrieved the dice from the floor, wouldn't you say? Carstares and I saw you make the exchange! Shall we break them for you?'

Ffolliot grabbed the dice. He was shaking, but tried to bluster. 'How…how dare you? I…I don't care for your tone, Carrington. Darleston has made no complaint!'

An expectant silence had pervaded the whole room. The assembled company looked with scorn at Ffolliot and with great interest at Darleston for his reaction.

His blazing eyes seemed to burn holes in Ffolliot's face, but his voice was as urbane as ever. 'I think this concludes our little game, Mr Ffolliot. You will hear from me in the next day or so to arrange the terms of payment for your debt.'

The host, Lord Bellingham, came forward to say icily, 'I am afraid I must ask you to leave, Mr Ffolliot, unless you are prepared to have those dice broken!' He waited a moment, but Ffolliot did not respond. Still clutching his dice, he stood up unsteadily and walked to the door. Men turned aside from him, disgusted.

Bellingham gestured to a footman. 'See that he leaves!'

Darleston rose to his feet, saying calmly, 'How very unpleasant. Ah, Bellingham! I do beg your pardon for this little contretemps! I shall also take my leave. Please accept my apologies.'

'Nonsense, Darleston, no need for you to leave!' said Bellingham. 'I'm sure Carstares or Carrington will join us for a game of cards! Why leave just because of that infernal little mountebank?'

Darleston resumed his seat, saying obligingly, 'Of course, Bellingham.'

When Darleston reached Grosvenor Square again it was four in the morning. He let himself into the house and found a candle burning on a small table. He picked it up and went upstairs to his bed-chamber where he proceeded to undress himself. Despite the acid comments of Fordham on the subject, Darleston insisted that he was perfectly capable of putting himself to bed at night.

The evening's events had done little to alleviate his temper, and the comment dropped by Carrington on the way home, that he very much doubted Ffolliot's ability to meet the debt he had contracted, had infuriated him. If it hadn't been for the loaded dice Darleston would have quietly cancelled the debt. Unfortunately the public exposure of Ffolliot's dishonesty made that impossible.

Ffolliot's suggestion that he himself had been using loaded dice also continued to rankle. Well, if Ffolliot couldn't pay the debt in one way, he should pay it in another! At this point the problem of Lady Caroline drifted back into his brandy-fogged mind. 'Blast

Caroline!' he said aloud. 'The only way to be safe from her is to marry someone else. But who?'

He pulled the nightshirt laid out for him over his head. What had George said? Marry the first eligible girl who can hold a rational conversation! Well, that was Ffolliot's sister! Damn! what was her name? Might have been Phoebe, but he couldn't really remember. It occurred to him that she would be made devilishly uncomfortable over the night's doings. That bothered him, he had been oddly attracted to her. Usually young girls bored him, but she had a spark of humour that appealed to him. Not on the occasion he'd danced with her at Almack's, to be sure, but in the park and at the concert she'd seemed a different creature entirely. And she had that unusual dog.

He was about to get into bed when the idea struck him. To his somewhat tipsy logic it seemed perfectly reasonable, although an irritatingly sober voice warned him not to do anything rash. Impatiently he thrust the warning voice aside to consider his idea. Then he pulled on a dressing gown, sat down at the writing desk in the corner and penned a brief letter. He read it through owlishly, nodded, and sealed it. That would take the trick! he thought triumphantly. Must get it off immediately!

A little unsteady on his feet now, he went back downstairs to leave the letter on the hall table for the post.

A glow of satisfaction pervaded his being as he returned to bed, convinced he had solved all his problems in the most sensible way imaginable. The idea seemed so neat and logical that he could not for the life of him think of a single objection to it: a circumstance which must be ascribed in great part to the quantity of brandy he had consumed.

Never, even when sober, prone to worry about a decision once it was made, Lord Darleston drifted off to sleep. His only concern was the devilish head with which he was bound to be afflicted when he awoke.

Chapter Four

Clad in sober grey muslin, Miss Ffolliot and Miss
Phoebe Ffolliot stepped off the terrace and moved
through the shrubbery towards the rose garden accompanied by a large Irish wolfhound. A basket hanging
from Miss Ffolliot's arm suggested that the pair were
engaged upon an expedition to gather flowers. The
scent of roses hung heavily in the early-morning air
and the cloudless sky gave promise of a lovely day.

Miss Phoebe took a deep breath, remarking, 'This
is the best part of the day. No one else about, just us
and the sun.'

Miss Ffolliot looked amused as she answered,
'Surely Mr Winton would improve the morning?
You'd scarcely notice if the sun disappeared, let alone
Gelert and I!'

Phoebe blushed, but said with spirit, 'You know
perfectly well what I mean, Penny. Gathering the flowers for Mama with you gives us a chance to be private,
and talk.'

'About Mr Winton?' asked Penelope, with a faint
smile.

'Oh, Penny, he's so wonderful!' said Phoebe, giving

up all attempt at dignity. 'I wonder why he is coming to see Mama…do you think he might possibly make an offer?'

'Not being in Richard's confidence, I can't say,' answered Penelope. 'But it does seem likely. Even Mama seems to think so, and certainly the fact that he went to town for the season last year, danced with you everywhere, took you driving, sent you flowers and came home when we did because of…of…Papa, and has danced attendance on you ever since, suggests that he takes an interest in you!' She gave her twin an affectionate hug.

This reference to the death of Mr Ffolliot put an end to conversation for several moments, and the twins gathered roses in silence. Phoebe selected the best blooms, cutting them carefully to place in her sister's basket. Penelope broke the silence, saying, 'I'm sure he would have spoken sooner but thought it would be in bad taste. As it is you will have to wait until we are out of mourning to be married. But that's only a month now,'

'Geoffrey doesn't let that stop him from enjoying life!' said Phoebe in disgust.

'Just because Geoffrey chooses to behave badly and gamble in every hell in town is all the more reason to act with some propriety,' said Penelope. 'Mama is very worried. She has no control over Geoffrey, even Papa didn't have much, and now he is without any restraint.'

'I wish he would come home,' said Phoebe. 'I mean, I don't, because he is always perfectly horrid, but we should at least know what he was up to.'

Penelope didn't answer immediately, but presently, after several more roses had been placed in the basket, she said reluctantly, 'Geoffrey is home. He arrived about four o'clock this morning.'

Phoebe stared at her sister. 'Are you sure? Does Mama know?'

'I'm quite sure,' said Penelope dryly. 'He made such a devilish noise coming up to bed that I woke up and heard the hall clock chime. He was not entirely sober and his language was most edifying. I'm surprised that you didn't wake up. As for Mama, Tinson knows that Geoffrey is home, and by now I am sure he will have informed Mama of the delightful treat in store for her.'

'Oh, dear,' said Phoebe. 'Poor Mama! Is it very dreadful, do you think, that we should be so uncaring about our half-brother?'

'No,' replied Penelope decisively. 'Geoffrey is an odious little beast, and considering the way he treats our mother it would be wonderful if we *did* like him!'

Phoebe was obliged to acknowledge the justice of this comment. Not only was Geoffrey appallingly rude to his stepmother, but he made it abundantly clear that he resented the existence of his three half-sisters, particularly Penelope, who frequently told him exactly what she thought of him with scant regard for her mother's remonstrances or Geoffrey's blustering threats. Phoebe glanced sadly at Penelope. It was hard to believe that the girl who moved so confidently beside her, one hand resting lightly on the dog's collar, was practically blind.

A serious accident four years earlier had left Penelope unable to do more than distinguish light and dark very faintly and perceive movement. Though perfectly confident in familiar surroundings, she had refused utterly to enter into last Season's festivities, declaring that she preferred to hear about them from Phoebe rather than have the strain of dealing with strangers and strange places. She had accompanied her parents and Phoebe to London but had remained mostly at home, so that few people even realised that Phoebe had a twin. From time to time she had attended concerts with a maid, but always veiled to avoid recognition.

By the time the roses were gathered it was nearly breakfast-time, so the young ladies turned their steps towards the house. They were met at the side-door by Tinson, the elderly butler. 'Shall I take the basket, Miss Penny?' he asked.

'Yes, please, Tinson, we'll arrange them after breakfast. Is Mama down?' asked Penelope.

'Mrs Ffolliot is in the breakfast parlour with Miss Sarah. She was wondering where you were, but I informed her that I thought you were in the rose garden and would be in shortly.'

'Thank you, Tinson. We will join them at once. I assume Mr Geoffrey is still abed?' said Penelope.

The butler's voice was impassive as he answered, 'Mr Geoffrey has not stirred since he went to bed and he did not express a desire to be wakened for breakfast.'

'Good!' said the twins in unison. They burst out laughing at their impropriety and Phoebe pulled Penelope's hand through her arm as they moved towards the breakfast parlour.

Mrs Ffolliot looked up, smiling, as her elder daughters entered the room. She deeply regretted that Penelope had refused point-blank to make her debut or even meet many people. Phoebe had been very successful, and Mrs Ffolliot knew that Penelope's lively personality would have been more than sufficient to overcome any disadvantage caused by her blindness. There was nothing to choose between the girls in terms of looks. Indeed, until Penelope's accident she herself had often not been able to tell them apart. They had the same curling dark red hair and grey eyes, were of identical height and figure and possessed the same charming countenance. But now, despite her usual gaiety, there was occasionally a withdrawn, shut-in look to Penelope's face, and if that had not been enough to distinguish the pair she was accompanied everywhere by the huge hound, Gelert, who acted as a self-appointed guide for his young mistress.

'Good morning, Mama; good morning, Sarah,' said the twins.

'Good morning, dears. Were there plenty of roses? We must have a good display in the drawing room for our guest, don't you think, Phoebe?' asked Mrs Ffolliot with a faint smile.

Phoebe blushed and Penelope chuckled. 'That's too bad of you, Mama. I've already made her blush and now you're doing it.'

Phoebe laughed at her twin as she sat down. 'Penny, how do you always know?'

'I told you, I can feel it. The room temperature just rose several degrees!' answered Penelope as Gelert guided her to an empty chair beside thirteen-year-old Sarah. 'Is there anything left, or did Sarah eat the lot?'

Sarah giggled at this reference to her notorious appetite and said, 'There's plenty. Shall I butter a scone for you?'

'Yes, please, love. I'm nearly as hungry as you!'

'Two scones for now, then, Sarah,' teased Phoebe. 'And I'll ring for Tinson to fetch another dozen!'

Breakfast passed merrily, without mention of Geoffrey or any other unpleasantness. The twins were perfectly aware that Mrs Ffolliot did not wish to discuss the situation in front of Sarah. They lingered over the teacups until it was time for Sarah to depart to the drawing room to practise the pianoforte.

When she had left Mrs Ffolliot sighed and said, 'Your brother is home again, Tinson informs me. I believe he arrived late last night, or rather early this morning. There is bound to be some unpleasantness, but he may not stay long and at least he does not have anyone with him this time.'

On his previous visit Geoffrey's friend Mr Frobisher had accompanied him. Mrs Ffolliot had considered that the young man's conversation was most unsuitable for the chaste ears of her daughters. She was also aware that he led her stepson into every low gambling hell in London.

Penelope had never revealed to anyone that he had attempted to take unwelcome liberties with her person, and had received a slap in the face in addition to being well bitten by Gelert. The incident was one she preferred to forget.

'It is a pity that he should come just now, but I dare say he will sleep until past noon, and anyway, Richard Winton is so well-acquainted with us that he will not be overly concerned. Phoebe, dear, a note came over this morning to tell me why he is visiting us today. He has made an offer for you, and begs my permission to pay his addresses to you. He is most generous and offers to house Sarah, Penny and myself if, as he puts it, our present situation should become untenable. You have only to consider your answer, my dearest.'

Phoebe stared at her as if unable to believe what

she heard. Her grey eyes filled with tears and she hugged her mother in joy.

Penelope contemplated her sister's future with real delight. Richard Winton was a close friend of the family, well-born and possessed of an easy fortune coupled with a good estate ten miles distant. He was passably good-looking, kindly, and he had been, in Penelope's opinion at least, in love with Phoebe for the last two years. He was one of the few people who had never had the slightest difficulty in telling the twins apart. For this reason alone Penelope had been disposed to favour his suit. As she had said once in a moment of candour to her mother, 'The idea of marrying a man who thinks you are your sister is not to be borne!' Absently she stroked Gelert's rough head, then rose to hug her sister. 'Oh, Phoebe, you'll be so happy together, and it's quite close so we shall see lots of both of you!'

'They might like to be alone!' laughed Mrs Ffolliot.

Phoebe protested indignantly, 'Of course we'll want you, Mama. Why, his letter says so!'

'Nevertheless, my love, I think we will give you time to become used to being Mrs Winton before we descend upon you for good. Now go and dry your face. You must arrange the flowers before he arrives,' answered Mrs Ffolliot.

Phoebe departed singing, but Penelope remained behind. 'Mama, do you have any idea why Geoffrey is home?' she asked.

'No, my dear. Why do you ask? I take it that you heard the noise? Tinson merely informed me that he was home. I gathered, from what Tinson *didn't* say, that Geoffrey was not at all sober when he arrived, but that is not unusual,' answered her mother.

Penelope was silent for a moment, and then said, 'I did wake up. Phoebe and Sarah didn't, so I...I...I went out into the corridor when I heard his door shut. Mama, something is really wrong. He was raving about Lord Darleston and...and some debt. He said, ''He'll take the lot, damn his eyes!'' Mama, do you suppose he has lost a terrible amount of money?'

Mrs Ffolliot went white, but managed to say calmly, 'We must suppose he has lost some money. Perhaps a great deal. You have not said anything to Phoebe?' Penelope shook her head. 'Good. Let us not spoil this day for her. Richard will be here in an hour or two, so we must put this out of our minds for now.'

'Yes, Mama, but what do you know of Lord Darleston? I met him once with Papa when we were driving, you know. He seemed...well, not the man to be found in the sort of hells we know Geoffrey frequents. Not at all like his odious cousin,' said Penelope, repressing a shudder with difficulty.

'When did you meet Lord Darleston?' asked her mother. 'Your father never mentioned it,'

'Oh, Lord Darleston thought I was Phoebe, and Papa didn't correct him because I kicked him under the driving rug. I think he had stood up with Phoebe at Almack's. Yes that's right, because I asked Phoebe about him and she said he was the most handsome man she had ever seen. That was before she fell in love with Richard, of course.' This observation was delivered with an absolutely straight face.

'Penny!' exclaimed Mrs Ffolliot, trying unsuccessfully not to laugh.

'Anyway, I thought his lordship was charming, and he admired Gelert! I suppose Papa didn't tell you because he knew you'd be cross with us for deceiving an Earl, so I warned Phoebe and that was that! Except that I met him again at a concert,' finished Penelope.

Despite herself, Mrs Ffolliot smiled. Genuine admiration of Gelert was a sure road to Penelope's liking. 'His lordship is very charming, and I would have been extremely cross with the pair of you for imposing on him like that!' said Mrs Ffolliot. 'I know very little of him except what the world knows, which is that he is a hero of Waterloo, that his first wife ran off with another man and that he has avoided marriageable women ever since. I remember his standing up with Phoebe; it was most unlike him. Someone told me later that he is considering remarriage because of the succession. And considering that his heir is that odious Jack Frobisher, one cannot wonder at his decision!'

Penelope laughed. 'Why, Mama, you are a positive fund of information. I must go and confer with Sarah on a suitable gift for the bride. Come along, Gelert.'

The pair left the room together, leaving Mrs Ffolliot alone to worry about the shortcomings and possible— or probable, as she admitted to herself—gambling debts of her stepson. She thought on reflection that it was entirely likely that Geoffrey had lost a great deal of money, and she wondered how, if that were the case, it was to be paid.

They were not wealthy. Phoebe's season had been paid for with money left by the twins' godmother specifically for that purpose. Penelope had insisted that her share be put aside for Sarah. Mrs Ffolliot and her husband had acquiesced because, despite her raillery and outward laughter, it was evident that the thought of braving a critical world she could not see frightened Penelope.

Mrs Ffolliot sighed, wondering if they had been

right in allowing Penelope to shut herself away. It would appear from what the child had said that she had met and liked at least one total stranger. This was encouraging, even if the pleasure had in part stemmed from a deplorable sense of mischief on the part of her daughter and, she had to admit, on the part of her husband. John Ffolliot would have enjoyed the joke as much as his eldest daughter. He would have been most unlikely to tell his wife of the meeting. Not from any fear of censure, but to spare her embarrassment when next she met Lord Darleston.

Casting her eye around the cosy breakfast parlour, Mrs Ffolliot wondered how much Geoffrey had lost this time. Last month it had been ten thousand pounds. She knew the estate would not be able to weather many such blows. Already their circumstances were uncomfortably straitened, and she thanked God that at least Phoebe was now provided for. Sarah was bidding fair to rival her elder sisters' beauty, and Phoebe could be counted upon to find a husband for her when the time came. It was only Penelope whose future exercised her mind. Perhaps if she stayed with Phoebe and Richard for a while, to meet people, it would rid her of this absurd notion that she was unfit to marry. After all, the blindness was the result of an accident, not something that she could pass on to a child!

A discreet knock at the door disturbed her thoughts. 'Come in,' she called.

Tinson entered. 'Excuse me, madam, but Mr Winton has called to see you. He is in the morning room.'

'To see *me*, Tinson, are you sure?' she responded.

'Mr Winton thought he should see you *before* he

sees Miss Phoebe,' said Tinson, with the ghost of a twinkle in his eye.

Mary Ffolliot burst out laughing. 'Oh, Tinson, where should we be without you? I shall come at once. Please tell Miss Phoebe that if she waits in the rose garden I shall send Mr Winton to her there. And you might tell Miss Penny to keep Miss Sarah occupied!'

'Certainly, madam, but as to Miss Sarah, she is still in the drawing room, helping Miss Penny to learn a new piece of music,' answered Tinson.

Richard Winton rose to his feet as Mrs Ffolliot entered the morning room and held out her hand to him. He bowed over it. 'Dear Richard, I received your letter. Need I tell you how happy this makes me?'

'Mrs Ffolliot, I can only say that I hope I shall be worthy of your good opinion and that Phoebe's father would have approved,' he answered. 'Perhaps even more importantly, does Penelope approve?'

'Of course she does!' answered Mrs Ffolliot. 'Apart from Tinson and their father, you are the only man who never had the slightest trouble telling them apart.'

Richard roared with delighted laughter. 'God help the man who takes her to wife. He'll never know a minute's peace!'

Noting the sudden sadness in his hostess's face, he said, 'I beg your pardon, that was clumsy. Does Penelope still favour the life of a recluse? Phoebe told me about it once. Perhaps once she and I are married Penelope can come to stay and meet new people. That might help her to gain confidence in herself.'

Despite the fact that her mind had been running along these lines, Mrs Ffolliot was taken aback. 'Richard, you are probably one of the kindest men alive. If anyone can help Penny it will be you and Phoebe. I am not quite close enough to Penny, dearly though I love her. The bond between those two is very strong and I think that Phoebe's marriage to you will give her the insight to help Penny. Now, Phoebe is in the rose garden and must be wearing away the turf, so you had better go to her, and we shall expect both of you for a nuncheon!'

The rest of the day passed very happily. Richard stayed until the late afternoon, finally taking his leave most reluctantly to receive his sister who was coming to stay. He and Phoebe were to marry as soon as she was out of mourning for her father. 'I wish it could be sooner, sweetheart,' he whispered as he kissed her goodbye in the hall. 'But society is terribly fussy about these things, even though your father is probably very annoyed at our sense of propriety!'

Phoebe floated back to the drawing room, to be brought down to earth by the presence of her half-brother. Never a prepossessing sight, Geoffrey, suffering the after-effects of the previous night, looked particularly repellent, in addition to which he reeked of brandy. Unshaven, with lank sandy hair and bloodshot eyes, he did not compare well with the just departed Mr Winton who, in addition to being impeccably turned out, had the advantage of a good pair of shoulders as well as a chin. Penelope had once said disgustedly that her brother reminded her of a mangy weasel, scrawny and slippery.

It appeared that Penelope had been voicing her opinion of his person in no uncertain terms, to judge from what he was saying. 'A fellow can have a drink in his own house, I hope, without being nagged by his sister! Damn it all, I need a drink with you about and after all I've been through! Anyway, don't preach to me about your mother's drawing room, it won't be hers for very much longer. It'll all belong to Darleston, blast his eyes!'

A stunned silence followed this announcement. 'Sarah, please go upstairs at once,' requested Mrs Ffolliot.

'Don't be silly Mama, she'll have to know soon enough,' said Penelope. 'Would you care to explain yourself, Brother?'

'Mind your own business, girl!'

'It is my business! How much did you lose this time?' she asked fiercely. Gelert growled menacingly in response to her mood, but Penelope gripped his collar firmly.

'Keep him off!' shrieked Geoffrey in panic. 'I saw what he did to Frobisher's arm!'

'How much Geoffrey? Or shall I let him go?'

'Penny!' gasped her mother.

'Thirty thousand pounds, and he wants it immediately!' answered Geoffrey as he rushed from the room.

Mrs Ffolliot and her daughters were too horrified even to gasp. The silence was eventually broken by Sarah.

'It sounds like an awful lot of money for an evening's fun, doesn't it?'

There was not really much more to be said.

Penelope awoke early the next morning after a restless night. Phoebe had cried herself to sleep but Sarah was too young to be alive to the full consequences of the affair. Penelope knew that her father would have been mortified at Geoffrey contracting a debt he could not meet and she herself writhed with shame. Darleston of all people!

She thought back to those brief meetings. He had certainly mistaken her for Phoebe the first time, for he had thanked her for the dance and asked how she was enjoying the season. At their second meeting they had merely spoken of the Mozart symphony they had just heard. The hint of humour in his deep, husky voice had appealed to her at once. Phoebe's description of him as tall, dark and excessively handsome had not told her nearly as much as that attractive voice.

The fact that he had been the only person to recognise her behind the veil had also made a deep impression on her. A man who could spot a near stranger like that was obviously very perceptive and observant.

Resolutely Penelope thrust that train of thought from her mind, forcing herself to concentrate on the current situation. How was Darleston to be paid? The estate could not bear a debt like that. Everything would have to be sold to pay it! Even then she doubted that the whole sum could be raised. Her musings continued fruitlessly until Phoebe awoke, but for the life of her she could think of no honourable way out of the tangle.

The three girls went down to breakfast in a subdued frame of mind. Even Sarah had realised from her elder sisters' attitude that the situation was disastrous.

They found their mother looking pale and worn. 'Good morning, dears,' she said, trying unsuccessfully to be normal. Her voice sounded tired.

Penelope frowned and said, 'The devil take Geoffrey! Mama, did you sleep at all last night?'

'Hush, Penny, you mustn't speak like that,' remonstrated Mrs Ffolliot gently.

'Did you?' pressed Penelope, ignoring the rebuke.

'Not very much!' admitted her mother.

'Well, Geoffrey won't be at breakfast anyway!' said Sarah, seating herself. 'At least, it would be unusual if he did come down this early!'

'What are we to do, Mama?' asked Phoebe in fearful tones.

Her mother smiled slightly, and answered, 'You at least needn't worry too much! Richard is to look after you!'

Phoebe's indignation spurred her into unaccustomed vehemence. 'Mama, how could you possibly think I would not be concerned about the three of you? Besides, if you are to be thrown out to starve I shall refuse Richard's offer and go with you.'

A burst of laughter from her twin greeted this announcement. 'Oh, for heaven's sake, Phoebe! I don't often hanker after my eyesight, but what wouldn't I give to see Richard's face when you told him! You pea-goose! He'd drag you to the altar before you could draw breath! And what's more, we'd help him!'

Phoebe had the grace to look a little sheepish. 'Was I being silly?'

'Very silly, love!' said her twin emphatically. 'What good would it be for you to starve with us when we are depending on you for the occasional charitable hand-out?'

'I trust it won't be quite as bad as that!' intervened Mrs Ffolliot. 'May I suggest that we leave this unpleasant discussion for now and eat our breakfast?'

The girls dropped the subject immediately, not wishing to upset their mother any further. Their chatter about the weather, music and whether or not Sarah should be permitted to read *The Mysteries of Udolpho* might not have been exactly cheerful, but at least it avoided the topic of Geoffrey and his disgrace.

After breakfast Sarah was sent off to the drawing room for her usual hour's practice and the twins and Mrs Ffolliot repaired to the Morning Room. They went over the situation carefully and decided that it would be possible for Mrs Ffolliot, Penelope and Sarah to manage in a small house, or cottage even. Mrs Ffolliot's jointure was not large but it would be enough.

These plans were thrown into complete disarray by the arrival of Richard Winton in a towering fury. He announced himself and told them without any round-aboutation that he knew the whole story, his sister having just come from London where it was the talk of the town.

'Elizabeth had heard something of the affair in town. She mentioned it to me when she arrived last night,' he said. 'Carrington and George Carstares caught Geoffrey switching the dice on Darleston and denounced him publicly. Unfortunately it was at Lady Bellingham's ball. Created the devil of a row, apparently. I'm afraid Geoffrey had already had to apologise for accusing Darleston of using loaded dice.'

'Dear God,' said Mrs Ffolliot faintly. 'I am afraid the debt will have to be met if Darleston insists.'

'I could see Darleston,' offered Richard. 'He might drop his claim if he knew that the position for you and the girls would be so disastrous. I don't know him well, but he is a decent enough fellow.'

'On no account! The debt will have to be paid, at least in part,' snapped Mrs Ffolliot. Phoebe and Penelope nodded in agreement.

'Besides,' said Penelope, 'if we get him out of it

this time, how long do you think it would be before it happened again? And most likely to someone who wouldn't care in the slightest. In fact I wouldn't put it past Geoffrey to trade on it!'

'True,' agreed Richard reluctantly. 'But how many gentleman would play with him, do you think?'

'None, I should hope!' answered Penelope, 'What about money-lenders, though? The estate will not bear what Geoffrey wants to spend. It is only a matter of time before he goes down that path.'

Her auditors looked shocked but did not bother to contradict her. They knew that what she said was all too true.

A knock at the door heralded the arrival of Tinson. 'The post, madam. And Mr Geoffrey is up.' This last rather apologetically.

Silence greeted the announcement, to be broken by Penelope. 'Never mind, Tinson, we know you couldn't help it!'

Despite the seriousness of the situation Phoebe could not repress a giggle, and even Tinson's well-trained mouth twitched. His voice gave no hint of this, however. 'Certainly not, Miss Penny.' He left the room with a dignified gait.

'Really Penny—' began Mrs Ffolliot, only to be interrupted by Richard.

'Anyway, there's only one thing to be done, Mrs Ffolliot. You and the girls are coming to live with Phoebe and myself. I'm damned if I'll have my wife's sisters and mother thrown into penury!'

'Oh, yes!' agreed Phoebe enthusiastically. 'How good of you, Richard!' She looked up at him with melting gratitude and adoration.

'Richard, you can't possibly want all of us foisted

onto you!' said Mrs Ffolliot. 'My jointure will be enough to support the three of us in a small establishment. We shall have to be careful, but no doubt we will manage.'

Richard's scathing reply was barely launched when the author of their misfortunes strolled in, saying airily, 'Everything's settled. Don't know what you were all in such a taking over!' Then he saw Richard Winton and looked scared.

Mr Winton eyed him forebodingly and asked in deceptively polite tones, 'And just what do you mean by that, Ffolliot?'

Geoffrey tried to bluster. 'None of your damned business, Winton. Private family matter, and I'll thank you to get out so we can discuss what has been decided!'

'Decided by whom, Geoffrey?' Penelope cut in.

'By me, miss! I'm head of the family!' was the reply.

'Then I'll certainly stay,' said Richard. 'Since I am to be a member of your family!'

Geoffrey shot him a scared and startled glance.

Mrs Ffolliot said quietly, 'We did not get a chance to tell you last night, Geoffrey, but Phoebe has accepted an offer of marriage from Richard. He has every right to be present.'

A crack of laughter from Geoffrey greeted this news, 'Marriage, eh? Well, they can forget that—unless Winton likes to put up thirty thousand pounds for her! She's going to marry Darleston! Got a letter from him. Cancels the whole debt in return for her hand in marriage! Told you it was all settled.' He brandished the letter in front of them.

The horrified silence was broken by Phoebe's incoherent wail of protest, and would have been further broken by Richard assaulting Geoffrey had not Phoebe cast herself into his arms, sobbing. As it was Richard had too much on his hands to do more than glare at Geoffrey and snap, 'Over my dead body, Ffolliot!'

'Geoffrey, you must see it is out of the question!' said Mrs Ffolliot. 'I will not give my consent to such a marriage!'

'Give me that letter!' Richard put Phoebe into Penelope's comforting arms and marched over to Geoffrey, who tried to protest.

'Nothing to do with you—!' He broke off and handed the letter over mutely, afraid of the expression on Richard's face.

Richard read aloud.

Dear Sir

I understand from mutual acquaintances that your estates will not bear the debt which you owe me. On the occasions when I chanced to meet your sister, Miss Ffolliot, I formed an agreeable impression of her person and character. I am prepared to forgo the entire debt in return for her hand in marriage.

If you are agreeable to this, please arrange the wedding for the fourteenth of July, by which time I understand she will be out of mourning, and let me know so that I may procure a special licence. Naturally I will let it be known that I have cancelled the debt due to my engagement to your sister.

I remain your obedient servant, etc. Darleston.

Richard crumpled the letter into a ball and hurled it from him. 'This is outrageous, but it changes nothing for you, Ffolliot!' he said evenly. 'Let me inform you that it becomes you neither as a man nor a brother to attempt to force your sister into marriage to clear your debts. And that would be my opinion whatever my own feelings towards her!'

'This is terrible,' said Mrs Ffolliot quietly. 'If this gets out we are ruined more than just financially.'

'Didn't he write "Miss Ffolliot"?' enquired Penelope suddenly.

'What does that matter? Yes, he did!' answered Richard irritably.

'It matters a great deal. I am Phoebe's elder by twenty minutes, therefore *I* am Miss Ffolliot. Moreover, Lord Darleston has met me twice, whether he knows it or not!' said Penelope triumphantly. 'I'll marry him, and that will settle Geoffrey's debt for once and for all!'

'Penny, you can't!' gasped Phoebe in shock. 'I won't let you do this for me!'

'Fiddle,' said Penelope. 'I liked the man, when I met him. After all, what can he do? He said "Miss Ffolliot". If he'd said "Miss Phoebe" it would be different; we'd have to tell him. As it is he won't know until it's too late. Which will serve him right for being so arrogant about it! He'd take more care over buying a filly!'

Geoffrey, stunned at first, finally found his tongue. 'You! What the devil do you think Darleston or any man would want with a blind wench?'

That broke the remnants of Richard's self-control. He took two swift strides and floored Geoffrey with a savage blow, just as Sarah came in to discover what all the noise was about.

She took in the scene and said delightedly, 'Oh, well done, Richard! That was a nice flush hit! You drew his cork beautifully!'

'Sarah! You mustn't use language like that!' protested her mother.

'Oh, but it was! Wasn't it Penny?' Sarah defended herself.

'Well, it did *sound* like a nice flush hit,' agreed Penelope. 'But I'll have to take your word that Geoffrey's cork has been drawn! Thank you, Richard!'

Geoffrey struggled to his feet, clutching a handkerchief to his streaming nose, and Richard, taking him by the shoulders, thrust him into a chair, saying, 'If you have any more comments like that, I suggest you keep them under your tongue or I'll take a horse whip to you!'

'Penny, no! You can't marry a near stranger!' said Mrs Ffolliot weakly.

'Mama, it's the only way. If all this gets out we are ruined. Think of Sarah, for heaven's sake!' pleaded Penelope.

'Darling, I can't let you do it!'

'Mama, don't be foolish. I'll be all right. Darleston is a gentleman, isn't he, Richard?' asked Penelope.

'I've always thought so, but I'm beginning to wonder!' said Richard. 'Mrs Ffolliot, you mustn't let her do this. I'll see Darleston, explain the situation. He won't force the issue.'

'No!' exclaimed Mrs Ffolliot. 'That would be intolerable.'

'Besides, I'll only do it on one condition!' said Penelope suddenly.

They all turned to her in surprise. She continued quietly to her brother, who listened in something akin to terror at the note of implacable determination in her voice. 'You will have the lawyers draw up a trust which gives you access only to the income from the estate and whatever is left in the funds. You will be not be able to touch the capital or sell anything without the consent of Mama and Richard or Phoebe, Sarah and myself as we come of age. Furthermore, if you die without issue then the estate must revert to Sarah!'

'Me? Why me?' gasped Sarah.

'Phoebe and Richard don't need it and neither will I. Darleston is so wealthy he could buy the whole county, let alone one estate!' said Penelope bluntly. 'Well, Geoffrey, those are my terms. If you don't like them find another way out! And don't think for a moment that you can bully Phoebe into it!'

Geoffrey stared at her in disbelief. He was caught and he knew it. Penelope's ultimatum was the only avenue of escape open to him.

'Damn you! What choice do I have?' he raged.

'None that I can think of,' she answered quietly. 'Well, do you agree?'

'Very well!' He rushed from the room in fury, slamming the door behind him.

'Mrs Ffolliot, you can't let her do this!' protested Richard. 'The whole idea is repugnant! She barely knows him!'

'What does that matter? Lots of marriages are arranged,' argued Penelope. 'And he doesn't know me! I should have thought you'd be much sorrier for him!'

'There is that, of course!' admitted Richard dryly. 'Nevertheless, this cannot be the only solution!'

'Probably not, but it does seem the neatest,' said Penelope. She turned to her mother, 'Well, Mama?'

'Penny, are you quite sure? The fourteenth of July is only a matter of weeks away.'

'Yes, Mama, quite sure.'

Chapter Five

Geoffrey Ffolliot tipped the brandy bottle up over his empty glass. A mere trickle came out. He stared at it blearily, then hurled the bottle from him with a curse as his brandy-fogged mind absorbed the fact that he had finished the bottle. He sniffed self-pityingly. No one cared that he sat drinking alone in his bedchamber! No one seemed to think that he deserved the slightest sympathy for getting so deeply into debt! And as for that little bitch Penelope! She had used the whole situation to make him sign that blasted deed consigning all control of his property over to the trustees! Damn her!

He groaned, remembering that it was her wedding day tomorrow. Had to give her away, didn't he? God, he felt sick! Get her out of the house at least! Good thing! Hah! Perhaps Darleston would teach her a thing or two about the respect due to a fellow! Geoffrey gloated over the thought for a moment. Better if it were Jack Frobisher, of course. He'd have known how to deal with the wench! Break her in the same way he'd break a rebellious filly! But it wasn't Jack; it was Darleston himself!

The memory of those scornful brown eyes boring into him at the Bellingham House ball made him shudder. Needed more brandy if he had to face both of them. Penny and Darleston together! Oh, God, where was the bottle. Finished it, hadn't he? Better ring for another! No! Old Tinson wouldn't bring one, most likely. Get it himself! Get two. Lots in the cellar! Go down now!

Geoffrey got to his feet very carefully and stood swaying for a moment. Then with unsteady steps he left the room. Fortunately he was so far gone that he completely forgot to take a candle. Otherwise he would have probably burned the entire house to the ground. As it was he made his stumbling way down to the kitchens, knocking over a number of chairs on the way.

He made it safely down the back stairs and into the kitchen. Now, where was the door to the cellar? Swaying giddily, he tried to get used to the darkness. Finally he thought he could find the door and walked very slowly and unsteadily towards it. His outstretched groping hand met the latch.

Ah! That was it! He pulled the door open. The blackness before him was absolute. Vaguely he thought about a light, but an odd thought of Penelope drifted into his mind. Didn't need a light! If that stupid wench could manage, then so could he!

He took one step down into the yawning blackness. No! He would need a light. Have to find the brandy, down there! Penelope wouldn't need to find the brandy but he did. Therefore, need a light!

It all seemed terribly logical. He swung around sharply, too sharply, and lost his footing. For a split second he teetered on the first step. His arms flailed wildly, trying to find something to grab and save himself. His fingertips caught the door frame and for a moment he hung there. Then his tenuous hold slipped and with a despairing scream he fell backwards into the waiting dark.

Penelope awoke to birdsong outside her bed-chamber window. She sat up in bed to stretch. For the past weeks she had been waking very early. The days had been so busy that this was the only time she got to think without interruption. Change had come into their lives with a vengeance after so many tranquil years. Tonight only Sarah would sleep in the room the three of them had shared for so long. Phoebe had been married a week ago. This morning she herself would marry the Earl of Darleston.

The ceremony promised to be very different from Phoebe's wedding, which, although rushed, had been a joyful occasion. Lord Darleston had waved aside the suggestion that he should meet his prospective bride again before the ceremony, though Mrs Ffolliot had insisted that he be given the opportunity to visit. If he had agreed Mrs Ffolliot would have told him everything, depending upon his generosity to accept Penelope openly instead of in the hole-and-corner fashion to which they were reduced. Phoebe therefore, was to remain very much in the background today, to avoid arousing suspicion. This would be helped by the fact that the Earl had requested his bride be prepared to leave almost immediately after the ceremony because of the distance to Darleston Court. This exclusion of her twin was, to Penelope, one of the worst aspects of the whole affair.

She was a country girl and had seen enough farm

animals to understand the mechanics of what marriage involved physically. According to Phoebe's panegyric it was simply wonderful. Also, from the sound of it, a great deal of kissing was involved. That seemed odd to Penelope. The only occasion on which a man had attempted to kiss her she had not enjoyed at all, except for the dubious pleasure of slapping Mr Frobisher's face and hearing his yells when Gelert bit him. Mama had told her only that in the marriage bed it was her duty to acquiesce to her husband and that in all probability she would enjoy it. Mrs Ffolliot had based this prophecy upon her own experience of marriage as well as her sneaking suspicion that Darleston was sufficiently experienced to know precisely what he was doing.

Geoffrey, of course, as her nearest male relative was to give the bride away. This, to Penelope, was not a pleasant thought. She felt far more like a sister to Richard Winton than to her own brother, who would have forced Phoebe into the marriage had he been able to get away with it.

Richard was such a contrast to Geoffrey. He was still shocked that Mrs Ffolliot was permitting the marriage to go ahead. Perhaps Penelope's likeness to his own bride had increased his sensitivity to the situation, but he had bowed to Phoebe's knowledge of her sister.

Phoebe had said thoughtfully, 'Penny has hated being blind, or nearly so, because she feels a burden to us rather than because it inconveniences her. Now she feels that she is doing something to help us. Also it has voluntarily brought her out of her seclusion, which is probably better than us trying to winkle her out by stealth.'

Mrs Ffolliot had concurred with this opinion, when

Richard had protested on the grounds of Darleston's approach to the whole business, saying, 'Darleston has been betrayed by one woman and treated very badly by one member of the Ffolliot family, yet he said in his letter that he had formed an agreeable impression of "Miss Ffolliot". Phoebe tells me that she barely spoke to him when he stood up with her, so I suspect any impression was made by his meetings with Penny. From that point of view we are not cheating him, and I have every confidence in Penny's ability to handle him. Losing her sight has made her very sensitive to people's moods and natures. She can tell more from a person's voice in one brief encounter than I can in several.'

'She will have her work cut out with Darleston, ma'am. He seems made of ice these days!' Richard had answered. 'I wish you will reconsider! He may be furious!'

'Penny described him as charming,' was all Mrs Ffolliot had said.

Penelope, of course, knew nothing of these discussions, but she had an idea that at least initially his lordship was going to be very angry when he was told about the switch. Richard had wanted to do it, but Penelope had said firmly that since it would be her husband and her marriage she would prefer to break the news herself. As she lay in bed she wondered how she was going to raise the subject. Obviously the change of name had not meant anything to Darleston. Perhaps he had never known what 'Miss Ffolliot's' Christian name was. Well, she would simply have to tell him the whole sordid story.

What really worried her was having to tell him that she was very nearly blind. Penelope hated being pitied.

The mere thought that he might pity her was galling. She would have to make it very clear that, with Gelert, she could be perfectly independent of his assistance once she knew her way about Darleston Court, which she understood to be huge.

She had got thus far in her ruminations when Sarah, who had been awake for a while but reluctant to dis-turb her, asked, 'Penny, are you scared?'

The question forced Penelope to think carefully. Honesty forced her to admit that she was. 'A little, Sarah. But don't you dare tell the others!'

'Why are you doing it, then?'

'Being scared is not a reason not to do something,' said Penelope.

'Don't be an idiot, Penny!' said Sarah. 'You don't even know him. It's hardly necessary to get married just to prove you aren't scared!'

Penelope hesitated. 'Sarah, we have tried not to talk about all this in front of you, but what Geoffrey did was very dreadful. He wrongly and publicly accused Lord Darleston of cheating and then cheated himself. The debt must be paid somehow. The scandal is already appalling. It could hurt Mama, Phoebe and you. I can stop all that by marrying Darleston.'

'Will he be very cross with you when you tell him?'

'I hope not, but if he is I dare say it will not be for long,' said Penelope, with a convincing display of confidence that she was far from feeling. 'Now, that's enough questions for the bride! Isn't it time to get up?'

'Yes, my lady!' answered Sarah, and was obliged to dodge a well-aimed pillow.

Tinson came downstairs especially early that morning, just as he had for Miss Phoebe's wedding a week earlier. All the Ffolliot girls were close to his heart, but Miss Penelope was perhaps the dearest. He was quite determined that nothing and no one should be allowed to spoil her wedding day.

He was fully aware that Master Geoffrey had been drinking late the night before, and it had occurred to him that the boy would need sobering up before church. When Tinson reached the kitchen, prepared to make some very strong coffee, he found the house-keeper, Mrs Jenkins, and Mrs Ffolliot's abigail, Susan, there before him.

As he entered Susan said, 'Here's Mr Tinson! He'll remember!'

'Remember what?' asked Tinson.

'The cellar door,' replied Mrs Jenkins. 'I'm sure it was shut before we went upstairs last night. But it's open now, or have you been down already this morning?'

Tinson shook his head and looked at the open door. 'No, Mrs Jenkins, I have not. And, yes, the cellar door was shut. I shut it myself.'

Susan nodded. 'There now! That's just what I said to Mrs Jenkins! ''Depend upon it,'' I said. ''Mr Tinson shut it. I saw him with my own eyes!'' I said.'

Tinson shrugged and said, 'No doubt the master came and helped himself to another bottle of brandy later on. I'd better see what sort of a mess he's made down there. Fetch me a light, please, Mrs Jenkins!'

She went into the scullery and returned with an oil lamp already lit. Tinson took it with a word of thanks and ventured through the door. He had only descended a few steps when the yellow glow of the lamp revealed Ffolliot's body lying sprawled at the foot of the steps.

His gasp of horror brought Mrs Jenkins and Susan through the door behind him.

'Oh, my goodness!'

'Is he dead?'

Tinson didn't bother to reply, except for a terse, 'Stay here!' but got down the steps as quickly as he could. He bent over his master and felt for the pulse in his throat. Slowly he straightened and looked up at the two women, shaking his head.

They stared at him as he came back up. The three of them went back into the kitchen, which was otherwise still empty.

'What will the mistress say?' asked Susan in shocked tones. 'And it's Miss Penny's wedding day and all! Why, she mightn't be able to get married today at all with this nasty business!'

Mrs Jenkins and Tinson exchanged a long glance. The rest of the staff would have informed any outsider that these two frequently disagreed. Despite this they were good friends and old allies, and there was one subject upon which they had but a single mind. Miss Penny was the finest, bravest lass you could wish for and they would have given their lives to spare her distress.

'Shut the door, Mr Tinson,' said Mrs Jenkins quietly. He nodded and did so.

Turning to Susan, he confirmed her sudden suspicion. 'Nothing is going to spoil Miss Penny's day! Say nothing to the mistress or to anyone! We'll lock the cellar door and I'll tell the mistress and Mr Winton *after* Miss Penny and her lord have left. I'll let them think only I knew.'

Susan glared at him and replied, 'Well, and it's a good idea, barring the bit about you getting all the credit for it! Shame on you, Mr Tinson! Mrs Jenkins and I aren't scared to own up! Are we, ma'am?'

'Not likely!' came the staunch reply. 'Silly old fool!'

As Lord Darleston was driven in his well-sprung chaise towards the church from the inn at which he had put up the night before, he wondered if he had taken leave of his senses. Certainly George Carstares, his groomsman, seemed to think so. He had protested vehemently when Darleston had first told him what he meant to do, the day Mrs Ffolliot's polite letter accepting his offer had arrived.

'For God's sake Peter, this is sheer persecution. Why, the girl may be in love with someone else but feel obliged to marry you! What if you take one another in dislike? She may be a dead bore, or find you a dead bore.'

'She's not a dead bore,' had said his lordship indignantly. 'I admit I thought her a little dull the first time I met her, but I dare say she was minding her dance steps. On the other two occasions that I met her she was very lively and showed a good understanding. You were the one who advised me to marry the first eligible girl I could talk to rationally! Besides, I like her dog!'

George had spluttered in his indignation at being cited as an influence in Peter's decision. 'What a wonderful basis for proposing to a girl! If you can call it a proposal! I made a joke and you like her *dog*? It's to be hoped the dog likes you, if it's the size you say it is. It's probably the one that mauled your cousin when he stayed with Ffolliot.'

Peter had remained silent. Not even to George could

he admit that he had still been as drunk as a wheel-
barrow when he wrote to Geoffrey Ffolliot and that he
had been completely and utterly dumbfounded when
he received an acceptance of his offer.

Carstares had been rather silent this morning since
they'd got up at the inn. He had done his best to dis-
suade his friend from what he thought must be a disastrous step but he could do no more on that head.
Now he shrugged mentally and said, 'Well, Peter, I
suppose I should stop being such a prophet of doom.
I hope it will all work out for you and I hope you
know I've only spoken out because I care about you.
All the same, I wish you would tell me why you are
getting married like this.'

Darleston was silent for a moment, and then said
evenly, 'You already know why. I married once for
love and look what happened. Even as we rompéd
Boney Melissa was betraying me with Barton. If it
weren't for the succession I wouldn't marry again, but
I'm damned if I want my cousin Jack to step into my
shoes. And I'm damned if I want to be dodging
women like Caroline for the rest of my life! This
seemed a good way of securing a sensible wife who
wouldn't expect me to dance attendance on her. I don't
mean to be in love with my wife and if she cuckolds
me I can divorce her without any qualms!'

George had enough sense to make no comment on
this explanation. They drove the rest of the way in
silence.

Just as they were about to alight at the church, Peter
turned to his friend and said, 'Thank you for bearing
with me, George. I don't mean to bully the girl or
make her the scapegoat for Melissa's sins, believe me.
I just don't want any emotional tie. But if you think

it best I'll speak to Miss Ffolliot before the ceremony to make sure she is not being coerced and that she perfectly understands the situation.'

George wrung his hand, 'Better late than never!' he agreed fervently.

They were greeted by the rector of the parish, Dr Pearson, who was a little surprised when the groom requested that he might be permitted to speak to the bride for a moment before the ceremony.

'My lord, with all respect, this is *most* irregular. However, if you will wait in the vestry I will tell Miss Ffolliot when she arrives that you wish to see her.'

'Thank you, sir,' answered Peter, and followed the sexton to the vestry, where he awaited the bride on a very uncomfortable chair.

He was not kept waiting long. The bride, veiled and all in ivory satin, was escorted into the vestry by Dr Pearson, who then stepped outside to wait. Darleston cleared his throat, glaring at George who promptly followed the rector.

Nervously he cleared his throat and looked at his bride. He had forgotten how slender she was, almost fragile, he thought, and a faint scent of flowers accompanied her. Silently she waited for him to speak.

'Miss Ffolliot, I realise this is a little late, but my groomsman has represented to me that you may have been coerced into taking part in this ceremony. I wished to ascertain that you had no prior claim to your affections and that you are indeed willing to marry me,' said the Earl stiffly.

Penelope listened very carefully and decided that candour was the best approach. 'My Lord, if I had taken you in dislike on the occasions upon which we met, or if my affections had been engaged, I should have sent you a note recommending you to go to the devil. As it is I am aware that my brother's behaviour has the potential to damage my family, so I am only too happy to marry you if it will save them pain. Like you I ''formed an agreeable impression''. On that basis I am willing to become your wife.' She felt a few qualms about her blindness and Phoebe, but told herself that his lordship would have expended more interest in selecting a new filly than he had on his marriage!

Peter blinked at his bride's blunt assessment of the situation, but told himself firmly that she was definitely sensible, which was all to the good. 'Thank you, Miss Ffolliot. George will be relieved that he is not assisting at a tragedy!' he said, and could have kicked himself, but the bride said nothing as she moved to the door, although he could have sworn the odd noise she made was suppressed laughter.

Five minutes later Peter Augustus Frobisher, Earl of Darleston, was awaiting Miss Penelope Ffolliot at the altar steps, feeling that he was in for some surprises where his bride was concerned. His groomsman, on the other hand, upon noticing the bride's twin sister in the church, had suddenly remembered an interesting piece of information about the daughters of the late Mr John Ffolliot. He wondered whether it was the part of a friend to warn the groom, but decided against it. That's what you get for buying a pig in a poke! he thought with a certain wry amusement.

Penelope proceeded up the aisle on her brother-in-law's arm, feeling extremely nervous about getting through the ceremony without making a fool of herself. She could see practically nothing in the dimly lit church. All her reliance was on the fact that she knew the place very well and had been walked through the ceremony a dozen times. And thank God it was Richard at her side, rather than Geoffrey, although just where Geoffrey had disappeared to was a complete mystery to her. The knowledge that Sarah was just behind her was an added comfort.

Penelope's confession of why she was doing this had touched Sarah's childish heart to the core. She had known her sisters loved her but, that one of them would do this to save her from scandal made the knowledge very real to her. Sarah was no fool; she knew Phoebe was protected by Richard and that the brunt of society's anger would have made it difficult for Mama to launch her into society. Sarah vowed to herself that there must never be anything she was not prepared to do for Penny.

So serious did she look that the groom was quite disconcerted by the frown on her face. He wondered if his bride was that solemn, but the memory of that stifled chuckle in the vestry reassured him.

The marriage service was brief and the bride and groom took their vows clearly. Penelope listened closely to the Earl's voice. It was just as attractive as she remembered. Their brief conversation in the vestry had confirmed that. He sounds a little nervous, thought Penelope, but she was aware few others would realise this. Her own nerves must be much more obvious!

The Earl thought initially that his bride was suffering no nervous jitters at all. Until, that was, her hand was placed in his by Richard Winton. Then he became aware that she was trembling slightly. George's comments on his behaviour rose mercilessly in his mind; he felt a cad. He could sense the girl staring at him and gave her hand a comforting squeeze. At least, he hoped it was comforting.

As for Penelope, she had become suddenly aware of the Earl's physical presence as he took her hand. The sun shone brightly through one of the windows and she was dimly aware of his height beside her, though his voice came from way over her head. She tried to stop shaking, but could not. Then, as she tried in vain to pierce her darkness and see him, she felt him press her hand gently. The trembling stopped and Penelope resolved to thank the Earl as soon as they were away from the church.

Darleston felt less guilty when his bride stopped shaking. He followed the rector through the service carefully, placed the ring on Penelope's now steady hand and heard them declared man and wife. *My God I've done it now. There's no going back!* he thought wildly, and then became aware that something was expected of him.

'You're supposed to kiss her, Peter!' came George's agonised whisper. The rector looked as though he were trying not to laugh.

Very carefully Darleston lifted the veil back from his wife's face to gaze into her dark grey eyes. *Strange eyes,* he thought. *They seemed to look straight through you, as though you weren't quite there.* He put a gentle hand under Penelope's chin and bent to kiss her lightly on the mouth. Her lips were warm and soft. The Earl decided that he would definitely enjoy kissing her again later on.

Penelope was unprepared for this. Although she had known it would happen it was the one thing that had not been rehearsed, and the strange feeling of yearning which swept over her at the touch of his lips was a complete surprise. She wondered if he had wanted to kiss her. George's whisper had been quite audible to her, and she was unsure whether to be amused or miffed. She felt the Earl draw her hand through his arm to lead her from the church and realised that the hardest part was still to come. She still had to tell him that he had been duped to a certain extent, and that was beginning to weigh heavily on her conscience.

The bridal party moved to the Rectory, where Phoebe, Sarah and Mrs Ffolliot whirled Penelope upstairs to change out of the wedding dress, which had been worn by Phoebe a week earlier. 'Darling Phoebe, thank you for letting me wear it. It was like being held by you all the time,' said Penelope, hugging her twin. 'Oh, Sarah! I couldn't have managed without you. You were wonderful!' Sarah blushed and blew her nose noisily.

'Penny, are you sure you don't want Richard to tell Lord Darleston?' asked her mother.

'Quite sure, Mama,' said Penelope. 'You see, if I don't tell him it will be because I am scared. Even if it is all a bit irregular I don't want to start by not trusting him enough to tell him myself.'

In no time at all it seemed she was being handed into the chaise. Some surprise had been expressed by the groom when he realised that Gelert was going to accompany them, and George had proved no help at all, saying enthusiastically to the new Countess of Darleston, 'Just the thing, Lady Darleston. Peter was telling me how much he admired your dog!'

Peter had glared at him and given in gracefully, thinking that as the dog was bound to join the household anyway it might as well be now as later. He followed his wife and her dog into the chaise, and the door was shut behind him by Richard Winton, who said in affectionate accents, 'Behave yourself, Penny,' then, in a more challenging tone of voice, 'Look after her, Lord Darleston.'

His lordship accepted this blunt command with commendable meekness, merely saying, 'I shall hope to receive both you and Mrs Winton at Darleston Court in the very near future so that you may assure yourself that I am doing so. Goodbye, Winton, and thank you.'

He noticed that as Winton stepped back from the chaise his arm was tapped by a nervous-looking old man who had sat at the back of the church with the Ffolliot's upper servants. Peter rather thought that he must be the butler. He dismissed the matter from his mind as his bride spoke.

'I am afraid Richard has become very older-brotherish since he became engaged to my sister,' said Penelope apologetically as the chaise rolled away.

'So it would appear,' said Peter. 'Are you tired, Lady Darleston? I dare say you were up early and have been very busy. Perhaps you would care to rest? We have some sixty miles to travel to Darleston Court.'

Concealing her surprise at the formality of his address, Penelope admitted that she had been awake early and that a nap would be welcome. Sleep was far away, however, so she settled herself back in the corner of the chaise to count to five thousand while she worked out how to start explaining herself to her husband. My husband, she thought. If only I could *see* him! I don't even know what he looks like, only Phoebe's description. She reached five thousand and sat up, ready to begin her confession, when a gentle snore informed her that his lordship was asleep.

It appeared to Penelope that a couple of hours passed before her husband awoke as they pulled into an inn-yard to change the horses. Lord Darleston procured a basket of food and they were on their way again. This was it, decided Penelope. She had to get it over with! Before she could start, however, Lord Darleston spoke.

'My lady, I think it is important that I make my position quite clear to you at the start. As you are possibly aware, this is my second marriage. My first wife disgraced my name and I would not have chosen to marry again except for the recent death of my cousin and heir. His death means that the title must go, after me, to a man I consider totally unworthy of it. To be perfectly honest with you I have married to beget an heir. I am sorry if you are shocked at my plain speaking, but I deplore deceit and you had better know that I have every intention of... of consummating our union as soon as possible.'

Penelope was speechless. She laid one trembling hand on Gelert's head and drew a deep breath. 'It is my turn to be honest now, my lord. I...I am not the person you think I am!'

Darleston was puzzled. 'What on earth are you talking about? You are, or rather were, Miss Penelope Ffolliot, aren't you?'

'Yes, but when you met me the first time, at Almack's, it wasn't me you met but my twin, Phoebe!' said Penny desperately, and a trifle incoherently.

Absolutely staggered, the Earl stared at her in disbelief. Then, as he recalled odd differences between the girl he had danced with at Almack's and the girl driving in the park and at the concert, he realised the mistake he had made.

'Phoebe…I *thought* that was the name! What in heaven's name were you two playing at, then? It was you, though, with your father that day and at the concert. I would swear it!' said the Earl angrily.

'Yes, that was me both times.' Privately she was amazed he was so sure.

'Why? Did you share your come-out to economise?' This in a menacingly quiet tone.

'No! I didn't want a come-out. I simply went to London to be with Phoebe. Hardly anyone knew about me; when you met me you thought I was Phoebe, so I let you continue to think it!' cried Penelope. 'Then Geoffrey lost all that money, and it wasn't the first time and we couldn't pay, so he tried to force Phoebe to marry you, even though she was betrothed…'

'He did *what*?' The shock and horror in the Earl's voice were unmistakable. She gasped in fright as he took her roughly by the shoulders. This was too much for Gelert, who rose, growling fiercely in warning.

'No, Gelert!' cried Penelope.

Darleston released her and said in a milder tone of voice, 'I beg your pardon. Please forgive me, I did not mean to startle you. You say your brother tried to force your sister to marry me?'

'Yes. We knew you meant Phoebe, but she had just become engaged to Richard so I said I would marry you. It was true what I said in the vestry, my lord. I would not have married you if I had not liked you. Anyway, you didn't seem terribly interested in whom you married or Mama would have told you. You shouldn't have bought a pig in a poke!' she finished, unconsciously echoing George Carstares's unspoken thought.

'Why the devil didn't you tell me all this in the

vestry?' demanded the Earl furiously. 'Good God! I shall be the laughing stock of town if this gets out! Well, it needn't alter my plans. You and your sister are so alike I dare say it doesn't make any odds which of you lies in my bed tonight! Is there anything else I need to know? God help you if there is, my girl!'

Penelope was shaking. This was far worse than she had imagined and she bit her lip to keep from crying. She still had to tell him she was blind, but she remained silent, terrified of bursting into tears if she spoke. Too late she realised that she had underestimated the insult to his pride in being so duped. It occurred to her that he had probably decided the whole family were cheats. Finally she asked in a very wobbly voice, 'Would you have married me if you had known that there were two of us?'

Darleston, already feeling guilty over his loss of temper, but by no means prepared to admit it, answered very angrily, 'Very well, *no*! it *wouldn't* have changed my mind!' He refrained from adding that it would have made a difference if he had been confronted with Phoebe. Mrs Ffolliot had been perfectly right in guessing that it was Penelope's stronger personality which had caught his attention. Goaded beyond endurance he added, 'And my intention to consummate this marriage stands, so I suggest you get used to the idea!' He then dragged the frightened girl into his arms and brought his mouth down savagely on hers.

Taken totally by surprise, Penny tried to struggle in vain. The Earl, however, had forgotten the presence of Gelert, who had become increasingly anxious about this stranger shouting at his mistress. He took instant exception to the situation and leapt at Darleston barking ferociously, forcing him to release Penelope. Half fainting, Penelope was unable for a moment to call Gelert to order, and she groped helplessly for his collar, finally dragging him back. Shaken with sobs, she slid off the seat onto the floor, her arms about the dog's neck, crying into his rough coat. Gelert whined and licked her face frantically, pausing only to direct a few warning snarls at Darleston.

Stunned by the dog's attack, Darleston sat back in his seat wondering just what he should do. His bride sat dishevelled and weeping on the floor of the carriage, her dog displaying every sign of flying at him again if he dared move towards her. He tried to apologise. 'My lady…I mean, Penelope, I'm sorry for losing my temper and frightening you…I hope you will forgive me.' Then, on a more practical note as she continued to cry, 'Would you care for a handkerchief?'

A choked voice answered, 'Thank you,' and a small hand was held out. He placed his handkerchief in it and then put his head in his hands in disbelief at the mess he had made of the whole affair. His temper had ebbed. He felt very guilty, but somehow still annoyed with Penelope for having witnessed it. He groaned inwardly. Tonight was definitely not the night to bed his bride. It would be tantamount to rape.

The rest of the journey was passed without conversation. The Earl had no idea what to say to ease the tension and Penelope was completely numbed by the thought of the night to come. She had been terrified when Darleston seized her. There had been no hint of gentleness in his embrace. His mouth had completely and brutally possessed hers and his arms had admitted of no escape. She began to feel sick with fear at the thought of being alone with him.

By the time they reached Darleston Court in the falling dusk Penelope was in such a state of fright that she could not stop shaking. When the chaise drew up at the front of the house a footman opened the carriage door and let down the steps. His Lordship leapt down, holding out his hand to assist Penelope to alight. Not realising, she attempted to get down unaided but completely missed the steps. She fell with a cry of fright and found herself once more in her husband's arms. 'Careful!' he said 'You will hurt yourself if you don't look out.'

There was real concern in his voice, and this undid her totally. Perceiving that she was about to burst into tears, he swept her up and carried her into the house, past the row of waiting servants, saying only, 'Dinner in fifteen minutes, if you please. I have something to show her ladyship in the study!' Closely followed by Gelert, he strode to the study door with Penelope in his arms. A footman rushed to open the door and close it behind them and Darleston deposited his wife gently on the sofa.

She turned towards him, saying shakily, 'Would you please ask one of your people to take Gelert to the stables for the night and feed him?'

Darleston blinked. 'Are you sure you would not feel safer if he remained?' he asked quietly.

'I would prefer to be able speak to you without worrying about his behaviour,' answered Penelope proudly. She suspected that her husband was going to be even angrier than before at what she was about to tell him. If Gelert attacked him a third time he might insist the dog be sent away. Besides, she was ashamed of her own fear. All her life her father had taught her to look her fears in the face and conquer them. She would not permit herself to hide behind Gelert's protection.

'As you please,' said Darleston. He tugged the bell-pull by the desk. The butler appeared and Darleston gave him his instructions, 'Meadows, please have her Ladyship's dog conveyed to the stables and fed.'

'Yes, my lord,' said Meadows.

Penelope heard the apprehension in his voice and said with tolerable composure, 'He will be good, I promise. Come, take his collar from me.' Meadows crossed the room to her side to grasp Gelert's collar. 'Go with him, Gelert,' she commanded. He obeyed reluctantly, giving a last growl as he passed Darleston.

'Thank you, Meadows. Her ladyship will ring for him when she wants him,' said the Earl.

Penelope turned towards her husband's voice and said nervously, 'There is one last thing I must tell you, my lord.'

'Yes? I doubt you can shock me any further, but go ahead.'

Bracing herself for the explosion, she said simply, 'I am blind.'

The silence lengthened, only to be broken by the Earl saying bitterly, 'I appear to have married into a family of cheats. Do you imagine I wish my heir to be blind? Dinner will be served in ten minutes. Ring for Meadows when you are ready to join me.'

Penelope heard his footsteps cross the room then the door slammed behind him. She realised too late what he was doing and sank back onto the couch in the knowledge that she would have to wait there until it occurred to him that she had no idea where the bell-pull was.

Darleston waited an extra twenty minutes for his

bride, before giving up and starting his own dinner. He was furious. Doubtless the staff was agog at the situation, and the wretched girl's last admission was the outside of enough. He ate several courses without even tasting them and downed a bottle of burgundy with no noticeable effect. Could he repudiate the marriage? Not without a shocking scandal which would leave him looking a total fool. Also, he suspected that the law was on the Ffolliots' side.

Blast the girl. Couldn't she even have joined him for dinner to make a show of wedded bliss for the servants? His conscience pointed out firmly that he had given her little cause to care what he wanted and that in all likelihood the girl was terrified of him.

Finally, after the footman had placed the brandy on the table, he began to consider the whole situation from Penelope's perspective. He tried to understand why she had done it. Obviously she must care for her sisters and mother very much. It occurred to him, on a wave of shame, that his behaviour would have terrified even a girl who could see. What Penelope must have felt appalled him. He thought it must have resembled a nightmare for her and found himself unexpectedly thankful that the dog had been there. The courage she had shown in sending Gelert out before making her final admission became plain to him. At least I didn't do anything, he thought, but that was small comfort as he recalled his final bitter comment.

He dismissed the footman and asked him to find Meadows. The butler arrived and said, 'The dog has been fed and suitably housed for the night, my lord.'

'Thank you, Meadows. Tell me, when you conducted her ladyship upstairs...'

'I beg your pardon my lord, but her ladyship is still

in the study, I believe. She certainly did not ring to be conducted upstairs.'

At this point the true reason for Penelope's non-appearance struck Darleston with all the force of a thunderbolt. He leapt to his feet in horror at his stupidity. 'My God! Meadows, please bring some hot soup and rolls to her ladyship's room in twenty minutes, do you mind? There's a good chap. I'll explain later and you can comb my hair for being such a fool!'

He raced out of the dining room across the hall to the study door. He recollected himself enough to knock lightly. There was no answer, so he opened the door and stepped in quietly. The inadequate words of apology died on his lips as he saw his bride, sound asleep on the sofa with traces of tears on her cheeks. He cursed himself silently for what he had done. All his anger had been unjust. The situation was his own fault for being arrogant. He would simply have to make the best of it and try to make the girl happy.

Softly he stepped over to the sofa and knelt beside it to take her hand. 'Penelope! Wake up,' he said gently. She did not stir immediately but when he spoke again, sat up in terror, trying to pull away from him. 'Penelope, it's all right. I have come to apologise and take you up to your room. Meadows is bringing you some food and then I shall leave you to sleep, I give you my word.'

He was horrified at the fear on her face but, to his relief, she relaxed slightly at his words. 'That's better. I cannot tell you how ashamed I am of the way I have behaved towards you. It was inexcusable, all of it. In truth it was my meetings with you, not your sister, which prompted me to believe ''Miss Ffolliot'' would be a suitable bride, so I can scarcely complain about which twin I received. As for your blindness, I can only say that my reaction was contemptible and I beg your pardon most humbly.'

Penelope was scarcely able to believe her ears at the change in his voice. She found her own voice with difficulty. 'It is I who should apologise, Lord Darleston. We played a shabby trick on you, especially with regard to my blindness. If you wish to repudiate our marriage I would not blame you.' She blew her nose and wiped her eyes, wishing that she could see him as she awaited his reply.

It surprised her. Peter put his hands on her shoulders and very gently pulled her into his arms. He held her lightly, resting his cheek against the auburn curls. 'That seems a little drastic, since I got the right bride through no fault of my own. Unless you prefer to have nothing more to do with me I suggest we get to know each other and try to wipe out this bad start to our marriage.'

Penelope listened with tears trickling down her cheeks and whispered, 'Thank you, my lord.'

Chapter Six

Penelope awoke the next morning to a gentle knock on her door. 'Come in!' she called. The door opened and she heard Gelert's bark as he bounded into the room. Delighted to find his mistress, he leapt onto the bed to nuzzle her face. The rosy-cheeked maid who had brought him said shyly, 'His lordship sent me to wait on you milady. I've brought some tea for you and his lordship's compliments. He will be at your disposal this morning to show you over the house.'

'Thank you,' said Penelope, finding it odd to be called 'milady'. She gave Gelert a last hug. 'Off now.' He jumped down beside the bed his tail beating a rhythmic tattoo on the floor. Penelope heard her maid approach the bed, and held out her hands for the tea. It was placed in her grasp very carefully.

'Have you got it safely, milady?' came an anxious enquiry. 'We were told that you're blind, and his lordship's orders are for all of us to be sure to help you find your way about.'

'That will be wonderful, thank you,' said Penelope, sipping her tea. She smiled in the direction of the pleasant, eager voice. 'What is your name?'

'Ellen, milady.'

'Will you be able to show me around until I know where everything is?' asked Penelope hopefully. 'Once I know the way to rooms and know the layout of the grounds I shall be all right with Gelert here. But if you are free to help at first, Ellen, I should be very grateful.'

'Oh, milady, it would be a pleasure. Shall I pull back the curtains now?'

Penelope nodded and heard the girl cross to the window. Light flooded in. She was instantly aware of the difference, probably the room faced east, she thought. Thoughtfully she finished her tea while Ellen busied herself around the room. It seemed that the Earl was taking some thought for her well-being. When he had carried her upstairs the previous night he had seen to it that she finished the soup and rolls, had all that she needed and knew she could reach the bell-pull from her bed, but after that her memory was vague, for she had been very sleepy. Suddenly she realised that she was wearing a nightdress and wondered how she had got into it. Frowning, she tried to remember, but all she could recall was someone with very gentle hands and a tender voice. It dawned on her that her husband must have put her to bed. She blushed hotly at the thought of him undressing her.

'Would you like to get up now milady?' Ellen's voice broke in on these embarrassing reflections.

'Yes, I should get up. What is the time?'

'Just after ten, milady. His lordship wouldn't let us wake you any earlier. He said to take the dog up at ten and not before, unless you rang.'

'Thank you, Ellen,' said Penelope as she got up. 'Did Gelert behave himself?'

'Oh, yes, milady, except for frightening one of the grooms half to death, being as he didn't know a dog was in that stall and he is such a size! Johnson, the head groom, told Mr Meadows that he'd had to persuade Fred not to give notice!'

Penelope laughed. 'You don't seem to mind him. I think someone made a lucky choice of maid for me!'

'Oh, no, milady! The master told Mr Meadows to line up all the maids and ask which ones liked dogs, without telling them why, and then to bring in your dog and see if they still liked dogs! I was the only one who did!' This last was said with great pride, and Penelope, after a startled moment, had to sit back on the bed, so hard did she laugh at this unorthodox method of selecting an abigail.

Half an hour later Ellen conducted her downstairs to the study, where Lord Darleston was awaiting her. She was a little nervous, both of her reception and of Gelert's possible reaction to her husband. Ellen was a good guide, explaining the passages and doors very clearly so that by the time they reached the study Penelope knew she would be able to find her own way back. 'Thank you, Ellen,' said Penelope as they reached the study door. She knocked, and upon hearing her husband call, 'Come in,' she entered.

Peter was sitting at his desk, looking over some estate business, 'Good morning, Penelope.'

Good morning, my lord.'

'Peter.'

'I beg your pardon?'

'Peter. My name is Peter. Peter Augustus, actually, but that's almost as formal as my lord. Unless you prefer not to, please call me Peter in private.'

Penelope listened very carefully. All she could hear

in her husband's voice was a friendly warmth. All yesterday's anger seemed to have disappeared. She relaxed visibly. Peter, watching her intently, could see the tension ebb from her slender frame and was immeasurably relieved. He had slept badly the previous night. Every time he had nearly dropped off, his conscience had pricked him back to wakefulness. His behaviour continued to appal him; he could scarcely believe what he had done and he had resolved to make every effort to help Penelope settle in.

Furthermore he had received a very disquieting letter from Richard Winton that morning, which had been delivered by a messenger who had ridden all night to reach Darleston Court. He did not quite know how to reveal the contents of the letter to his wife. With any other girl he would have simply given it to her to read, but that was obviously impossible.

He decided to approach the matter obliquely. 'Tell me, Penelope, were you very much disappointed that your brother did not appear to give you away?'

Penelope flushed and hesitated. She could not lie and say she *had* been upset when in reality she had been relieved! On the other hand it seemed so improper to tell Darleston—oh, dear, Peter!—just how much she disliked her half-brother.

Eventually she said quietly and without rancour, 'I am afraid, Peter, that I was not in the least upset. My half-brother and I share a mutual dislike. I was far happier for my brother-in-law to give me away. Indeed, given the circumstances of our marriage, I should not be surprised to learn that Geoffrey was too embarrassed to face the pair of us!'

Peter was not really surprised. He could not imagine that there could have been much affection between young Ffolliot and his proud sister. For she was proud, not arrogant or above herself, it was just that she had a certain dignity and gallantry in her bearing. The contrast with Geoffrey's whining and somewhat shady character could not have been more marked. It occurred to him that she must have been bitterly galled by the knowledge that her brother was a cheat.

In his turn Peter hesitated, then he said simply, 'Then I hope you will not be too upset to hear, that one of your grooms followed us here bearing a letter from Richard Winton. In it he asks me to break the news that your brother must have fallen down the cellar steps the night before last. Your mother's butler found him early yesterday morning with a broken neck. He decided that it was better to wait until after our wedding to inform your mother. He did not wish to spoil your wedding day. I am sorry, Penelope.' Peter could think of nothing further to say to his bride.

Her mouth dropped open in amazement. She looked to be completely stunned, and then shook her head, saying in disbelief, 'Geoffrey is dead? Oh, dear God! And on our wedding day! I married you to avoid scandal! Not to inflame it! Whatever will people say?'

Peter had already thought about this and he had a ready answer. 'We will just tell the truth. Accidents do happen, you know, and we can emphasise the story of the faithful old retainer not wishing to ruin his young mistress's happy day!' No need to tell the world that the bridegroom had seen to that without any outside assistance, he thought ruefully.

Penelope looked unconvinced. 'Sell them a Banbury story, do you mean? Does Richard happen to mention just what Geoffrey was doing down in the cellar? Not that I need ask. No doubt he was in his cups as usual!'

Her husband nodded in embarrassment, and then realised how useless that was. 'Er, yes, Winton does say that it appears Geoffrey was a trifle bosky.'

'Bosky? A *trifle* bosky?' was the scornful rejoinder. 'I'm only surprised that he could get as far as the cellar!' Then she recollected herself and said shame-facedly, 'I beg your pardon, my lord—I mean Peter. But Geoffrey could be simply horrible. When your letter came he tried to bully Phoebe into marrying you even though she was already betrothed to Richard! And he wouldn't even wear mourning for Papa! The kindest, most loving father!' Tears stood in her eyes as she said this.

'He didn't bully you, I hope?' asked Peter in real horror.

'Certainly not!' she retorted. 'I would have told him to go to the devil if it had been just the debt. It was more the stigma for my mother and sisters. Besides, I used the situation to force Geoffrey into putting the whole estate under the control of a trust so that he could not continue to waste it. Under that trust it now goes to my little sister Sarah, since Phoebe and I don't need it!'

'I see,' he replied slowly. 'Then we need only consider the practicalities of the situation.' Thoughtfully he eyed the gown of grey muslin in which his bride was arrayed and said, 'I shall send to London for some new gowns for you. You are out of mourning—for your father, of course. And for a half-brother I believe a month's half-mourning will suffice. So, since we are spending our time here quietly at Darleston Court, it should not be necessary to be terribly strict. Just as long as you don't dash about the countryside in bright colours! Yes, some new gowns definitely!' He hoped this would change the subject, since Penelope was obviously chafed by it.

It certainly did effect a change of subject, but not quite in the way he had intended. Penelope flushed even more vividly than before. What must he think of her, not having suitable clothes for her new status? Well did she know that the simple gowns Phoebe and Mama had fashioned for her were out of place here. She lifted her head and said proudly, 'There is not the slightest need, my lord. I have quite enough clothes for my needs.' It occurred to her that she had been a trifle ungracious, and she stammered, 'I...I mean it is very kind of your lordship, but I do not require new clothes or wish you to be spending a great deal of money upon me!'

Peter was taken aback. It was the first time in his career that an offer to supply new finery to a woman had been refused. Most of 'em, he thought cynically, would have presented him with a detailed list! Belatedly he remembered that the Ffolliots were not well off and that there had been very little time for Penelope to acquire any new gowns. He realised that his offer had sounded like a condemnation of her attire. Careful now! he thought.

'Of course not!' he said cheerfully, ''Twas just that I thought since you'd had no time to buy new clothes since you came out of mourning for your father it would give me great pleasure to do it for you! You can trust me to know what colours will suit you. I shall avoid pink. Something tells me that it will not be one of your favourites! And since you are to be in half-mourning initially, perhaps deep blues, even pale colours such as a lemon-yellow will be acceptable!'

Self-consciously Penelope raised a hand to her au-

burn curls and admitted, 'Indeed, pink is not a favourite! Neither Phoebe nor I ever wear it! We both
prefer blues and greens.' With an effort she smiled at
her husband, saying, 'I beg your pardon, my lord. If
you wish to buy me some new gowns, I should like it
very much.'

He smiled in relief. 'Excellent. Ask Ellen to take
your measurements and leave the rest to me.' She
could hear the smile in his voice.

'Oh, one other little thing, Penelope...'

'Yes, my lord?'

'I think you are cheating.'

'Cheating!' The outrage in her voice was unmistakable.

Peter grinned at the reaction and continued, 'Yes,
cheating! I distinctly recall asking you to call me by
my Christian name. You are being extremely disobe-
dient, and if I do anything about it your dog will probably try to bite me again!'

'Oh!' She stopped in confusion. 'I'm sorry he was
so badly behaved, my...I mean, P-Peter. He is generally very good, but...'

Peter interrupted her, saying seriously, 'You must
not apologise for his behaviour, Penelope. I deserved
it. I shouted at you and then tried to force my attentions on you. I'm glad he was there. Which brings me
to something else.'

'Yes, Peter?' It was much easier as you went along,
she discovered.

She heard him clear his throat. He sounds nervous,
she thought in amazement.

'Our relationship,' he said carefully. Oh God! How
to put it? He rustled some papers. 'At the present I

have no intention of insisting upon my…my rights as a husband.'

And just what, wondered Penelope, does the well-bred bride reply to that? To her absolute horror she heard herself asking, 'Why not?'

Peter was also rather taken aback. That was the last response he had expected! 'Well, we don't know each other very well yet. I…I don't wish to force myself upon you.'

'Because I am blind.' It was not a question, but a statement. She flushed in embarrassment. It was the same old problem. Someone unable to accept her affliction without pitying her. Perhaps he even found it distasteful.

Peter heard the pain in her voice, saw the crimson stain her cheeks and was puzzled. What had he said to hurt her? 'Yes,' he said gently. 'I think it would be unfair for me to insist you share my bed before you have learnt to know me and trust me, especially after yesterday.'

All she could hear in his voice was sincere concern. Yes, he was kind, this husband of hers, despite his loss of temper the previous day. He was not extending patronage or pity, but simply behaving in accordance with the dictates of his honour. 'Thank you, Peter.' She did not know what else to say, how to apologise for her suspicions.

He looked at her carefully, not really understanding what had upset her. It occurred to him that it would be just as important for him to understand her, to avoid future mistakes.

Diffidently he said, 'I thought that today I should perhaps show you over the house and part of the gardens. Ellen, your maid, will also help you. Unfortunately she has not had much experience as a lady's maid, but…'

'She likes Gelert!' Penelope finished his sentence with a chuckle. 'Thank you, Peter. Ellen told me about how you chose her. If you have time to show me around today that would be lovely. Once I know where everything is Gelert will be able to guide me.'

'Gelert? What on earth do you mean?'

A demonstration was always most effective in Penelope's experience. 'You are sitting down, aren't you?'

'Well, yes.' How the devil did she know?

'At a desk. Is the desk between us?'

'Yes.'

She walked straight towards him in absolute confidence with her hand on Gelert's collar and stopped about eighteen inches from the desk. 'The desk is about a foot and a half away, isn't it?'

'Good God! How did you do that? You even knew I was sitting!'

'Your voice, of course. The height is wrong for you to be standing. And I heard you move some papers so I thought you must be at a desk. As for knowing where the desk was, Gelert stopped me.'

Peter stared at them in disbelief. 'And he does that all the time?'

'Yes. It makes it much easier if I don't have to wait about for people or take them away from whatever they are doing. I prefer to be as independent as possible.'

Good heavens! Here he'd been thinking that he was tied to a girl who would need constant help and attention. He began to revise his ideas very quickly. This was no helpless child to be nursed over every obstacle.

She would probably give him a sharp set-down if he tried!

He wondered what to say, and then thought, When in doubt, be direct!

'I find myself in an awkward situation, then, my dear. My instinct is to shepherd you around every chair, make sure you never take a step without an attendant, but something tells me you would not appreciate this!'

Penelope smiled. 'Not at all, Peter. It would drive me quite demented! I like my privacy and I prefer to know that someone has sought my company for pleasure rather than a sense of duty or charity.'

'I take your point, Penelope, but there may be times when you will need my assistance which may not occur to me. I would like to think that you will have no hesitation in asking for help.'

'Thank you, Peter. I will remember that.' There was still a certain reserve in her voice and Peter realised at once that she would probably find it difficult to ask him for help. He wondered how much of this was due to his own behaviour and how much to pride and—well, to put it bluntly, sheer cussedness!

Wisely he dropped the subject, resolving to leave it to time. 'Shall we start our tour in the breakfast parlour, then, Penelope? Are you hungry?'

'Yes, please, Peter.'

He moved to her side, wondering how the dog would react, but Gelert, sensing no alarm on the part of his mistress, merely looked at him indifferently. 'Will you take my arm, Penelope?' Wordlessly she held out her hand. He kissed it and tucked it through his arm to lead her out. Penelope wondered at the odd thrill that ran through her at the touch of his lips.

After breakfast Peter began their tour of the house. After careful thought he had decided to concentrate on making sure she could find her way about. The servants had been warned that nothing must be left lying about and nothing moved without warning their mistress.

He told her this as they entered the study. 'Thank you, my lord—I mean, Peter. But they needn't worry too much. Gelert would never let me fall over anything. He has been my eyes for the last four years. It would have been much harder without him. As it is I have been able to retain some independence of movement.'

Peter stopped in surprise. 'You were not always blind, then?'

'Oh, no. It was an accident. Geoffrey let off a gun near my horse one day. When I was thrown off my head hit a tree root. I was unconscious for days. When I did come to I had the most dreadful headache and couldn't see. I can distinguish light from dark a bit, and I notice movement, but that's about it.'

Peter said nothing but his mind was relieved of one worry. Repudiating the marriage was out of the question, but he had been concerned about the possibility of his wife passing on her affliction to a child. At least now he had only to consider the best way of wooing the girl so that he could start a family.

Despite his discretion on this subject, Penelope sensed his slight change of mood and was quick to realise the reason. 'Peter, it was bad enough that we didn't tell you about Phoebe, or that I was blind, but I would never have married anyone if there had been the slightest possibility of passing my blindness on to a child. Please, you must believe that.'

Peter stopped dead, staring at his wife, utterly amazed. 'How the devil did you know what I was thinking?' he demanded at last.

'I…I don't know, your voice or something. I can do it with Phoebe all the time, because we are so close. I always know when something is wrong and she always knows about me.'

Peter looked at his bride in consternation. 'I shall have to behave myself if you are going to read my mind like that. Even my thoughts will have to mend their manners!' Certainly some of his thoughts would have to be put firmly to the back of his mind for a while. Looking at Penelope, he realised just how hard it was going to be stopping himself from making love to her. The memory of the softness of her lips in church and putting her to bed the previous night was vivid. He had restrained himself nobly on that occasion, but hoped to God that the situation would not arise again.

Honesty compelled him to admit that the chances of him showing a similar level of self-discipline another time were about zero! The delicate curves of his wife's body would have been a constant temptation under any circumstances, but to know that he had the right to take her and make love to her made his decision to wait doubly hard. Hoping devoutly that she couldn't sense what he was thinking now, he concentrated on his description of the study. It was a very masculine room, furnished with comfortable leather chairs, a large desk and walls lined with books. All the Frobishers had enjoyed collecting books, and this library was justly famous for its collection of seventeenth century manuscripts of poetry.

Penelope, listening to her husband, was perfectly

aware that something was bothering him, but this was one subject on which she could not possibly understand his thoughts. With no experience of love it did not occur to her that she could be the object of his desire. She supposed that he would tell her when he wanted to consummate the marriage, which made her a little nervous. Would he just come to her room one night and get into bed with her? Of course, Phoebe had thought it was wonderful. But then Phoebe and Richard were in love; surely that made a difference. Still, even Mama had said she would probably enjoy that part of married life. Suddenly she realised that she had not heard a word Peter had said for several minutes and dragged her mind back to the study.

After the study came the State Dining Room followed by the Small Dining Room, which were both on the ground floor, after which they descended to the kitchens where Penelope was introduced to the French cook, François, and his minions. François excelled himself in his Gallic address, assuring his new mistress that he would be inspired by her presence to create new dishes for her delectation. Penelope responded delightfully, thought Peter, quite unaware that his feelings for his wife were not at all along the lines he had intended.

Finally they repaired to the Morning Room, where a light meal had been laid out. Over this Darleston told his wife a great deal about the history of the house and his family. The Earldom went back to the Restoration of King Charles II. The then Viscount Darleston had fought bravely for his King and had been duly rewarded upon his return from exile. The house itself had been built in the following century, after the Elizabethan manor house burned down.

Penelope could hear the passion in Peter's voice as he told her all this. She could understand his pride in the title and his reluctance to permit it to go to one who would soil its lustre. Jack Frobisher, she thought, was the last man Darleston would wish to have to acknowledge as his heir!

In the afternoon Peter took her back over the part of the house he had shown her in the morning and was amazed to realise that she could find her way about without much difficulty. She laughed at his surprise, saying only that she had become very quick to remember things like that. 'You are quite incredible, my dear,' he insisted. 'Why, George got lost between his bedroom and the dining room the first time he stayed here!'

'You and George are very close, are you not?'

'Yes, we fought together under Wellington in the Peninsula, and at Waterloo. Both of us came back here to recover after we were wounded at Waterloo. George's parents are dead, his sister was close to her confinement and I had no desire to be alone at that point—' He broke off, not wanting to mention his first wife's disastrous flight with her lover when she'd heard of his return from war.

Penelope heard the bitterness in his voice so she changed the subject adroitly. 'Did you admire Wellington very much? Papa used to read all the newspaper reports aloud to us for my sake. I always felt that Wellington sounded very aloof and unapproachable. Did that make it hard to serve under him?'

'Not at all,' answered Peter. 'We knew he was out to get the job done and that he would do it. Also I assure you, my dear, that you will not find him in the least unapproachable when you meet him, as you are bound to do!' Peter knew quite well that his erstwhile commander would be fully appreciative of the charms of the new Lady Darleston.

They moved out into the garden together with Gelert. Peter was fascinated to see how the great dog guided his mistress, protecting her from any mishaps. He always stopped before steps, pushed her to the centre of any doorway and guided her safely around obstacles. 'Did you train Gelert on purpose, Penelope?'

'Not really. We hoped for a while that my sight would return, or at least improve, but it didn't. Gelert was about a year old then. Papa gave him to Phoebe and me when he was a puppy and we shared him, but after the accident he spent more time with me and gradually began guiding me about. I couldn't do without him now.'

Peter took her to the herb garden, where an almost tangible cloud of fragrance greeted them. He said, laughing, 'I've no idea what they are all called, but I know which ones smell the loveliest.' To his surprise Penelope could identify most of them by their scent or texture, and it was obvious that she took a great deal of pleasure in the garden.

Peter began to realise that his wife's other senses appeared to be highly developed. If he stepped away she had no trouble locating him from the sound of his voice. He also began to have an inkling of the extent of her independence and pride. She did not cling to him nervously in the new environment she faced, but rather stepped out boldly into the unknown with a courage that left him wondering how he would acquit himself under a similar affliction.

'Do you ever long for your sight?' he asked abruptly

as they left the herb garden to wander through the shrubbery.

She hesitated before answering, 'Yes. Very often, when I meet new people, but I try to avoid that because they annoy me by being pitying and patronising.'

'Was that why you didn't come out with Phoebe?'

'Yes, meeting lots of people all at once is terribly confusing. I can't see them and the headaches come back because I get scared of the crowd. My parents took me to a local Hunt Ball but it was awful. You see, I can't dance any of the figured dances, only the waltz. None of the men wanted to dance with me, so Phoebe pretended to be me for half an hour and I had some of her waltzes!'

Peter roared with laughter. 'So I wasn't the first victim after all! Was that your idea, to dance for your sister?'

'Goodness, no! Phoebe dared me to do it, but Mama was very cross with us and I didn't really enjoy the ball, so I refused to go to any more. I suppose it was cowardly but it seemed much easier to stay at home.'

Peter thought he detected a note of sadness in her voice, but her face told him nothing. 'Do you find it frustrating not knowing what I look like?' he asked unexpectedly.

'But I do know! Phoebe described you in great detail after our first meeting. Tall, about six foot two, with black hair, brown eyes and an olive complexion. You have a fine figure and are very handsome, according to her.'

Peter chuckled at the unmistakable mischief in Penelope's voice. The chit was teasing him! Thank God his behaviour hadn't frightened her off.

When they stopped to sit on a garden bench Penelope said shyly, 'Perhaps when we are...are a little better acquainted, you would permit me to...to touch your face. You s...see that way I can *feel* what you look like.'

The request startled Peter. He had seen how she had touched a rose and explored its petals. The idea that those gentle, soft hands might touch him in the same way was very pleasant.

She was facing him with that odd listening look on her face, but his silence disconcerted her and she flushed, saying, 'I'm sorry, I didn't mean to offend you.'

'You have not offended me at all,' he assured her, adding, 'Would you like to do it now, while we are alone?' His voice told her that he was perfectly sincere, so she lifted her hands to his face, gently tracing the strong line of his jaw and chin. The nose was finely modelled, his cheekbones high, his mouth warm and firm. His hair curled crisply and she liked its texture. In fact she liked what she found very much.

Peter sat utterly still as her hands moved over his face. It was very like a caress, and he found himself deeply aroused, although he was aware she had not intended it thus. Her face was turned up to his as she concentrated, her dark red hair curling around her brow, her lips slightly parted. Finally Peter could deny himself no longer. Very gently, so as not to scare her, he slipped one arm about her waist to draw her nearer. Those soft fingers quivered, were still, and her listening look intensified.

Not taking his eyes from her face he said huskily, 'May I join in, Penny?' The diminutive disarmed her and she nodded mutely, not trusting her voice.

He raised his free hand to her face and stroked her cheek lightly, enjoying its soft smoothness. The column of her white throat was equally soft. He could feel her trembling in his arms yet she did not try to draw away from his embrace. His fingers passed gently over her tender mouth and with a groan of pleasure he bent his head to cover her lips with his own. This time Penelope made no attempt to struggle, rather she melted against him, returning his kisses as best she could. From the moment he had put his arm about her waist she had known he would kiss her and had schooled herself not to draw back, but the sensations his mouth aroused took her completely by surprise. Her heart was pounding erratically, something seemed to have happened to her breath, and she was conscious of a spreading weakness in her body.

As for Peter, he found his wife's innocent response to his advances a revealing experience. The relationship he had enjoyed with Lady Caroline and other even less respectable partners since his first wife's defection; had not prepared him for the protective instinct aroused by Penelope's timid return of his embrace. Her mouth was unbelievably sweet. He was ashamed when he recalled how brutally he had taken it the previous day. Now his mouth moved gently yet passionately over hers as his arm tightened around her waist. The other hand slid over the curve of her breast under the muslin gown and he felt her gasp in surprise. Reluctantly he released her. He wanted to bed her, most certainly, but for her sake he did not want to rush his fences.

'Thank you, Penelope. I...I...think we should return to the house,' he said. His voice betrayed his confusion. Dear God, he wanted her so much. It would be torture to know she was asleep in the bedroom next to his, that all he had to do was walk through the connecting door and get into her bed. He remembered how lovely he had thought her when he'd put her to bed last night, still with the tears on her cheeks. It had been impossible to resist the temptation to caress one of those delicate white breasts, and she had smiled so tenderly in her sleep!

Penelope rose slowly to her feet, rather surprised to discover that her legs would still obey her commands. She did not know what to say. His kiss had left her shaken physically and with her emotions in a whirl. The feelings he had aroused in her were beyond her comprehension. Her gasp when he touched her breast had been one of pleasure, and she wondered if her response had disgusted him. On the whole she thought not, he had released her very gently, not at all as though he were angry.

Peter's thoughts were also in turmoil, but of a different kind. A nasty suspicious voice in his mind was warning him to watch his step, that he was becoming interested in his wife as a person, perhaps even as a lover. Better not to care, just be civilised, keep a distance. Remember Melissa. You don't want to make the same mistake twice. But she's not like Melissa, he argued. Melissa had been a virgin, certainly, but she had not been the total innocent this girl was. The nagging doubts persisted. Perhaps it would be better to keep some emotional distance between them.

By the time they reached the house Penelope was aware of Peter's change of attitude. His manner towards her was still friendly but he made no attempt to win her confidences, merely speaking of the route they

were taking back to the house. She was a little sad-
dened by this, assuming that somehow she had caused
his withdrawal, and decided firmly that she had better
not become too attached to her incalculable husband!

Chapter Seven

A month later Darleston sat in his sunny breakfast parlour consuming a plate of ham and eggs, wondering if he would see his wife at breakfast or indeed at all that day! In the time since their wedding the couple had made very little progress in their relationship. Peter acknowledged to himself that this was his fault.

For perhaps a week Penelope had tried very hard to get to know him and he had politely rebuffed her every time. Then she had given up and had appeared to avoid his company. After a week of being effectually ignored, Peter had begun to feel piqued and had made tentative advances, hoping to mend the breach.

Penelope it seemed, had other ideas. She had made it quite clear that she had plenty to do and was not pining for his company! She spent a great deal of time with his housekeeper, learning the ways of the house, and even more time in the drawing room, playing the piano. He had frequently paused outside the door to enjoy the music, knowing from experience that if he went in she would not continue past the end of the movement.

'Good morning, Penelope,' said Peter now, looking

up from his letters as his wife entered the breakfast parlour with Gelert. 'Did you sleep well?'

'Very well, thank you, Peter.' answered Penelope.

Peter rose to his feet to help her to a chair and bestowed a pat upon Gelert, who had completely accepted him as a friend. 'Would you like a cup of tea?'

'Yes, please.'

He poured one for her, saying as he passed it to her, 'There you are, my dear. Are you very busy today? I thought we might go for a drive together.'

'That is very kind of you, Peter, but I will be in the stillroom for much of the day. Perhaps another time.'

'As you please.'

Having seen that Penelope had everything she needed, Peter continued reading his correspondence, feeling that he had perhaps been too thorough in avoiding any emotional involvement with his wife! Despite the fact that she generally used his Christian name in private, the polite formality of her manner always made it *sound* as though she were calling him my lord.

To make matters worse for Peter, he was having a great deal of difficulty remaining on his side of the door which connected their rooms. He was not sleeping particularly well, and when he did sleep he was disturbed by dreams which made it even harder not to be able to go through that door. He had not attempted to kiss her since that first day in the garden and the memory of her response haunted him.

It was difficult to believe that the remote girl on the other side of the table had responded so sweetly to his embrace. She seemed as distant and cool as the moon. Peter gazed at her in frustration as she sat in the sunlight from the window, munching a scone and sipping her tea. Her dark red hair showed gleams of copper in the light and there was a slight tinge of pink in her usually pale cheeks.

Penelope was perfectly aware of Peter's scrutiny, as she always was. It was not distaste for his company that made her avoid him, but a profound distrust of her own feelings. She was uncomfortably aware it would be only too easy to fall in love with her husband. Obviously that was the last thing he wanted. He had made no further attempt to kiss her, or to do anything else a marriage should involve, so she must assume that either he was not attracted to her or that she had disgusted him. Therefore it would be most unwise to indulge in any affection for him. She continued to sip her tea, conscious of her husband's regard but utterly unconscious of the fact that he was jealous of the teacup.

'I have received a letter from George Carstares. Would you object if he came to stay, Penelope?'

'Not at all, Peter. I should like to know your friends. When will he arrive?'

'I shall write telling him to come when he likes, which means he will come as soon as he receives my reply, in all probability.'

'Then I shall inform Mrs Bates and ask her to have a room made ready for him at once. I am glad you will have some company.' Having finished her breakfast, Penelope arose. 'If you will excuse me, Peter, I will go about my day now.'

'A moment please, Penelope, if you would not mind.' Peter had made up his mind swiftly; he must try to breach the gap between them.

She turned towards him with a questioning look on

her face, said, 'Very well, my lord,' and sat down again.

He winced at the chilling formality of her response, which made it quite clear she waited from duty, not inclination. For a moment he hesitated, before saying, 'I would very much like you to come for that drive with me, my dear. We seem to see very little of each other and I grudge your company to the stillroom and Mrs Bates. Besides, Gelert will enjoy the run!' Gelert, hearing his name coupled with the word 'run', uttered an enthusiastic bark and wagged his tail.

'You really want me to come out with you?' Penelope was surprised. Always before he had accepted her refusals with equanimity, which had reinforced her belief that he preferred it that way and merely requested her company out of duty.

'Yes, I do want your company, Penelope. I think it is time you met some of my tenants. As my wife that is one your duties,' he said, wondering just how he should go about convincing her that it was time she fulfilled all her wifely duties.

'If that is your wish, Peter, of course I will accompany you. When do you wish to set off?'

'I should finish reading my letters and reply to some of them... an hour from now shall we say?' answered Peter, glancing idly at the rest of his letters.

One of them caught his attention. 'Oh, here is a letter for you, Penelope, from your mother!'

'From Mama? Please read it to me, Peter!' said Penelope in unabashed delight.

'Read it to you?' It had not occurred to Peter that he would have to read his wife's correspondence.

Misunderstanding his exclamation, Penelope blushed. 'I beg your pardon, my lord. I will ask Ellen to read it for me if you are too busy.' She went to Peter's side and held out her hand for the letter.

Realising that he had unintentionally hurt her, Peter ignored her outstretched hand and slipped his arm about her waist. 'Silly child, of course I'm not too busy! It was just that I had not really thought about how you were to read your letter. Come, sit down again and I'll read it for you at once.' Before she could protest he had pulled her onto his lap. 'There! Comfortable? I do hope your mama hasn't written anything too personal! What should I do if she has, my dear?'

Stunned to find herself sitting in her husband's lap, with his arm around her waist, Penelope was taken off her guard and answered without thinking, 'Don't listen, of course!' Peter burst out laughing.

'I suppose I could try that, or shutting my eyes might help!' He opened the letter and began to read aloud.

'"Dear Penny, Thank you for your note letting us know you are well—" Did you write, Penelope?' Peter was very surprised.

'Yes, just a short note to say I was well. I can write if I am very careful and don't rush. Ellen addressed it for me. I asked her to post it when she went to the village. Should I not have done so?'

'You most certainly should not!' said Peter. 'Why didn't you get a frank from me, and leave it on the table in the hall, you silly girl? Your mother will think I won't let you write to her!'

Penelope blinked. 'A frank! Oh, dear, I forgot you could give me one. I hope she didn't think that you are a sort of Bluebeard! Perhaps I'd better write again.'

'I think you should, or I'll have that ferocious

brother-in-law of yours down upon me!' teased Peter. 'Now, where was I? Ah, yes. "Could his lordship not give you a frank?''—see! "Or did you merely forget that he could do so? Sarah gives it as her opinion that Darleston has you locked in a dungeon and that you were forced to write the letter. I think it was a mistake permitting her to read *The Mysteries of Udolpho* and Richard has apologised for giving it to her. I suggested that if Darleston had wished to behave in such a dastardly fashion he probably would have franked the letter and made you write more, but she informed us that criminals always make one fatal error and that this is his. She was more convinced by Richard's comment that Darleston would have chosen a really wealthy victim like Emily if he'd wanted to behave like Montoni!'''

Peter had to stop reading at this point, to regain some control over his voice. 'Good God, what an imagination! Penelope, you are to write immediately! I intended to offer my services as your amanuensis, but no doubt that will afford your sister fresh grounds for suspicion. Stop laughing, girl, this is my reputation at stake!'

Penelope tried to contain her mirth, but failed totally. Peter was delighted to see her quiet reserve shattered and continued with the letter.

> Phoebe and Richard are very well. They have spent a great deal of time with us and are very happy but I believe Phoebe is writing to you, so I won't spoil any of her news.
> Ariadne has had her foal and it is a filly. Richard thinks she is very promising!
> Sarah sends her love and she is also writing, al-

though I believe she is uncertain whether to address a letter of encouragement to you, Penny, or
threats to Darleston. She is consoling herself with
the thought that Gelert will probably take the first
opportunity of dealing with the situation!
I am glad Darleston was not out of reason cross
about the affair. You must now show yourself to
be equally generous. Be a good girl, Penny darling, and a kind and loving wife.

Your Devoted Mama.

Peter was silent for a moment after finishing the
letter. Penelope was leaning confidingly against him,
smiling tenderly at her own thoughts. He studied her
delicate profile, delighting in her proximity. Gently he
reached up to stroke her cheek, marvelling at its softness. Startled out of her thoughts, she turned to him
enquiringly. He gave her a hug and said, 'Perhaps we
should write to your family this evening to allay the
fears your little sister entertains.'

Unable to resist the temptation to tease him,
Penelope said, 'Goodness no! She'll enjoy it far more
if we fuel her suspicions. It will be a very good idea
for you to write the letter and me merely to sign it!
Think what a thrill for her to be the heroine and to
dream of rescuing me from your clutches!'

'Thanks very much. My clutches don't seem to be
that unbearable to you!' said Peter in amusement. 'If
we do that she will probably disguise herself as a boy
and run away to rescue you. I shall give her a copy
of *Northanger Abbey* at the first opportunity!'

'What's that about?' asked Penelope curiously.

'A young lady who reads too many sensational nov-
els, *The Mysteries of Udolpho* in particular, and allows

too free a rein to her fancies! It was written by the same woman who wrote *Pride and Prejudice* and *Mansfield Park*. Do you know them?'

'Mama read *Pride and Prejudice* aloud to us. We all liked it.'

'Good! I shall recommend *Northanger Abbey* with a clear conscience.' He stood up and set Penelope gently on her feet. 'Come along, Penelope. If we are to go for our drive I had better finish the rest of these letters and write to George at least. That is, if you really don't mind him visiting us. Shall we invite Sarah later on as well—just to lull her suspicions of course!'

Penelope's face plainly mirrored her delight. 'Could we. Peter? I mean, I'm sure she doesn't really believe you are a villain, but I should like to see her.'

'Of course you may invite her,' said Peter, happy to have hit on such a simple way of pleasing her. Surely now they would go on better than they had been doing. He held the door open for her and watched her departure with Gelert, an odd smile on his face. Slowly he walked to the study, still chuckling at the letter Penelope had received.

Penelope came to seek him out an hour later, ready to go for their drive. She had spent a great deal of time discussing her bonnet with Ellen and was feeling particularly frustrated that she could not judge the effect for herself. She knocked at the study door shyly, amazed at the slight feeling of breathlessness that took hold of her as she heard his deep voice. 'Come in, Penelope.'

Peter looked up from his desk as she entered and smiled. 'Ready, my dear? My letters are finished, so we shall go?' He added, 'You look charming in that bonnet.' She did. The bonnet framed her face and the dark green ribbons that were tied under her chin emphasised the fairness of her complexion.

Penelope did not really know how to respond to the compliment. She wondered why he was being friendly again and how long it would last. 'Thank you,' she said at last, feeling that she must say something.

Peter led her out to the waiting phaeton and lifted her up into it effortlessly. Penelope trembled as she felt his hands encircle her waist. She told herself fiercely to stop being silly. After all he was only lifting her into a carriage!

Peter told himself exactly the same thing, and reminded himself that an open carriage, especially with a groom up behind, was not a good place to make love to a girl, even if she was your wife.

He leapt up into the vehicle, trying very hard not to think about the delicious curve of Penelope's waist, or how she had sat in his lap while he read her letter. It would be positively dangerous to dwell on such thoughts while driving a high-couraged pair like his matched greys!

The drive was very pleasant. They called at several farms on the estate, and while Peter discussed the crops and harvest with the farmers Penelope was entertained by their wives. She discovered that Peter was looked up to as a good landlord and that he was genuinely concerned with the welfare of his tenants. The last farm they visited was particularly interesting.

'We may not be able to stay long here, Penelope,' said Peter. 'Jewkes got married last year and his wife is expecting their first baby very soon. As a matter of fact she is Ellen's sister!'

'Peter, if only you'd told me I could have brought a note from Ellen,' said Penelope.

'I'm sorry, dear, I didn't think. But at least you may take a message back,' he apologised.

Jewkes was in the farmyard when they arrived and was extremely proud that the Earl had brought his new Countess to be introduced. 'Proud to meet ye, milady. My Martha's in the 'ouse. Come y' in to meet 'er. She'd be that sorry to miss ye! Take my arm, milady. Ellen tells us ye're blind but once ye know the way ye never forget!'

'I'll wait with the horses, Tom, and not intrude on Martha,' said Peter.

'Why, she'd not think it a trouble, milord!' expostulated Jewkes, but Peter insisted, thinking that the two women would talk more easily without him.

Tom Jewkes rejoined him a moment later. 'Goin' along like winkin', they are! Cheers Martha up to have a visitor, not that she's gloomy, but we'll both be glad when it's all over.'

'Hoping for a fine lusty son, are you, Tom?' asked Peter.

The farmer thought about it and said, 'Well, in a manner of speaking, yes. But bein' a farmer ye get so used to wantin' a heifer, it's hard to break the habit! And I'll tell ye summat, milord, I'll be glad whichever it is just so long as Martha's all right! And so will you be when it's your turn, if ye'll forgive my speakin' so bold!'

Peter gripped his shoulder and the conversation turned into agricultural topics.

Presently Penelope appeared at the kitchen door and Gelert, who had waited with Peter, bounded across the yard to her side. She placed her hand on his collar for him to guide her to Peter and Jewkes.

The latter was highly impressed. 'Ellen said as how ye had a dog to be guide ye, which I couldn't believe, but Martha says if a dog can herd sheep and cattle, why not guide a human?'

'He is very good at it,' said Peter. 'And now I think we should be getting back for our nuncheon and letting you get on with your work, Tom. We'll call again to see how Martha is going on. Mind you let us know if you need anything.'

'Oh, Mr Jewkes,' said Penelope. 'I told Martha that I would send Ellen over for a few days when she is…confined. Just send a message when you need her.'

The farmer flushed. 'Why, milady, I know Martha will be easier in her mind if she knows that. Thank ye.'

Penelope smiled and said, 'It's nothing, Mr Jewkes. I know I should like to have my sister with me, and so I thought Ellen had better come. Goodbye.'

Peter lifted her into the carriage and leapt up beside her. They drove off at a spanking trot, Peter negotiating the turn out of the yard with ease. 'That was kind of you, Penelope. I know how much you depend on Ellen.'

Penelope was silent for a moment, and then said, 'Martha is so glad to be having a child, but I thought she sounded a little scared. She didn't say much but I know she was glad when I said Ellen would be coming over.'

They drove on in silence for a mile, but it was not an awkward silence. Peter was thinking of his wife's generosity in volunteering to do without her maid. He realised guiltily that he had spent so little time with

Penelope recently that she must be doubly dependent upon Ellen for company. Yet she never complained, although she had admitted that she found her blindness to be frustrating in company. But, no! It was not the actual blindness which had bothered her but people's reaction to it. What had she said? *They annoy me by being pitying and patronising...*

Almost without thinking, he asked her, 'Penelope, what frustrates you most about being blind?' She did not return an answer immediately and he said gently, 'I'm sorry. I didn't mean to pry. Forget it.'

'I'm not offended, Peter,' she said, laughing. 'It's just that there are so many things which frustrate me that I didn't really know where to start!'

'But you never say anything!' he said in surprise.

'Well, what good would it do?' she answered. 'I suppose the thing I miss the most is reading. But even then my family were always happy to read aloud. Reading music too. My sisters used to help me to learn new pieces. Sometimes we would learn them together. One of them would practice and I would learn the piece by ear! They helped me to learn lots of poetry by heart too, so it's always there when I want it.'

Peter suddenly understood fully just what a leap of faith she had taken to marry a total stranger for the sake of her family. He felt a surge of tenderness for her, an urge to look after her. Transferring the reins to one hand, he slipped his arm around her shoulders and said, 'Well, I can't help you with new music, but I can certainly read aloud to you!'

'But I don't wish to make demands on you!' protested Penelope, trying to ignore the odd fluttering of her heart as she felt his hand caress her shoulder.

'My sweet, it is merely a fair return for all the pleasure your music gives me! I often listen outside the door,' he admitted with a smile. 'I love music, you know, Penelope.'

'I…I thought it would disturb you!' she said in surprise.

'The only thing that disturbs me is that you won't let me sit down in comfort to listen!' he said. 'I have to skulk around the door because you always stop if I come in, you silly child.' He gave her a light hug and returned his full attention to his horses. The last thing he wanted was to tip his wife into a ditch because he couldn't keep his hands off her!

Penelope did not know what to say. She could not understand his change of mood. Not that he was ever unkind or rude. Simply distant, so that she hesitated to approach him. Did he really wish to be friends now? Or would he revert to his formal coolness? It was lovely when he was being kind and approachable. Then she felt that there was nothing she could not ask him. But be careful, she warned herself. Just respond to as much as he offers, when he offers it. It occurred to her that it would be easier said than done to switch her feelings on and off.

Falling in with her abstracted mood, Peter drove home swiftly. He did not resent her silence, rather it was refreshing to drive out with a woman who did not feel obliged to fill up every moment with chatter. He hoped that he had managed to at least partially bridge the chasm he had created.

'Gelert seems to have enjoyed his run,' said Peter, as they walked into the Great Hall. 'We must take him out more often, I think. Did you enjoy yourself my dear?'

'Yes, I did, thank you, Peter. Gelert is used to more

exercise. P…Papa and I used to drive out together.' The slight hesitation told him how much the loss of her father had hurt.

'You miss him very much, don't you?' asked Peter, touched.

'Always. We were very close, you see. But I am glad now that he died when he did. He would have been so ashamed of what Geoffrey did.' She turned and faced him. 'I have been meaning to apologise to you for his behaviour, but I just didn't know how to bring the subject up…'

'There is no need, Penelope. I was also at fault for not calling a halt to that damned game of dice when I had the chance. Don't give it another thought, I beg of you.'

Penelope went into her nuncheon feeling much easier in her mind over the whole matter. Perhaps things were finally sorting themselves out, she thought hopefully.

The rest of the day passed peacefully. Penelope spent the afternoon in the stillroom, helping her housekeeper to sort out and dry herbs. Her mind drifted over the morning's drive and she wondered again why Peter had suddenly become friendly. Perhaps he was just moody, she thought. Then, as she relived the visit with Martha Jewkes, another possibility occurred to her. He wanted an heir, didn't he? Was all this kindness a ploy to get her into his bed willingly? She blushed at the idea, but the more she thought about it, the more likely it seemed.

Having reached that conclusion, she examined her own feelings. She had to admit to herself that she was fond of her husband, despite his recent coolness towards her. In fact, if she were honest with herself, she liked him very much. He was unfailingly polite to her, and the respect and liking she had observed in his tenants were indicative of a fine man. Finally she came to her physical reaction to him. When he touched her in any way she enjoyed it. The time he had kissed her in the garden she had not wanted him to stop. Why had he stopped? Should she not have kissed him back? Had she disgusted him? Perhaps he didn't find her attractive but felt he must do his duty and beget an heir!

She took extra care over her toilet that evening, asking Ellen to dress her in a gown of dark green silk which had arrived from London. Ellen had taken great pleasure in describing all the lovely new gowns which had been ordered. They all suited Penelope's colouring perfectly, setting off the glowing curls and the fairness of her complexion.

By the time she joined Peter for dinner Penelope was so nervous that she had withdrawn behind her barriers again. Peter noticed the change immediately and set himself to drawing her out once more. He teased her about the suspicions her brief letter had aroused, suggesting ways they could reply to Sarah's letter when it arrived. Gradually Penelope relaxed, forgetting her worries and simply enjoying her husband's company.

For his part Peter was more than content with his companion. His eyes dwelt appreciatively on her slim figure, not missing a single curve. The silk of her gown clung to every contour and he thought with pleasure of the softness of her body when he had lifted her into the carriage. Mellow candlelight caught highlights in the dark red hair, which seemed to glow with an inner fire. The memory of the sweetness of her mouth was a constant temptation, but he controlled himself nobly. Surely it could not have been quite so yielding, so responsive!

After dinner they sat in the drawing room and Penelope played the piano for him. She played with a sensitive touch and Peter listened with real pleasure. His bride never ceased to amaze him with the things she could do for herself, despite her blindness.

By the time she had played through a Haydn sonata he had come to a decision. He could wait no longer; he wanted her so much it hurt. Surely after a month, he told himself, she would not mind! After all, he had warned her that he wanted an heir.

Penelope finished the sonata and stood to close the piano. Peter went to help her. Standing so close to her was too much for his self-control. His hand caught her wrist and he pulled her gently but inexorably into his arms. Startled, Penelope froze, instinctively turning her face up to his.

Peter felt her stiffen. His conscience told him to release her, but the sensation caused by holding her against him made short work of this gentlemanly impulse and he pressed his lips firmly upon hers. One hand slid up her back while the other caressed her throat and cheek. For a moment Penelope fought the urge to respond, but when that wandering hand moved to stroke her breast she gave an involuntary moan of pleasure and yielded to his embrace, slipping her arms around his neck to cling to him.

Peter felt her response and tightened his arm to support her. Her lips, so incredibly tender and soft under his, parted slightly and, unable to resist the temptation, Peter slid his tongue into her mouth. He groaned as he fully tasted her sweetness. Dear God, he thought wildly, I could take her right here on the floor!

His hand slipped into the bodice of her gown and Penelope thought for a moment that the world had turned upside down. Her whole body trembled and she wondered if she were about to faint. The straying fingers in her bodice teased and caressed the tender flesh, his mouth possessed hers completely.

He released her mouth, only to murmur against her cheek, 'Penny, I cannot wait much longer. I want you in my bed. Do you understand?' He took her mouth again, gently at first, then more insistently as his desire for her took control. Scarcely knowing what he was doing, he lifted her in his arms and carried her effortlessly back to the sofa. He sat down with his wife nestled in his lap to continue his assault on her already weakened defences. Again his hand slid into her bodice and he stroked the velvety flesh as his mouth moved over her throat, making her shiver in delight.

Penelope was lost on a sea of sensation; his hands and mouth were igniting a blaze which threatened to consume her utterly. She stroked his face and returned his kisses shyly, unsure of herself. Peter felt a surge of tender affection. She was so sweet and lovable in her innocence, he thought. Then, realising that he was about to lose control of his emotions completely, he suddenly released her, saying harshly, 'Penelope, I think you should go up to bed now. If you do not I cannot be responsible.' His hands were shaking as he put her from him and stood up. He told himself that he didn't want to rush her, but in truth his own feelings were frightening.

Penelope couldn't believe her ears. What had she done wrong? Confused by Peter's rejection, she stood up slowly and moved to the bell pull. She heard Peter cross swiftly to the door, heard it open and slam as he left. Her body still trembled from his caresses. She yearned for more. Why had he left? He had said he wanted her. Surely he hadn't thought that she was unwilling! Unable to answer her own questions, she pulled the bell and waited for Meadows.

He came almost immediately. 'Meadows, please send Ellen to me in my room. I am ready to retire for the night.'

'Yes, milady.'

Slowly, sadly she went out of the room with Gelert and made her way through the house to her bedchamber. She wondered where Peter had gone. Probably the study, she thought. It was his refuge and she never sought him out there.

When Ellen came she found her mistress abstracted, even depressed. This was surprising; Lady Darleston was generally very cheerful. Tonight she was not at all inclined to talk, indeed she seemed close to tears. Ellen had been told already that she would be going to stay with her sister and was very grateful to her mistress for thinking of this. She chattered gaily as she brushed Penelope's hair and readied her for bed. Perhaps the mistress had disagreed with the master over some matter, she thought as she put away clothes.

'Goodnight, milady. Come along, Gelert,' said Ellen as she prepared to leave. She noticed that the connecting door was open and wondered if she should shut it. No, if the mistress and master had argued it would be better to leave it open. You couldn't make up through a shut door!

Penelope lay in her great bed, feeling frustrated and depressed. She was quite sure she had annoyed Peter by responding to his advances so willingly. Well, then, next time he kissed her, she wouldn't respond. At least, not if she could help it! She was obliged to admit to herself that it might be very difficult not to respond to her husband's sensuous embrace. His mouth and hands were so very persuasive, she thought as she drifted off to sleep. Perhaps she could simply pretend not to enjoy his advances!

Coming up to bed an hour later, Peter stood at the open connecting door to gaze at his sleeping wife. He too was feeling frustrated, and the confused look of pain on Penelope's face when he thrust her away refused to be banished from his mind. Why, he asked himself, couldn't he initiate a physical relationship with his wife without all these unwelcome emotions creeping in? Perhaps it would be safer not to take her to bed if it was going to stir up feelings best forgotten? But he had to take her to bed if he wanted an heir! Blast it all, why did she have to be so sweet, so damned responsive and yielding? He didn't want to care for the girl. He liked her very much; she was a charming companion. That was all he wanted to feel!

Chapter Eight

Penelope entered the breakfast parlour the next morning determined to try and recapture the friendliness of the previous day. She had taken particular care with her choice of gown, selecting a dark blue morning dress which Ellen and the housekeeper assured her was most becoming. Her efforts were not entirely wasted.

Peter looked up as she entered and caught his breath. The deep blue emphasised the fairness of her complexion. Her hair was caught at the nape of her neck with a wide blue bow and lay carelessly over one shoulder, the burnished curls blazing against the dark fabric. An affectionate smile hovered around the delicately cut lips. He remembered how they had yielded to his demands the evening before…soft, trembling… Hell and damnation! He wouldn't think of it! He would not be undone by a pretty face again!

'Good morning, Peter.'

'My lady.' He rose and pulled out a chair for her. 'I trust you slept well?'

'Er…yes,' she lied gallantly. In truth she had not slept well at all. Nervously she seated herself. The formality of her husband's greeting chilled her. His tone was simply arctic.

'Would you like a cup of tea?'

'Thank you, my lord.'

He poured it and passed it to her, trying to ignore his conscience, which told him that he was behaving badly. He retired into his newspaper.

Penelope tried again. 'I did enjoy the drive yesterday, Peter. If you are going again, may I come?'

'I will be going on horseback today. It will waste less time.'

He looked into her face. For one fleeting instant he thought he saw her mouth tremble, but then an expression of cold indifference settled over her face. 'I beg your pardon, my lord.' She would not try again; his rejection hurt too much and it was too much like begging. Next time he invited her out he could go to the devil!

The following hour found Penelope in a restless mood, longing to go out. She tried to concentrate on her music but found the charms of Handel were nothing compared to the prospect of exercise. A ride would have been enjoyable, even on the inevitable leading rein. She told herself firmly that it was merely for Gelert's sake that she wanted to escape from the house. Innate honesty forced her to admit to herself that she had wanted to spend time with her husband.

The memory of his passionate kisses the previous night had disturbed her sleep. He had been so gentle, yet demanding. He had even said that he wanted her! Her fingers slowed on the keys as she dwelt on the memory. What had she done wrong? She longed for the courage to ask him, but his greeting at breakfast had been so distant and icy. A waste of time! What on earth was wrong with the man? One moment he behaved as though he liked her, the next as though she were a nuisance.

A rebellious thought crept into her mind. Why should she not go out? After all, she did not have to wait on Peter's pleasure for her entertainment! One of the grooms could just as easily escort her! Her decision made, she closed the piano, and went to change.

Ellen was predictably horrified. 'Riding? But, milady, what will the master say?'

'The master,' said Penelope between her teeth, 'may go to the devil! Please just find my riding habit.'

Ellen did as she was bid, reflecting that her mistress surely couldn't come to much harm on a leading rein. The head groom, Johnson, was very reliable. But what the master was going to say she hardly dared to think!

The master, having spent a busy morning visiting tenants and discussing improvements to his estate and crops for the coming winter, was startled to say the least at the sight which met his eyes as he rode homewards across the park. His wife, atop his favourite retired hunter, with his head groom and her dog in attendance, was cantering off goodness knew where!

Good God, what the hell did Johnson think he was up to? Swearing under his breath, Peter galloped his mare over to intercept them.

Hearing the hoofbeats, Johnson turned around and immediately said, 'We'd best stop a moment, your ladyship. The master is back and he's coming this way.'

Penelope bit back the very unladylike rejoinder which rose to her lips and merely said, 'Very well. Perhaps his lordship wishes to join us.'

Observing the grim look upon the Earl's face, Johnson could think of nothing less likely. Gloomily he wondered just why he had let his mistress cajole him into this foolishness and whether the master would give him a reference or not.

Penelope on the other hand was quite calm. She was determined to give as good as she got. After all, he had not told her that she might not ride any of his horses! It occurred to her that Johnson might be in a certain amount of trouble, however.

'Don't worry, Johnson. It will be me he'll be annoyed with. I'll tell him you didn't like the idea,' she said encouragingly.

'I'd appreciate that, milady!'

Peter pulled the mare in beside his errant bride and her escort and glared at them.

'What the devil do you think you're doing?'

His head groom wilted at the outrage in his voice, but Penelope faced him squarely with her chin up and answered in dulcet tones, 'Riding, my lord. Do you care to join me? I understood you to be otherwise engaged this morning, but if you have finished your business early and would not be wasting your time of course you are most welcome.'

He stared at her and said angrily, 'I do not consider it safe for you to be on horseback, my lady. You will please oblige me by returning to the stables at once. And as for you, Johnson, you must be out of your mind!'

Penelope sniffed disdainfully. 'My lord, I have been riding since I was a little girl. If my parents saw no need for me to stop when I lost my eyesight, I can see no reason for you to concern yourself with my safety. Johnson merely obeyed my orders in saddling a suitable horse and accompanying me. You had given no contrary orders, so you can scarcely blame him.'

Unable to think of a single answer which would not shock his servant, Peter was at a loss for a moment. Then he said curtly, 'Change horses with me, Johnson. Griselda is too lively to lead another horse from. I will take your mistress for a ride.' He suited the action to the word and dismounted.

Johnson obeyed, and gave the reins of his quiet hack to the Earl, who vaulted effortlessly into the saddle. He took the leading rein and said, 'You may return to the stables, Johnson.' Then, seeing the woebegone look on the man's face, 'Oh, for heaven's sake man! You can't imagine that I'd sack you for obeying orders!'

'Yes, sir! I mean, no, sir. Thank you, sir!' Johnson mounted and set off, leaving the Earl and his unrepentant Countess confronting one another.

Peter drew a deep breath and said, 'Shall we go, my lady?'

'Certainly, my lord.'

Peter pressed his mount into a trot, observing that his bride sat the old hunter with easy confidence.

'In future, Lady Darleston, I would appreciate it if you checked with me before setting my household by the ears!' The fury in his quiet voice was unmistakable. Inwardly she quaked but lifted her chin even higher, facing him defiantly.

'Indeed, my lord? I cannot conceive what concern it is of yours how I choose to spend my time, always provided I do not waste yours, of course!' she replied.

'You are my wife! Of course I am concerned with your safety!' he said furiously.

'Oh. I'm afraid that didn't occur to me, my lord. I was not aware that you had any interest whatsoever.'

Her air of calm detachment galled him. Damn it,

the impertinent chit had as good as told him to mind his own business! Despite his anger he had to acknowledge that her seat on a horse was magnificent. She rode so well that he could understand her reluctance to give up after her accident. He decided that there was nothing to be gained in arguing the point. Obviously she was quite capable of controlling a horse and he was making a fool of himself.

'Well, you are obviously able to handle a horse. As long as you ride with either myself or Johnson you should be safe enough. Believe it or not, I do take an interest in your well-being!'

'How kind of you, my lord. However, I beg that you will not concern yourself with me. I shall be more than happy to ride out with Johnson. You must have a great deal of estate business to occupy your time.' Her voice spoke volumes of indifference she was far from feeling. The thought that he would offer to spend time with her as an unwelcome duty stung her pride unbearably.

Peter immediately realised that he had offended her deeply. He changed the subject at once. 'How do you find Nero's paces, Penelope?'

'Very comfortable, my lord.'

He winced at the formality of her reply but forbore to comment upon it. After all, he had started it!

She continued, 'Johnson informed me that Nero is practically retired but is the most reliable mount in the stables.'

'He certainly is,' said Peter with a fond glance at his old friend. 'I rode him at Waterloo. But for him and George Carstares I should have been killed.' He was silent for a moment, reliving the battle, lost in a haze of smoke, the roar of guns and the screams of dying men and horses. He shook his head to dispel the hellish vision.

'What happened, Peter?' Her voice was gentler, drew him back. Something in his voice had told her that the horror of the things he had seen that day would live with him for ever.

After a moment he went on. 'I was rallying my men. They were in a square, holding their ground, but the French columns kept coming. There were shots flying everywhere but Nero was as steady as though he'd been in his stable. Finally a musket ball hit me. All I remember is a pain in my side and lying in the mud, staring up at Nero's belly. The men said it was the strangest thing they ever saw. Any other horse would have taken to his heels, but he stood right over me until our men managed to beat back the French. Otherwise I would have been trampled.'

'And Mr Carstares?' prompted Penelope softly.

'George saw it happen. When he could, he fought his way to me and got me back on Nero, had one of the men lead me to the rear.'

Penelope was silent for a moment. Perhaps his anger had simply been at seeing her on a horse he must regard as very special. Eventually she said, 'I'm sorry I rode Nero without your permission, Peter. I can understand that you would prefer no one else to ride him.'

'It's no matter Penelope,' said Peter in embarrassment. 'He needs to be ridden, and since he is getting on a bit now I don't ride him as much as I used to. If you will exercise him I shall be glad of it. I still ride him occasionally, for old time's sake, but otherwise please consider him as your own.'

'Thank you, Peter.'

They rode on in silence. When Peter spoke again he had reverted to formal indifference. With a sigh Penelope gave up trying to regain lost ground. If his lordship wished for a relationship distinguished by cool propriety he should have it!

The following morning Penelope arose and sent a message to the stables to find out when it would be convenient for Johnson to ride out with her. The answer came back before she was out of her bath that Johnson would be at her disposal whenever she wished.

Penelope thought about this carefully as she dried herself. 'Very well, Ellen. Please lay out my riding habit, and then when I am dressed you may send someone to tell Johnson that I shall be down directly after breakfast.'

'Yes, my lady.'

'And, Ellen.'

'My lady?'

'I think I will go for a good long walk after my ride and take something with me to eat. Just fruit, bread and cheese will do, and whatever you would like to eat if you will come with me.'

Ellen blinked in surprise. 'Don't you think you'll get tired, my lady?' Then, remembering her place, 'I mean, of course I'll come, but...'

Penelope set her jaw and said firmly, 'No buts. Just lay out my habit and think about what you'd like to eat for lunch!'

Ellen did as she was told and shortly, arrayed for riding, Penelope made her way down to the breakfast parlour. As she passed along the corridors and galleries she told herself firmly that she would *not*, absolutely would *not* give her husband the slightest reason to think she cared about his attitude towards her. If he felt like being friendly, or even amorous, she would simply be polite. Constant rejections when she overstepped some invisible boundary were too hurtful.

It did not occur to her that Peter was the one who kept on stepping over the emotional boundaries which he had set for their relationship.

Peter rose to his feet at her entrance and laid down his morning paper. 'Good morning, Penelope. Would you care for a cup of tea?'

'Thank you, my lord, that would be lovely.' She congratulated herself silently on the cool, but polite tone of her voice.

It was on the tip of Peter's tongue to remonstrate with her for being so formal but he decided to let it pass. Something in her face warned him to tread warily. She was wearing what her mother and sisters would have described as 'Penny's keep-out look'.

He poured her tea and set it down before her. Observing the snugly fitted habit, he enquired, 'Were you planning to ride this morning Penelope?'

'Thank you, my lord. Yes, I have sent a message down to the stables and Johnson is expecting me after breakfast.'

Peter sat down and thought about this. He knew perfectly well that he had behaved badly the previous day and that he should offer to escort his wife, but her very next words showed how little that would be appreciated.

'I think I shall enjoy riding out with Johnson,' she said sweetly. 'He seems very easy to talk to. And afterwards Ellen and I are going to take Gelert for a long walk with a picnic lunch.'

'Good heavens, girl! You'll be exhausted!' he exclaimed before he could stop himself.

Penelope looked amused and replied, 'You must not concern yourself about me. I am perfectly capable of judging how far I can ride or walk.' And, changing the subject, 'How are you spending the day, my lord?'

'Estate matters. I have to see a tenant. If you would care to join me...'

He got no further. 'How kind, my lord, but I am sure that Johnson will prove an acceptable escort. And of course I would not wish to be in your way.'

The cold indifference in her voice stung, but Peter merely shrugged and said, 'As you please, Penelope.' Having finished his breakfast, he excused himself politely and left to go about his business.

As the door shut behind him Penelope relaxed with a sigh of relief. It had been far more difficult than she'd expected to maintain a pose of icy formality. She was annoyed to realise that her hands were trembling slightly as she finished her cup of tea. Silly little fool! she told herself crossly as she made her way to the side table and helped herself carefully to a boiled egg. Somehow her appetite seemed to have deserted her.

Johnson met her as soon as she entered the stable yard. 'Good morning, my lady. Nero is saddled and ready. The master said as how you would be riding him in the future. For which we're all glad. He's a nice old chap and he does get a bit bored not going out as often.'

Penelope smiled and said, 'Well, I'm afraid that I won't be providing him with too many thrills, just a quiet ride every day or so!'

'Just the thing for the old fellow,' said Johnson

cheerfully. 'Fred! Bring Nero out for her ladyship, and Misty for me.'

'Yessir!' Penelope heard the clatter of hooves on the cobbled yard and then a voice saying respectfully, 'Here they are, Mester Johnson, sir. Will that be all, sir?'

The voice sounded just a little nervous, and something stirred in Penelope's memory. 'Ah, would this be Fred who got such a terrible shock to find Gelert here in a supposedly empty stall?'

'Aye, that's him, my lady. Silly clunch! Well, say something, lad!'

'Good morning, my lady. I'm sure 'e's a nice dog, but I'd never seed sech a big un afore!'

Penelope smiled and said, 'I don't suppose Mr Johnson had either! Never mind, Gelert really is quite harmless, I promise! Now, shall we be going?'

'If your ladyship is ready,' said Johnson. He brought Nero around to her and, taking her foot, threw her into the saddle. She settled herself quickly, sorting out her skirts and finding the stirrup. Carefully she gathered up the reins so that she could just feel Nero's mouth and waited quietly while Johnson mounted.

He did so and asked, 'Are you ready my lady?'

'Yes, Johnson.'

They trotted out of the yard together, with Gelert bounding around them, and Johnson said, 'There's a pretty ride through the park towards the village, my lady. Plenty of room for a canter if so be your wish, and we can circle back around the Home Farm and through the woods. About an hour and a half it would take.'

'That sounds excellent, Johnson,' said Penelope

cheerfully. 'You pick a ride that you would enjoy, it doesn't really make much difference to me.'

Johnson glanced at her and said slowly, 'Well, I suppose not, my lady, but when spring comes around again and the violets are out in the Home Wood, or even now when all the birds are about and the smells are nice anyway…well, that's why I thought we'd go this way. Ellen was saying how you like the herbs and we thought you'd like this.'

Penelope turned towards him and said, 'Thank you, Johnson, for giving it so much thought. I do appreciate that.'

Penelope enjoyed the ride very much. Johnson was an excellent guide, telling her all about the route they were taking and describing the scenery. It was a glorious day and she could feel the sun warming her as the horses trotted along. To her great delight there was even a lark swinging high above them in a rapture of song. They halted the horses and she listened entranced for several minutes, and Penelope then said, 'You know, Johnson, a neighbour of ours at home, Mrs Knighton, had one trapped. She put the poor little thing in a cage in her drawing room and it just drooped and fretted. Wouldn't eat, wouldn't sing. My sister and I got into the most awful scrape because we let it out into her garden and of course it was gone. When it took off and realised it was free again…oh the song! You'd have thought its heart had been breaking in that horrid cage!'

Johnson snorted and said, 'Them as puts any wild bird, leave alone a lark, in a cage needs to be caged theirselves. 'Tisn't right for a lark, of all birds! They need the sky and the wind, my lady. And anyway, do you think as how a lark singing caged inside would sound like this one?'

Penelope shook her head and said softly, 'No, he'd sound stunted, like his soul would be.'

'That's right,' said Johnson. 'And I'll warrant you and your sister didn't care much about the trouble you got into!'

His mistress grinned engagingly. 'Not very much!' she admitted. 'Mama promised all sorts of dire retribution in front of Mrs Knighton and revoked it all when we got into the carriage to go home!'

The groom gave a shout of laughter. 'That's the way. I dessay she was a-wishing she'd done it herself!'

The rest of the ride passed agreeably. Johnson, who had known the Earl since boyhood, like all the older servants, had had little time for the previous Countess. This one he reckoned to be a far better bargain! Old Meadows had it right when he said she was quality through and through. A real lady she was. Not too high in the instep and had a brain as well as a heart. As they turned to ride homeward Johnson silently congratulated his master on a good choice!

Penelope returned to the house to discover that Ellen and François between them had contrived an extremely hearty picnic lunch which included a large bone for Gelert. Despite Ellen's misgivings Penelope still felt fresh after her ride, and was determined to go for a walk. Quite apart from her genuine desire to get out of the house and give Gelert enough exercise she was unwilling to give his lordship the slightest reason for thinking she was moping about or pining for his company.

They set off together through the kitchen garden and orchards with the lunch split between two small satchels and Ellen further laden with a rug. Ellen said she knew a good spot for a picnic about a mile and half away, where the stream dropped several feet in a tinkling cascade to a deep pool. It was, she said a sheltered, sunny spot and would save them having to carry any water. They reached the place after about forty-five minutes of steady walking and spread out the rug in the filtered shade of a spreading oak close to the pool.

Myriad sounds came to Penelope's ears: the plash of the water falling into the pool, a constant ripple of birdsong and the occasional splash of a leaping trout. Contentedly she sat on the rug and helped Ellen set out the lunch. Cold pasties, a cold chicken, bread rolls, cheese, a very large slab of plum cake, and fresh fruit. Fortunately François was adept at simple meals of this sort, being as how, said Ellen, the master often liked to come out like this with a gun or fishing rod.

'He's not much of a one for ceremony,' said Ellen, completely forgetting that it was not her place to pass comment on her master to his wife. For her part Penelope didn't care. If she couldn't get to know her husband and his likes and dislikes one way then she would have to resort to more devious means!

The afternoon passed peacefully and Penelope found out a great deal about Ellen's family, especially her sister, Martha. Ellen was terribly excited about becoming an aunt for the first time. Occasionally she stopped and begged pardon for rattling on, but her mistress simply laughed and said she liked to hear it all. And indeed Penelope was finding, in Ellen's stories of her family life, some surcease from a homesickness she had hardly dared to admit to herself.

Separated from her mother and sisters for the first

time in her life, without anyone to really talk to or confide in she had begun to feel almost unbearably lonely. If only Peter was consistent, they could be friends, she thought. There was a great deal about him that she liked, and it was obvious that his servants held him in considerable affection as well as respect. This to her mind was indicative of a fine man! With a smile she remembered the scene in *Pride and Prejudice* where Lizzy discovered how wrong she had been about Darcy by listening to his housekeeper praise him to the skies. Firmly Penelope put aside the reflection that Lizzy then proceeded to fall very much in love with her erstwhile enemy! Love, thought Penelope, was definitely out of the question!

Chapter Nine

Over the next few days Penelope continued to ride out in the mornings or go out with Ellen. She saw very little of Peter except at breakfast or dinner, when their conversation was limited to polite enquiries about each other's health and activities. Even breakfast she tried to avoid, only coming down when she was fairly sure that Peter would have left.

When it rained heavily one afternoon she found plenty to do helping Mrs Bates in the stillroom. That lady said that the mistress was a great deal more helpful than some fine ladies who couldn't tell one herb from another even with their eyesight! Together they brewed simples and arranged herbs for drying while through it all Mrs Bates gossiped comfortably about the house and its traditions. Penelope heard all about the wonderful parties the previous Earl and his lady had given, and how broken up the old Earl had been when his wife died of a wasting disease.

'He only lived a twelvemonth my lady, just didn't seem to care any more. Master Peter was in the Peninsula then, but the Earl, he wouldn't call him home. In the end Mr Meadows wrote to Master Peter and told him just how things was without his lordship knowing. He sold out and got home within a month but 'twas too late. His lordship died and Master Peter married eighteen months later. Ah, 'twas a bad business.' She sighed lugubriously, but went on more cheerfully, 'Well, it's all different now, dearie—my lady, I should say! Now, I'll just go to the sewing room and find some more muslin bags for this lavender. Such a lot we've got this year!'

She bustled out of the room and the door shut behind her. Penelope mused over what she had been told. She wished she had known Peter's parents. They sounded rather nice. Her thoughts were interrupted by the door opening and she swung around quickly. The footsteps were not those of Mrs Bates. Then a distinct odour of shaving soap reached her and she could hear Gelert's tail thumping the floor enthusiastically.

'Good afternoon, my lord,' she said politely.

Peter had long since stopped being openly amazed at her uncanny ability to know who had entered a room so he just answered, 'Good afternoon, Penelope,' and wondered how the devil she did it.

'Mrs Bates will be back very soon if you wish to speak to her,' said Penelope.

'Actually, Penelope, it was you I came to find,' said Peter steadily, as he tried to remember just how long it was since he had seen his wife alone. At least four days he thought, and then it had only been by chance that she had come to breakfast before he'd left. It was almost as if she were avoiding him!

Penelope looked a trifle surprised and said, 'You wish to speak to me, my lord?'

Peter took a deep breath and said, 'Er, yes. I thought that I had better inform you that my cousin Jack has arrived unexpectedly. He tells me that he is on his way to visit a friend and simply stopped to wish us happy, but I felt obliged to offer him lodging.'

He looked keenly at his wife. She suddenly looked very pale and her voice was not quite steady as she said, 'I...I...thought you did not like your cousin.'

'No, I don't, but he is my heir and I cannot in all honour refuse him the hospitality of this house without a better reason than that,' Peter replied. 'Has something disturbed you, Penelope? You are acquainted with Jack, I believe. Was he not a friend of your brother's?'

'Yes. Yes, he was. He stayed with us once,' answered Penelope, making a tremendous effort to calm herself. She felt that it was impossible to tell Peter the truth: that she feared and loathed his cousin. She would simply take good care never to be alone with him. 'Will he be staying for long—and when does Mr Carstares arrive?'

'Jack will only stay two or three nights, and I had a letter from George. He is staying a little longer with his sister to bear her company while Fairford is away. He'll be along in a week or so.'

'Very well, my lord. I will see you and Mr Frobisher at dinner, then,' said Penelope politely.

Peter was suddenly piqued at this cool dismissal. Damn it! She can't just dismiss me like that! He reached out and took her hand, firmly pulling her towards him. She stiffened and tried to pull away, but he ignored this and with his free hand pushed her chin up. She stopped resisting but the expression on her face was cold. Nevertheless he could feel that she was trembling and he bent his head to kiss her, expecting the same warm response that she always gave him. It was not there. She stood submissively in the circle of his arm and remained seemingly aloof.

In reality Penelope was finding it extremely difficult to control her instinctive desire to respond to Peter's gentle kiss. As always her heart pounded, and she felt that her knees would give way at any moment, but somehow she clung to her resolution and remained outwardly unresponsive. Just when she thought she could bear it no longer and must return his kiss, he stopped and released her.

Unhurriedly she stepped away and asked steadily, 'Will that be all, my lord?'

Puzzled, Peter looked at her. Her whole body seemed to radiate relief and her expression suggested that she did not find his attentions in the least bit agreeable. After a moment he gathered his wits and answered slowly, 'That was all I had to tell you. I beg your pardon, Penelope. I will see you at dinner.'

He left the stillroom in some confusion and returned to the study where, instead of settling to the work he had intended to do, he sat wondering what on earth he had done wrong. It did not really take him very long to work it out. Penelope *was* avoiding him, and she had obviously taken his hints that he did not wish for a close relationship. That, he told himself firmly, was all to the good. The only problem was that he did not really enjoy making love to a statue, especially when the said statue had hitherto responded to his advances with a tantalising mixture of innocence and passion.

But that's just the problem, he thought irritably. You found her too appealing, too—he flinched at the word—lovable. Surely now you can simply get on with it and...? *No!* He couldn't do that! He couldn't force himself on the child if she found his attentions distasteful. But did she? he wondered. Then he understood fully. His wife was protecting herself from being hurt in the only way she could: by retreating behind a barrier of complete indifference.

He cursed as he realised what he had done. The only way he could break the impasse was to confide in her, apologise and explain his odd humours. And to do that he would have to step out from behind his own barriers, thus creating the very situation that he wished to avoid: a relationship of emotional intimacy with his wife!

As he had expected, Peter did not see Penelope again until dinner time. He heard her in her bed chamber, chatting away to Ellen as she changed for dinner. Briefly he considered knocking on the door and escorting her down to the drawing room, but then decided against the idea. After all, he'd got what he wanted, hadn't he? A wife who would make no demands on his time or feelings.

His thoughts turned to his cousin as he tied his cravat. What did Jack want this time? Money, no doubt. Peter already made his heir a generous allowance, but it never seemed to be quite enough to support Jack in the lifestyle he enjoyed. Idly Peter wondered what Jack would do when he was cut out of the succession by a child. I'll have to settle some money on him, thought Peter, and he certainly won't be happy about it! Oh, well, plenty of time before we need to consider that!

He went on down to the drawing room, where he found his cousin lounging in a wing chair. 'Good evening, Jack. I hope the staff have made you comfortable,' said Peter in a friendly manner.

'Oh, yes, Cousin, I always feel quite at home here,'

replied Frobisher. 'But where is your bride? I am looking forward to renewing my acquaintance with her.'

'No doubt she will be down shortly,' answered Peter, wondering why the thought of his cousin meeting Penelope was so distasteful. He began to ask Frobisher about his journey, and for how long they were to have the pleasure of his company, when Penelope entered the room.

The first intimation that he had of her arrival was an utterly blood-curdling growl from the doorway. He swung around in consternation to see Penelope with her hand gripping Gelert's collar firmly. And just as well! The dog was snarling viciously. What on earth had got into him? Only once had he seen the beast react like that, in the chaise on his wedding day. Suddenly he realised that Gelert's attention was focused on Frobisher, and turned to look at his cousin, who had whitened and was backing away.

Penelope spoke quickly. 'I am sorry, my lord. Perhaps you might ring for Meadows and I will ask him to take Gelert down to François in the kitchens. We will wait in the hall.'

'That seems an excellent suggestion Penelope, if you think François won't mind,' said Peter in relief.

'Oh, no, he and Gelert are good friends. He says Gelert is the only dog he has ever known who doesn't try to steal in the kitchen,' said Penelope as she dragged the still snarling dog out of the room.

Peter turned back to Frobisher, unsure of what to say. He could only think of one reason why the dog should react so savagely. It also made sense of Penelope's evident upset at the news of Jack's arrival. Peter was stunned by the fury which arose in his breast at the mere suspicion that Frobisher might have taken advantage of Penelope's blindness. Somehow he managed to mask his anger and turn the dog's behaviour off with a casual apology. He couldn't accuse his cousin on the basis of a dog's testimony—however much he might wish to!

Penelope returned alone and Peter immediately went to her and took her arm. Damn her independence! He was determined that she should not feel any fear of Frobisher just because she had sent Gelert out. He remembered the other occasion when she had refused to hide behind Gelert's protection and paid silent tribute to her courage.

'Penelope, I believe you are already acquainted with my cousin Jack Frobisher.'

He led her up to him reluctantly, but Penelope was in complete control of herself and responded cheerfully, holding out her hand. 'Indeed, yes. How do you do, Mr Frobisher? I do beg your pardon for keeping you waiting. Perhaps we should go straight into dinner, before François's creations are quite ruined.'

'What a marvellous idea, fair cousin. But first I must extend my condolences to you on your recent sad loss! I was very much distressed to hear of it!'

Penelope looked rather puzzled at first, but then answered, 'Oh! Yes, of course. Geoffrey's death. Thank you, Mr Frobisher.'

'And on the very morning of the wedding, I understand,' continued Frobisher. 'No doubt Peter has been at pains to console you in your…er…time of grief. On a happier note, do permit me to welcome you to the family, and to congratulate Darleston on acquiring such a charming bride!' Frobisher bowed low over her hand but did not kiss it. Not with his formidable cousin standing right there. He looked at Penelope appraisingly. Just as appetising as ever, he thought nastily. All that fresh loveliness, but not for him! Darleston got everything, damn his eyes!

They went into dinner and Frobisher exerted himself to try and charm his companions. He missed very little and was quick to notice the constraint between the couple. Good! he thought unpleasantly. It certainly suited him if they were ill at ease with each other! It was delightful to think that all his cousin's reputed skill with the ladies had not helped with this one! He asked his cousin about the estate, and even managed to conceal his boredom at Peter's answers.

Turning to Penelope, he said, 'It sounds as though my cousin is spending a vast deal of time on his estate! How do you contrive to occupy yourself?'

Penelope answered easily, 'Oh, I go for walks with my maid and Gelert, or I ride out with Johnson—the head groom, you know. That is if the weather is fine. Otherwise I find there is plenty to do in the house.'

'You ride out?' said Frobisher, surprised. 'I'm surprised Darleston permits such a thing! Most unsafe isn't it? And with only a groom!'

'Penelope is quite capable of deciding what is and isn't safe for her to attempt without my interference, Jack,' said Peter, annoyed that Frobisher's comment so closely tallied with his own initial reaction. He also suspected that Penelope was about to deliver a blistering set down!

'Of course,' said Frobisher hurriedly. 'And where do you ride, Lady Darleston?' Something told him that it would be as well not to assume terms of familiarity with his hostess.

Penelope answered politely, Peter's interjection having given her time to recall the impropriety of administering a severe snub to her husband's cousin and guest. 'Oh, I let Johnson decide. We usually go through the park and into the village and then swing around to come back around the Home Farm and the woods.' She left it at that. Not for anything would she have shared the joy of those rides and Johnson's descriptions of the countryside with someone like Jack Frobisher!

'Ah, yes,' said Frobisher smoothly. 'And back over that picturesque old bridge into the park. How very pleasant.'

'That's right,' said Penelope. 'You must know it well, of course.'

'Indeed I do,' was the reply. 'Well, it seems with all this activity on your part, Lady Darleston, that Peter's company is entirely superfluous!'

Over the next couple of days Penelope had no difficulty in avoiding Frobisher's company. Gelert's behaviour on that first evening had seen to it that he was just as eager to avoid her when he knew the dog to be with her.

Nevertheless it was with real relief that she saw him off two days later. For one thing, good manners had dictated that she must put in an appearance at the breakfast table and not simply disappear for a walk in the middle of the day. Peter, of course, was being hospitable as well so that meant they'd had to be together a great deal more than she would have liked. His manner remained politely distant, and although this was what she expected and told herself she preferred a nagging ache persisted.

Frobisher left immediately after breakfast and Penelope, having sent a message down to the stables for Johnson, set off with a light heart for her morning ride, her first in three days. It was a pleasant day, with the sun going in and out, but there was a fresh wind blowing which added a nip of autumn to the air.

They took their usual route and came out of the woodland path just near the bridge over the stream. Johnson leaned forward to unclip the leading rein from Nero's bridle. The bridge was too narrow to ride abreast and he generally let Penelope ride over first, knowing that of all horses Nero was one he could trust to behave.

Penelope pushed Nero into a trot, knowing that the wise old fellow would head straight for the bridge. She was taken completely by surprise when, at the first rumble of his hooves on the planks, the horse stopped dead in his tracks and tried to pivot around on his haunches, snorting nervously. Controlling him with hands and heel, she soothed him. 'There now, you old idiot! What's the matter? Come on then. You know this bridge!' Firmly she gave him the office to go ahead, and reluctantly, snorting at each step, the old horse obeyed.

Suddenly an ominous creak was heard. Nero, whinnying in fright, tried to back off the bridge but it was too late. Johnson, spurring forward with a terrified yell of warning, was helpless as he saw the horse pitch forward as the bridge collapsed under him, flinging his rider over his head into the rocky stream.

Horrified, Johnson threw himself from the saddle and leapt into the stream, slipping on boulders in the fast-running water in his efforts to reach his mistress, who was lying between two rocks with her face in the water. Gelert beat him to it. The great dog was there with a mouthful of his mistress's hair, dragging her clear of the water.

'Good lad,' gasped the groom as he got to the pair. 'Here now, let me lift her. That's it!' He made his way carefully to the opposite bank with his limp burden and laid her down on the grass. Quickly he loosened the buttons at her throat, turned her onto her front and began pressing on her ribcage rhythmically. Water poured out of Penelope's mouth and in a moment she began coughing weakly as she tried to drag air into her lungs.

'Thank God!' whispered Johnson, and helped her to sit up. She appeared dazed, but by some miracle seemed to have no major injuries. Far more worrying was the fact that in the brisk wind she was already beginning to shiver violently. Shock too, thought Johnson. He had to get her home, fast!

Thinking quickly, he stripped off his coat and put it on her. 'Just stay right there, lass—my lady. I'll be back in a brace of shakes!' Swiftly he waded back across the stream to get his own horse. Old Nero had scrambled to his feet and was making his way over, but both knees were badly cut up and he was limping on his near hind. Johnson's heart contracted at the old horse's plight, but he had to help his mistress. Cursing, he went on and caught his quiet mare, leading her back to Penelope.

Gently he helped the shaken girl to her feet, talking to her encouragingly, and somehow managed to get her into the saddle. She swayed dangerously and Johnson realised that she could not possibly remain there with the amount of support he could give from the ground. Praying that she would not fall off, he vaulted up behind her and eased her forward so that

he could get into the saddle himself. Once he was sure
he had her safely he set out slowly for home. Sparing
a brief glance back, he saw that Nero was limping
along behind. Gelert trotted just ahead.

They were halfway home on that torturously slow
journey when a startled shout was heard to the right.
Johnson looked around with a sigh of relief. It was the
master, galloping towards them on the mare Griselda.

He pulled her in beside them and asked furiously,
'What the devil happened, Johnson? Is she all right?
You're supposed to look after her!'

'There's no need to tell me that, my lord. I think
she'll be well enough, when we can get her home and
into a warm bed. Bridge collapsed, and, yes, 'tis my
fault for not thinking fast enough that Nero would
never have baulked at a bridge without a damn good
reason!'

Peter was silent for a moment while he took this in,
then, 'I'm sorry, Johnson. Don't blame yourself. I'll
ride on, and bring a carriage back for her. Can you
manage for now, or shall I take her and you ride in
on Griselda?'

'Better if you take her, my lord. My arm is going
numb for all she's such a slip of a thing. Begging your
pardon, my lord.'

Peter brushed this aside and leapt off his mare. He
steadied Penelope while Johnson dismounted carefully
and then vaulted onto the gentle Misty. Johnson was
in Griselda's saddle and riding fast before Peter had
Penelope fairly settled in his arms. He put Misty into
a walk and continued the slow ride home. Penelope
leaned against his shoulder and he could feel the shiv-
ering which shook her whole body. 'Home soon,
sweetheart,' he said encouragingly, and wondered if

she was even aware that he had taken Johnson's place. She seemed only half conscious.

Talking quietly to her, he came to the conclusion that she was aware of him, but simply lacked the strength to reply. She had turned her head slightly so that her cheek rested on his chest in an attitude of trust.

With a mile to go across the park, his travelling coach came to meet them down the ride, driven hard by Johnson himself with Fred beside him. Another groom leapt out as the coach pulled up. Fred jumped off the box and ran to the horses' heads.

'Well done, Johnson,' said Peter in relief.

'I sent for Dr Greeves, my lord. And a message up to the house. They'll be expecting us at the main entrance. 'Tis easiest for the carriage. Jim here can bring Misty and Nero back.'

'Nero!' said Peter. 'I forgot all about him!' He looked around. The old horse was still limping along behind, his head nodding at every painful step. Peter winced as he realised that his old friend was badly hurt.

No time to think of that now. Johnson was waiting to help him with Penelope. Together they got her off Misty and into the coach. Peter got in with her and settled her along the seat, wrapping her in the rugs he found, then knelt on the floor himself to steady her against any bumps. Gelert jumped in beside him and Johnson closed the door.

Johnson drove back to the Court as quickly as he could without too much jolting. He drew up at the front door and found Ellen, Meadows and Mrs Bates anxiously awaiting them. The Earl carried his semi-conscious wife up to her chamber where Mrs Bates and Ellen took over, shooing him from the room with scant respect which spoke whole volumes about their regard for the mistress.

Peter left obediently and went down to the entrance hall to receive the doctor who, to his relief, arrived very soon. He escorted Greeves upstairs and left him at Penelope's door, saying, 'Her ladyship's maid and Mrs Bates are in there. I shall wait out here for you.'

Greeves nodded. 'Very well, my lord,' he said, and went in.

Peter sat down on a chair in the corridor and waited impatiently. He was reasonably certain that Penelope had taken no serious injury, but, like Johnson, the wetting and cold wind frightened him. A lungful of water too!

It seemed a very long time before Greeves reappeared, although it was actually only half an hour. 'Sorry to keep you waiting, my lord,' said Greeves, who was experienced with distraught husbands.

'How is she?' asked Peter at once.

'She'll do well enough. Strong constitution although she looks so fragile.' Peter heaved a sigh of relief. The doctor continued, 'A wee bit of concussion and a fair few bruises. The main problem will be the wetting she got and the water she took in. You can be grateful to that groom of yours for thinking so fast or she'd not have had a chance. As it is you can expect her to be unwell for about a week, I'd say. And keep her quiet for another week after that. Just carriage exercise, no riding or walking, and keep her well rugged up and out of draughts. I've left some medicine. Mrs Bates and Ellen know what to do. Someone had better sit up with her for a couple of nights. She's a bit feverish and may become disorientated at times. Nothing to worry about, just reassure her.'

'Thank you, Greeves,' said Peter.

'Not at all, my lord, and congratulations on your marriage,' said Greeves. 'I'm just sorry to meet her ladyship in these circumstances. I'll come again tomorrow to check on her. Now, don't come down with me: I know my own way after all these years! You go in and see her ladyship. And for heaven's sake relieve her mind about the horse. She's badly worried over him. Lie if you have to, but make it convincing! Goodbye, my lord!' He held out his hand.

Peter gripped it warmly and said, 'Thank you again, sir. I'll see you tomorrow.'

Pausing only for a perfunctory knock, he went straight into Penelope's room, where he found her propped up in bed with several pillows and Ellen carefully spooning the last of some chicken broth into her.

Mrs Bates came to him and said, 'Oh, Master Peter, what a terrible thing!'

'Never mind, Bates,' said Peter kindly. 'The doctor says her ladyship will be quite well very soon. He wants us to sit with her for a couple of nights, so if you or Ellen can be with her until after dinner I'll take over then.'

'If that's what you want, my lord, that's what we'll do,' said Mrs Bates. 'Her ladyship seems inclined to sleep at the moment, but if she wants you earlier we'll send for you.'

'Of course,' said Peter. 'I'll be in the house all day, and I'll make sure Meadows knows where I am. Now I'd better speak to her.'

He went over to the bed and leaned over his sleepy wife. 'Warmer now, little one?'

She opened her eyes and smiled up at him, 'Much warmer,' she said weakly. 'Just very tired.'

'You sleep, then. I'll leave you with Ellen and Mrs Bates for now and come back to sit with you later,' said Peter gently.

'Nero, is he hurt badly?' she asked. 'He didn't want to go onto the bridge but I made him. He tried so hard to stop!' There were tears in her eyes.

'A few cuts and bruises,' lied Peter, who had no idea just how badly hurt the horse might be. 'He'll be fine by the time you're out and about again, so don't worry. Now, settle down and go to sleep.' He bent over, kissed her gently and left.

Returning after dinner, he found Ellen with Penelope. There was a fire burning brightly on the hearth which cast a dim glow over the room. Ellen put a finger to her lips and he nodded in acknowledgment.

The maid tiptoed over to him and spoke softly. 'Her ladyship has just gone back to sleep. I've given her some broth and her medicine. She needs it again in four hours, or when she wakes up. Doctor says she's not likely to sleep more than a few hours at a time. There's a full kettle by the fire to make her a hot drink if she coughs. Mrs Bates left some valerian and chamomile in the little blue jar on the mantel. She says 'twill help the mistress sleep better. Just put a little in the hot water.'

Peter nodded. 'Thank you, Ellen. I'll go through to my room to change for the night and come back. I won't be long.'

He went out quietly and returned ten minutes later in his nightshirt and dressing gown. He dismissed Ellen with a kindly word of thanks and went quietly over to the bed. Penelope was sleeping soundly enough, although her breathing sounded a little laboured. A small table had been pulled close to the bed. On it he found the medicine, a jug of lemonade with a tumbler and a bowl of lavender water.

Reassured that he had everything he might need, he walked around to the other side of the bed and carefully got onto it. Might as well be comfortable, he thought, sliding under the eiderdown. As he lay there listening to Penelope's breathing he wondered about the bridge. His bailiff, Stanwyck, had gone out with Johnson to look at it. He had come back to say that some of the supports had worked loose and was threatening all sorts of dire punishment for the man he had sent out to overhaul it at the start of the summer. Peter was a little puzzled. The bridge had apparently been in good repair; he could see no reason why a previously reliable man should suddenly skimp on a job, especially when it might cost lives, not to mention his own employment.

Eventually Peter dozed off. He awoke shortly before midnight to find Penelope stirring beside him. She was coughing badly and seemed a little confused.

He spoke immediately to reassure her. 'It's me, Penelope. Peter. How are you feeling?'

Unfortunately this only served to confuse her further. She could not for the life of her think what her husband was doing in her bed. 'Peter? Why? What do you want?' Her voice sounded scared and Peter resisted the impulse to inform her that it was not unusual for a husband to spend the night in his wife's bed.

'Er, I'm the night nurse, Penelope,' he explained.

Penelope thought about that carefully. Night nurse? Why should she need a night nurse? Gradually her mind cleared of all the odd dreams she had been having and she remembered what had happened. 'Oh, I...I fell off Nero, didn't I? And got wet.' She stopped to cough again and tried to sit up.

Peter helped her, saying, 'Just wait a minute and I'll get you a drink.' He climbed over her carefully and poured a tumbler of lemonade, putting it into her hand. She nodded her thanks, unable to speak for the coughing. Peter racked his brains and remembered the kettle. Quickly he went over to the fire to put the kettle on the hob. It was quite warm already, and in a moment he had a tisane of valerian and chamomile ready for her.

He took it across to her and said, 'Try this—Mrs Bates's recommendation, a tisane. Then I'll give you your medicine.'

'Thank you,' she said as she took the cup from him. She sniffed it. 'Valerian and chamomile. This will make me sleepy!'

'At midnight that's probably not a bad thing,' observed Peter with a tinge of amusement in his voice.

M...midnight? But you were in my bed!' She sounded absolutely shocked.

This time Peter said dryly, 'There's nothing improper about *that*, my sweet. We *are* married, you may recall!'

'Yes, b...but,'

He interrupted her, half-amused and half-annoyed. 'Rid yourself of the notion that I am harbouring any villainous designs upon your person, Penelope. I am merely concerned with your health and trying to make sure that Mrs Bates and Ellen get enough rest!'

'I...I beg your pardon, my lord,' said Penelope stiffly, extremely embarrassed both at finding Peter in her bed and at having been so rude.

'Very well. Now finish that tisane and you can take your medicine.'

She did as he bade her and took the dose, screwing up her face in disgust as she tasted it. 'Ugh! How horrid!'

'No temptation to stay sick, then,' said Peter unsympathetically as he settled himself in an armchair by the fire.

Startled at the direction of his voice, Penelope asked, 'Why are you in the chair?'

'I thought you objected to me in your bed,' was the blunt reply.

'Yes, but... I mean, no! I mean... I didn't mean to ...' She stopped, tired and uncertain about just what she *did* mean!

Peter looked up sharply at the tone of exhaustion and confusion in her voice. Infamous of him to tease her when she was ill and needed his kindness! 'Never mind, Penny,' he said gently. 'If it will not disturb you I will come back to bed.'

'Yes, please,' she whispered, half asleep.

By the time Peter reached the bed she was sound asleep again. Very carefully he got into bed and made himself comfortable.

His slumbers were disturbed by some very detailed and delightful dreams in which Penelope had obviously quite overcome her shock at finding him in her bed. Eventually one of these dreams was so vivid as to jerk him out of sleep. He woke up completely to discover that Penelope had rolled over in her sleep and was snuggling up to him in a confiding manner which made his heart pound and his blood seem several degrees warmer. That spelt the end of sleep for Peter. He spent the remainder of the night with gritted teeth, reminding himself that his wife was sick and moreover that he had foolishly assured her that he had no villainous designs upon her person.

When Penelope awoke again it was to find Ellen with her. His lordship, Ellen informed her would come back to sit with her during the afternoon, while she and Mrs Bates would sit up in turns at night. Penelope tried not to feel hurt. After all he was a busy man and theirs was only a marriage of convenience.

Chapter Ten

~~~~~~~~~~~~~~~~~~~~~~~~~~~~~~~~~~~~~~~

Ten days later, shortly after tea, George Carstares's
curricle bowled up the driveway drawn by a pair of
chestnuts. Penelope, much recovered, was in the drawing room playing the piano when she heard the com-
motion in the Great Hall. A cheerful voice was saying,
'Hello, Meadows, you old rascal. Where's his lordship? Out? Shooting rabbits? Oh, well, I suppose we'll
get a rabbit pie out of it.'

She walked out onto the gallery overlooking the
Great Hall feeling very nervous about greeting her
guest. Did he know she was blind? What had Peter
told his friend about the marriage?

Just as she was wondering whether to call out
Carstares looked up and saw her. 'Good evening, Lady
Darleston. I hope my arrival won't inconvenience
you.'

'It's Mr Carstares, milady,' explained Meadows.
'Now let me take your coat and hat, Master George,
then you can join her ladyship. Master Peter—his lordship, I mean—won't be very long.'

'Do come up, Mr Carstares,' said Penelope with a

friendly smile. 'Unless you would prefer to rest in your room.'

'Rest? Good God, no, ma'am!' said George. He came up the stairs to her and said, as he saw Gelert, 'That hound of yours is even bigger than I remembered! How are you, Lady Darleston? Recovered from your wetting and fall, I hope!'

'I'm much better, Mr Carstares. Shall we go into the drawing room?' She moved towards the door with Gelert, and George, who had received a long explanatory letter from Peter, leapt to open it for her. She smiled and thanked him.

'Please make yourself at home, Mr Carstares. There is a brandy decanter on a side table, I believe, or I can send for some tea if you would prefer that.' Penelope seated herself on the Queen Anne sofa and Gelert lay down, resting his head on her feet.

'Thank you, but I'll wait for Darleston. How is he?'

'Very well, but the estate has been keeping him rather busy.' In sober fact Penelope had been very little in her husband's company for the last few days. And since he had most uncharacteristically exerted his authority with her to confine her to the house she had been extremely bored.

George heard the constraint in her voice. He remembered what Peter had said about not wanting any emotional involvement and correctly deduced that his friend had achieved his aim. Rough on the girl, he thought sadly. She was a pretty little thing, and if Peter was doing his well-known impersonation of an icicle it must be rather uncomfortable for her.

He asked politely after her family, and when Peter came in ten minutes later he found them roaring with laughter over a letter Penelope had received that morning from Sarah. Neither one noticed him at first, and he stood watching them from the doorway. He had not seen his wife in so merry a mood for days. Penelope felt the draught and turned towards him with a questioning look on her face. It seemed to him that all the animation died out of her face to be replaced with a look of guarded enquiry.

George followed her gaze and said, 'Hello, Peter! Your sister-in-law seems to have the most unflattering notion of your character. Read this!'

Peter came forward and took the proffered letter. 'May I, Penelope?'

'Of course, Peter.'

He read aloud.

Darling Penny

I hope you are better. Why didn't Lord Darleston frank your first letter? It seems awfully mean to me. Mama says you probably forgot, but I think that is a hum. It's a pity that he's so mean, because he looked quite nice at the wedding. It just goes to show, you can never tell.

I have been reading *The Mysteries of Udolpho* and Mama says I have let it prey upon my imagination too much. I suppose Darleston hasn't really got you locked in a dungeon, has he? And where was he when you fell off your horse? It would be too good to be true, but even Richard doesn't think it's very likely. He and Phoebe are very well and absolutely sickeningly in love. I hope you aren't. It would be nice to have one sister in possession of her senses.

At this point Peter stopped to laugh a little awkwardly. Nothing seemed more unlikely than that

Penelope should even like him, let alone love him! If anything he would have said that Penelope had settled into dislike of him. He handed the letter back to her, saying lightly, 'Well, my dear, I suppose I had better live up to my reputation and find a nice damp dungeon for you! How are you, George?'

'Very well, thanks, Peter. Penny has been looking after me admirably. You know I don't think I congratulated you sufficiently at your wedding, you lucky dog!' said George, laughing even while he groaned inwardly at the obvious discomfort between his hosts. *Peter, you idiot,* he thought. *You've made a mess of this all right and tight!*

Penelope blushed as she rose to her feet. 'I must go and change for dinner, if you gentlemen will excuse me,' she said. Peter attended her to the door and opened it. 'Thank you, Peter. Did you shoot any rabbits?'

'Three,' he answered.

'Oh, good. George, you'll get your rabbit pie!' said Penelope with a chuckle as she went out.

Peter followed her into the hall and shut the door. 'Penelope?'

'My lord?'

'So formal, my dear?'

There was a wistful note in his voice which pierced her defences, but she replied steadily, 'I find it preferable to maintain consistency in our relationship, my lord.'

She was aware of his closeness, but jumped when she felt his hands grip hers gently. 'Penny, this is foolish...' he began.

Her fingers trembled in his. As always his touch

drew a response from her. He drew her closer, gazing into her wide grey eyes with their incredibly long lashes. His gaze dropped to her mouth. The delicately shaped lips looked softer, more inviting than ever. Desire flared in him. He leaned towards her, but at the last moment she pulled away from him.

'I…I must change for dinner. Please excuse me, my lord.' He released her hands reluctantly and watched her go, longing to undo the damage he had done.

Dispiritedly Peter returned to George and said, 'You and Penelope seem to have taken to each other.'

'Delightful girl,' said George. 'A pity she's blind, but it doesn't seem to stop her doing much. How do you get along with the dog?'

'Fine, now,' said Peter.

'Oh, don't tell me he went for you!'

'Only when I richly deserved it,' said Peter, in the sort of voice which suggested that he would prefer not to discuss the subject. 'A brandy, George?'

They talked casually about mutual acquaintances for a while, and then Peter said, 'Well, what's bothering you, George? You said in your letter that you had something to tell me that you preferred not to commit to paper. Out with it.'

George looked worried. 'Yes. If it wasn't for that I wouldn't have dreamed of butting in at the moment.'

Peter was puzzled. 'Why on earth not?'

'Why not? For goodness' sake, Peter, as if it wasn't bad enough having to remind you to kiss the bride in the church! The best man doesn't usually come along on the honeymoon!'

'Oh, rubbish. We're not exactly lost in love, you know. Get on with your story or whatever it is.'

George took a deep breath, 'I'm concerned about

your cousin Jack Frobisher. There are some very ugly rumours going around.'

'George, there are always nasty *on dits* circulating about my cousin! You should ignore them. I do!' said Darleston in amusement.

'Seems he's getting desperate. The money lenders have got their claws into him, apparently. A couple of weeks ago Frobisher attempted to elope from Bath with Carrington's sister, Amelia.'

'Good God!' exclaimed Darleston in distaste. 'Don't tell me that this is common knowledge!'

'No, it was all hushed up,' said George reassuringly. 'In fact that's the main reason Carrington didn't call him out. These things always get about, and naturally it wouldn't do the girl's chances much good. Told me in confidence because he wanted you to be warned. Thinks Jack did it in response to your marriage. You know, being cut out and all!'

'But you said there were rumours about Jack!' Darleston pointed out

'The rumours are not about him but spread by him. At least, so I suspect.' George cleared his throat, uncomfortably aware that he was venturing onto dangerous ground. He continued. 'Peter, Frobisher was there the night you had your turn-up with Ffolliot. He probably knew quite well that Ffolliot's estate would never bear a debt of that size. He was furious about your marriage, you know. Been saying that you only did it to spite him and that he'll make you regret it. He's been stirring up all sorts of gossip about Penny too. Saying the marriage was a put-up job to clear Ffolliot's debt. Which is true. But you don't want everyone to know it!'

Darleston stared at him in shock. 'Good Lord! Are people taking him seriously?'

'Well, you'll admit the story makes good telling! People are listening, Peter. The most popular version is that the whole thing was a plot to entrap you into marriage. Which, if you ask me, is a little hard on your wife! I should say she has enough problems without that! If anyone was trapped into marriage she was!' said George bluntly.

'Is there anything more?' asked Darleston, ignoring this rider.

'Well, there is one thing.' said George reluctantly. 'Carrington thinks Frobisher is in enough of a mess to try and dispose of you. You must know he made no secret about the fact that he didn't expect you to re-marry.'

'George, are you seriously suggesting that Jack is going to try and kill me so that he can inherit? You must be crazy!' burst out Darleston. 'This is nine-teenth-century England, not medieval Italy!'

'I know! I know it sounds mad. But it's just possible he might be desperate enough to do it. Trying to elope with Miss Amelia was pretty desperate! Another thing,' George continued, 'if you'll forgive me for touching on a private matter. If Frobisher wants to inherit, it's possible he might also try to harm Penny.'

Darleston stared in amazement. 'Penelope? Why?'

'Well, she is your wife, you know. An heir and all that,' said George, extremely embarrassed. This was delicate ground for even the closest of friends.

'You needn't…' Darleston only just stopped himself informing George that the chances that Penelope might be carrying an heir were zero. 'Does anyone else know about this?' he asked

'No. Only Carrington. He said I should warn you at once. Knew something about the lender Frobisher went to. From what Carrington said, if your cousin is in his clutches it could be very serious.'

Darleston took a turn around the room. 'This sounds like pure nonsense, but I suppose I had better look into it. Don't say anything to Penelope just yet, will you? If Jack does try anything his only hope of getting away with it is to make it look accidental, and I have every confidence in Gelert's ability to protect her. Something will have to be done about the gossip, of course. I won't have anyone gossiping about my wife!'

'You said accidental,' said George slowly. 'What about that fall she had? Didn't you tell me that Jack was staying with you just before it happened? Could he have tampered with the bridge?'

'Good heavens! I doubt that he even knew she was riding at all, let alone where she… Wait a minute, maybe he did know! I recall something being said about her riding at dinner one night. That's right! He thought it was dangerous. Penelope would have bitten his head off if I hadn't interrupted.'

'Did he know where she would ride?' asked George. Peter racked his brain but couldn't remember. 'Goodness knows. Anyway, this is too fanciful! It was sheer fluke that Penelope rode onto the bridge first.'

'Might have been worse if she hadn't,' George pointed out thoughtfully. 'Your letter said that Nero refused to go on. Now, if Johnson had gone ahead, and then Penelope got Nero to go, the bridge could have collapsed under the pair of them!'

'Maybe. Come on, we'd best change for dinner. François gets very angry if we are late!'

Dinner that night was a far more cheerful meal than

it had been for the previous few nights. George and Penelope were in a way to becoming fast friends. It was obvious to Peter that his friend admired Penelope and that she treated him with much the same open friendliness she had once shown to her husband. She even unbent towards him a little, but he was uncomfortably aware of a demon of jealousy gnawing at him. That he had only himself to blame for her air of polite indifference did nothing to reconcile him to it.

George and Penelope were discussing the late war with France. It was evident that Penelope had followed it very closely and Peter was conscious of a twinge of pride at the intelligence displayed in her questions and comments. 'I wish more women had an understanding of the war!' said George. 'Some of them say such stupid things!'

'Oh, come, George! So do lots of men!' protested Peter.

Penelope smiled and said, 'Yes, like my brother's friend Mr Frobisher. He thought that it was a lot of fuss about nothing and bemoaned the fact that he couldn't go to Paris.' It suddenly occurred to her that Jack Frobisher was her husband's cousin and heir. Perhaps it was not quite the thing to be rude about him. She flushed and said, 'I…I do beg your pardon, my lord. I had forgotten that Mr Frobisher is your cousin.'

Darleston gave a short laugh, saying, 'You needn't worry about that, Penelope. My opinion of my cousin is well-known to George, who fully agrees with me. I would greatly prefer the entire world to forget that he is my cousin.'

There was an awkward silence which George tried to fill. 'By the way, Penny, do relieve my curiosity!

What happened to Frobisher's arm when he stayed with your family? It was bandaged for weeks and all he'd say was that he'd been bitten by a dog.'

'Gelert didn't like him,' said Penelope, and refused to elaborate.

George didn't press the issue and Darleston had a shrewd idea as to what must have happened. 'Jack Frobisher is a toad. He probably deserved it!' he said, feeling again that unexpected rage at the thought of any other man touching Penelope. He looked at her closely. Her expression was often difficult to read, but he thought she had paled at the mention of Frobisher's arm.

Penelope left the gentlemen very correctly to enjoy their port, and retired to the drawing room. When they came in she was playing the piano. She stopped, but they begged her to continue and disposed themselves to listen. The instrument sang under her fingers, and it was obvious that she was completely absorbed in the music. Darleston thought to himself that she looked particularly lovely when she was concentrating hard on something.

He ran a distracted hand through his hair, trying desperately to concentrate on something other than the soft enticing curves of her figure. He raised his eyes to her face. The dark red curls were piled high on her head to fall in soft ringlets; they jostled for position, caressing her neck in careless abandon. One particularly vagrant lock tickled her cheek in a way that made Peter's fingers itch to stroke it back.

He nearly groaned aloud in frustration and dropped his gaze to her hands which drew rippling magic from the instrument. He tried to focus on the music, but found himself remembering the occasions when she had touched him. Good Lord, he was behaving like a lovesick schoolboy! With a massive effort of his will he turned away and wrenched his mind from contemplating Penelope.

He thought over what George had told him. Would Jack really try to murder him? Surely not! And yet the notion could not be dismissed. It occurred to him that it was even more a matter of urgency for him to consummate his marriage. The sound of George's voice roused him from his thoughts. Penelope had finished playing and George was offering to read to her. He had the *Gazette* in his hand and Penelope was delighted.

Darleston began to feel annoyed. Dash it all, she didn't have to be that friendly! And why was George so damned assiduous in his attentions? To be calling her Penny as though he had known her for ever! The contrast between the polite, reserved manner Penelope kept for him and the way she treated George was marked, and although he had encouraged her reserve he was piqued. By the time Penelope excused herself for the evening he was determined to visit her room for the express purpose of telling her plainly to behave herself!

George and Darleston remained chatting for a while, the former cheerful and unrestrained, his host a little gloomy. Finally George decided to put the cat among the pigeons. He was quick to observe and understand the demons which drove his best friend. The tension between the pair was not lost on him and he thought he could make a shrewd guess as to the cause of it.

'Peter, you're a lucky dog. If I organised a marriage for myself, as you did, it would be a total wash-out. She'd turn out to be a half-wit, or bad-tempered, or worse. But you! You end up with the most charming, intelligent girl imaginable! Even has a nice dog! I take it all back. You couldn't have chosen better if you'd known the girl for years. Nothing like Melissa either, thank God!'

Peter looked a bit startled at this panegyric. He didn't answer for a moment, but finally said, 'Yes, I suppose you're right. It could have been a lot worse.'

George left it at that. Hopefully Peter would give it some thought. It was obvious to him that Peter was annoyed by the ease with which he had made friends with Penelope. With a bit of luck it might make him realise that the girl wasn't a dangerous charmer, like Melissa, and that he could treat her as a friend, rather than a distant and not overly liked acquaintance, without disaster.

George excused himself early, saying the drive had tired him and that he would see Peter in the morning. Peter said, 'I'm unfortunately obliged to see my bailiff in the morning. Do you mind entertaining yourself? We might take guns out in the afternoon.'

'Of course I can entertain myself. Might even take Penny riding. She tells me you let her ride old Nero and that she's back in action after the accident.'

For some reason the thought of Penelope riding with George enraged him. Why, when he had offered to take her out yesterday she had refused. No doubt she would accept George's invitation with alacrity! Angrily he pushed away the knowledge that his own offer had been less than inviting. He was more than ever determined to suggest to his wife that she should be more reserved with George. With this in mind he changed himself for bed and then knocked firmly on the connecting door.

A brief silence followed his knock, and Peter wondered if his wife were already asleep. Then a startled voice bade him enter. Penelope was sitting up in bed brushing her hair. He walked over to the bed to stand looking down at her. She faced him nervously, uncertain of what he wanted. A pulse hammered in her throat and she realised to her annoyance that she was trembling.

'Peter?' Her voice was commendably steady, but her husband caught the hint of uncertainty.

'May I speak with you, Penelope?'

'Of course.' Was that *all* he wanted, drat him?

Darleston didn't mince words. 'I'm pleased, of course, that you like George, Penelope, but it is scarcely necessary for you to be quite as friendly, or to be on Christian name terms with a man you have only just met! With any other man I would be very angry indeed. Please remember that I require discretion in my wife and would prefer her to maintain a ladylike reserve with other men.'

Penelope was stunned. 'Are you seriously telling me that you expect me to be boring with everyone just because *you* happen to have a preference for it? Don't be an idiot, Peter!'

It had not occurred to Peter that she would argue with him. Surprised, he snapped back, 'If that is how you see it, yes! I'm not prepared to be cuckolded twice!'

Penelope's jaw dropped in amazement. For a moment she was rendered utterly speechless at the implied insult, and then she lost her temper. Before she could stop herself she was out of bed, standing before him shaking with hurt and rage. The angry words spilled from her, 'How *dare* you? Just because I am pleased to see someone who treats me as a…a *friend*, rather than an unwelcome guest! You are suggesting that I would be unfaithful to you? If that's what you think of me, I'm not surprised you go to such pains to avoid me. I hate you, Peter. Get out!'

It had not dawned upon Peter that his gentle bride had a temper, and he was startled to say the least. He had rather expected a continuation of her polite reserve. What he might have said in response would never be known. He found to his horror that the extremely diaphanous nightgown in which Ellen had arrayed her mistress did little, if anything, to conceal her charms. On the contrary, it displayed her slender figure to admiration. He stood staring at her, with desire rising in his blood, unable to think of anything save that he longed to tear the flimsy silk from her with a minimum of ceremony.

Furious that he was still there, and totally unaware that she might as well have been naked, Penelope repeated her command. 'Get out, Peter, and leave me alone!' She accompanied this with a stamp of her foot and pointed to the door. Peter, observing the lift of one delectable breast under the almost non-existent nightgown, forgot he was meant to be having a fight with his wife. He grasped her by the shoulders, pulled her against his body and kissed her fiercely.

The ringing slap he received across the face, coupled with the fact that his wife stood on his foot very hard indeed, brought Peter to the realisation that he had chosen an inauspicious moment to kiss her. He released her at once and stepped back, saying angrily, 'I beg your pardon, ma'am. I will relieve you of my presence! Goodnight!'

He left the room immediately, slamming the door

behind him. Penelope got back into bed slowly, buried her face in the pillow and cried herself to sleep. Darleston, standing silently cursing himself on the other side of the door, heard the muffled sobs but was too mortified to go back and apologise. The memory of the hurt on her face lashed at his conscience. Blast the girl!

Chapter Eleven

The following morning Peter was not surprised to be informed by Meadows that the mistress was breakfasting in bed, having passed an indifferent night. He merely nodded and returned to his perusal of the morning papers.

George looked up and said, 'Meadows, please ask her ladyship if she would care to go riding with me this morning. Or driving if she prefers.' Turning to Peter, he said, 'Driving might be better, do you think?'

'Probably,' was the unconcerned reply.

George took the hint and concentrated on his breakfast. As he ate he wondered how long it would take Peter to relax and at least trust his wife. He was quite aware that Peter was annoyed at the ease with which he and Penelope had struck up a friendship. 'Damned fool that he is!' muttered George under his breath.

'I beg your pardon?' said Peter.

'Oh! Er…just talking to myself!' George excused himself hurriedly, startled to realise that he had spoken aloud.

Peter nodded and left it at that, but he had very little doubt of the identity of the 'damned fool'! He was beginning to agree with George. What on earth was wrong with him? Surely he could manage to be consistently kind to the chit and not keep losing his temper? It wasn't as though she was annoying in any way. She was attractive, even beautiful, she was gentle, but with plenty of spirit. He grinned reluctantly as he recalled how she had turned on him last night.

He was physically attracted to her, no doubt of that! It would be very easy to be extremely fond of her. And that, he admitted to himself as he sipped his coffee, was just the problem. He didn't want to care at all. If he didn't care, then he couldn't be hurt by her. But she can be hurt, his conscience nagged. Why should Penny be hurt because of Melissa's sins?

His mood had lightened considerably by the time he had finished his breakfast. He was still confused, but his innate sense of justice was forcing him to the realisation that he would have to do something permanent about his behaviour. It wasn't in anyone's interest for him to continue blowing hot and cold on Penelope's feelings. He would only succeed in driving her into estrangement, if indeed he had not done so already.

Meadows came into the room just as they were finishing. 'Her ladyship is at your disposal whenever you would care to go, Master George. She would prefer to drive with you, if you have no objection,' he said.

'Thank you, Meadows. Please send a message to the stables for my chestnuts to be harnessed and tell her ladyship that I will be ready as soon as the horses are. Sure you can't come, Peter?'

'Quite sure,' said Peter with genuine regret. 'But why don't you try the paces of my new greys? They need exercise and your own team could probably do with a rest after your journey.'

George correctly deduced from this that Peter was trying to apologise for his earlier bad temper, and he suppressed a grin with some difficulty. 'With pleasure, dear boy. I'll try not to lame 'em for you. The greys, then, Meadows.'

'Very good, Master George, but don't tire her ladyship! She has been extremely unwell!' With that Meadows departed on his errands.

Peter stared after him in some bewilderment. 'Good Lord! Next thing you know Meadows will be calling her ''Miss Penny'', just as if he had known her from childhood! How amazing!'

'Not at all!' said George, amused by Peter's surprise. 'Very lovable girl, Penny. Reminds me of my sister!'

Half an hour later George and Penelope were bowling along behind Peter's prized Welsh greys with Gelert running beside them. Penelope was rather quiet at first, and George noted the faint circles under her eyes. She cheered up a bit when George told her that Peter had offered to lend them his greys. Surely if he would lend his beloved greys he wasn't too angry with her, she thought.

'Where shall we go, Penny? Your choice.'

'Oh, could we visit the Jewkes farm? Martha's baby will arrive soon and I should like to visit her. I have a note from Ellen for her, and some clothes for the baby. Do you know the farm?'

'We'll find it. I've been there once with Peter.'

A child gave them directions to the farm, and as they drove along George wondered if he should try to explain something of Peter's confusion to Penny. Peter would be furious if he knew, but the sight of Penelope's troubled face decided him. 'Penny?'

'Yes, George.'

'Hope you won't be offended, but could I talk to you about Peter?'

'About Peter?' echoed Penelope.

'Mmm. Odd fellow, Peter. Seems very moody at the moment. Thought it might be easier for you to handle him if you knew more about him. Generally he's the kindest chap alive, but after we got back from the War he changed.'

'Melissa?'

'That's it. You see, he married her for love, despite the fact that everyone else knew she married him for his money. When she ran off with Barton and got killed it was pretty hard on Peter. Of course he knew before he rejoined what she was like. She wasn't very discreet. Probably volunteered hoping he'd be killed. But the fact that she dragged his name in the mud, well, he just can't seem to forget about it. Don't know if you knew any of this.'

'Peter told me a little,' said Penelope. 'But he is so withdrawn most of the time, and then sometimes he is quite friendly. I find it very hard to understand his moods and…and I don't think he likes me very much.'

George's heart ached at the sadness in her voice as she said this. 'Thing is,' he continued, 'Peter finds it almost impossible to trust a woman now.' He refrained from mentioning Lady Caroline Daventry and her connection with Peter. 'But if you can just bear with him until he comes to his senses…don't let him upset you too much…' he left the sentence unfinished and they drove on in silence for a while.

Finally he said with difficulty, 'When Peter said he

was getting married again I thought he'd gone mad, the way he went about it. Think now that he couldn't have chosen better. Told him so last night. Must be plain as a pikestaff, even to him, that you're not like Melissa. Probably he'll be a bit easier to live with soon. He's the very devil when he's moody!'

Penelope thought over his words of advice as the greys cantered along in the autumn sunshine. Would Peter become more predictable? George was his best friend, so presumably he understood him. She did not want to be estranged from Peter. Surely they could be friends, even if they weren't in love!

And that, she realised, was her problem. Despite all her efforts to remain aloof, Peter's charm and kindness, when he was not being disagreeable, had got past her guard. She had, almost without knowing it, fallen in love with her husband! A husband, she told herself, who only wanted her to provide an heir, who didn't really care twopence for her. More than anything in the world she wanted to prove to him that she was worthy of his trust and respect, even if he never loved her.

She groaned inwardly at the mess she was in. Well, she thought, it's too late to back out now!

Their arrival at the farm interrupted her thoughts. As George swung the curricle into the farmyard she realised that she had ignored him for at least a mile.

'I beg your pardon, George, I didn't mean to be so dreadfully rude. I was thinking over what you said about Peter. I'll keep trying. I know he can be kind…he was so good about finding out that I am blind and that it was really my sister he thought he was marrying—' She broke off in horror. 'Oh, dear, I shouldn't have said that!'

George laughed. 'Peter told me in his letter what had happened. Serves him right. But from what he said to me on the way to the church it was actually you that he meant to marry!'

Penelope was startled. 'He said that, but I thought he was just being polite!'

'No, one of the things he liked about you was Gelert!'

Penelope giggled. 'Did he tell you how he chose a maid for me? He had Meadows line up all the housemaids to ask them if they liked dogs. Then he showed them Gelert and they picked the only one who was left!'

George chuckled and said, 'One of the things that gives me hope about Peter is that he has never completely lost his sense of humour. He'll be all right! Also, Meadows likes you. He couldn't stand Melissa! Peter takes a lot of notice of Meadows because the old boy looked after him as a child. Meadows was quite insistent that I mustn't tire you out this morning. Made Peter think a bit!'

'Meadows has been very kind to me,' said Penelope. 'And I notice that he nearly always calls you "Master George" and quite often calls Peter "Master Peter." He's like our old butler. I'm sure Tinson will never call me Lady Darleston!'

'Probably not. In fact I wouldn't be surprised if Meadows forgets himself one day and calls you "Miss Penny"! He nearly did this morning,' said George with a grin, 'Gave Peter something to think about. Meadows was so correct with Melissa that it was embarrassing!'

A cheerful hail from the farmhouse put a stop to their conversation. Jewkes had heard them and come out to see who was there. He was brimming over with excitement, and as he rushed towards them his words became distinguishable '...on'y sent a lad ten minutes ago! Took ye at yer word, my lady. It's a boy, and he come so fast I barely 'ad the midwife 'ere in time. Ellen will be real disappointed, but we was all caught short as ye might say!'

'Jewkes, is the baby here already?' gasped Penelope. 'Oh, how dreadful! I promised to send Ellen! Poor Martha! George, we must go home at once to tell Ellen. One of the grooms will bring her over immediately, Jewkes. I'm terribly sorry!'

Jewkes roared with laughter. 'Why, there's no call to feel bad, my lady. We didn't expect the little lad for another week. An' it's right kind of ye to send Ellen at all. I'll tell Martha. She's asleep now. Tired her out it 'as, for all it 'appened so quick. Ye'll forgive me if I get back to 'er?'

'Why of course you must, Jewkes!' said Penelope warmly. 'Here, I've a letter from Ellen and some clothes for Baby. We'll go back now and send Ellen over. Goodbye—and congratulations!'

George turned the curricle out of the yard and said, 'Home, then, Penny?'

'Yes, please, George. I must send Ellen to her sister as quickly as possible. She was so anxious about Martha, and excited about being an aunt!' said Penelope. 'You do not mind, George?'

'Of course not! We can go out again, if you like, once you have given the message,' said George obligingly. 'Pity to spend a day like this inside if you don't have to!'

'We could ask the lodgekeeper to send the message

up to the house!' suggested Penelope. 'That way we won't waste any time or get caught up.'

'Good idea! There's a very nice drive around the edge of the park, which should exercise the greys nicely and get us back in time for a late nuncheon!'

The greys quickly covered the distance back to the lodge and the message was delivered. The ten-year-old son of the lodgekeeper was only to happy to earn a penny by going up to the Court.

That done, George set the greys in motion again. They were eager to be off, yet they responded willingly to his light touch on the reins. He steadied them as he said cheerfully, 'Peter stole a march on me over this team. He used to own the prettiest team of chestnuts, knew I admired them and offered to sell them to me. Next thing we know Camley sells up and Peter's got his greys! Don't know how he hears the news so fast. He offered to let me call him out, but he's too good with a pistol for me! And he's not bad with a sword either.'

Penelope laughed. 'I can just see you calling him out because he sold you a pair of horses that you coveted. He'd have simply said that he thought you wanted the chestnuts so he gave you first refusal, since he didn't need them any more!'

'You know him uncommonly well, Penny,' said George in amusement. 'That's exactly what he did say!' They lapsed into a companionable silence. George Carstares thought that for all her liveliness Penelope didn't seem to feel the need for constant conversation. He knew she needed time to think over what he had said earlier. It sounded as though Peter was very confused about his marriage. He suspected that

Peter was fonder of the girl than he was willing to let on.

Penelope enjoyed the swift rhythm of the hooves on the road and the swing of the curricle. Before her accident she had been taught to drive by her father. The easy motion of the carriage and the steady pace of the team told her that George was a good driver. She found herself wishing bitterly that she did not have to sit passively, but could take the reins.

Generally she did not waste time sighing over what could never be, but several times just recently she had caught herself in the middle of what felt suspiciously like a wallow of self-pity. Stop it! she told herself with a mental shake. Then she realised that it would be far better to work out the reason for her mood and face it.

That was how she had reconciled herself to the loss of her sight. She had faced her fury with Geoffrey and conquered it with the help of her father. He had made her see that bitterness would harm only herself. He had forced her to be as independent as possible, refusing to pity her. Above all he had understood the pride which made pity a totally unacceptable reaction to her affliction.

So why, after all these years, should self-pity creep in? Frustration, yes. She often felt frustrated, but she had discovered long ago that it was better to consider a problem dispassionately to see if there was a solution. If not, then it was best to move on to something else.

Peter. She wanted to see Peter. She wanted to know what he looked like, this man she had married and so foolishly fallen in love with. That he was handsome, she knew. Phoebe's description had told her that. At first she hadn't minded, hadn't even thought about it. Now it was suddenly important. She felt at a complete emotional disadvantage not being able to see him. Well, bad luck, she thought, there is no solution.

Having made her way through the tangled skein of thought, Penelope set herself to thinking about how to win Peter's trust and liking. Slapping him in the face and stamping on his foot was probably not a good start! She considered apologising for her loss of temper but rejected the notion. It wouldn't harm him to realise just how angry and hurt she had been. Besides which she was *not* going to emulate 'Patient Griselda'!

The pounding of another set of hooves disturbed her thoughts. A rider, approaching at a gallop from the rear, by the sound. She felt George turn to glance over his shoulder as the newcomer drew close.

'Chap's in a big hurry.' He pulled over a little.

The next few seconds were filled with confusion. There was a shattering explosion, swiftly followed by a startled yell from George. Something hurled her from the seat to the floor of the curricle.

'Stay down Penny!' Another explosion mingled with George's frantic command. She could hear the terrified neighing of the horses as George fought to control them. The curricle swung madly as they plunged in fright, attempting to bolt. Penelope clung to George's legs as she crouched on the floor. Gelert was barking furiously and she could hear the other horse galloping away at top speed. Gelert's barks receded into the distance.

Gradually George calmed the greys until they stood sweating and restless in the road. He looked around, but their assailant had made good his escape. Gelert had chased him, but his instinct to stay with Penelope had obviously prevailed and he was coming back. George looked down at Penelope.

'Are you all right? He's gone. You can get up.' He helped her back onto the seat. Then he caught sight of her bonnet. The left side of the brim was in tatters. He stared in horror and swore savagely. Penelope, still confused and uncertain about what had happened, was taken aback.

'What happened, George?' she asked in shaky tones.

'Someone shot at us. Or rather, at you!'

'Shot at me? Have you gone mad? What on earth for?'

George did not answer immediately. 'We'd better go home and tell Peter,' he said, and put the greys into a trot.

'George! Why did someone shoot at me? You must tell me!' Penelope was close to tears of fright and anger.

Resigning himself to the inevitable, George glanced at her and said, 'I suppose I'd better, but Peter isn't going to like it.'

'Did Peter know about it?'

'Well, obviously neither of us thought there could be any danger on the estate!' said George defensively. He continued, 'How much did Peter tell you about his heir, Jack Frobisher?'

'Not much. Peter told me that he doesn't like him. That was why he married me. To stop Mr Frobisher inheriting the title.' Penelope blushed as she said this.

'That is probably the explanation for this attack. Frobisher is in financial difficulty. He's counting on Peter's money. You, as Peter's wife, could be a danger to his plans. I warned Peter last night that the pair of you could be in danger, but we didn't think there could be any trouble here. Or that an attack would be so direct. Don't worry, Penny. We'll get home and Peter will sort it out.'

'He wasn't a very good shot,' said Penelope, trying gallantly to lighten the atmosphere.

George laughed shortly. 'If he'd been any better Peter would be a widower again! Feel the brim of your bonnet, Penny!'

Chapter Twelve

'Peter, may I speak to you for a moment?'

Darleston looked up from his desk, surprised at his wife's entrance and the note of distress in her voice. She rarely sought him out willingly. He looked at her closely. The slim hand resting on Gelert's collar was trembling slightly. He rose and went to her, taking her hand to lead her to the sofa.

'Come, sit down, Penelope. Something is upsetting you? Tell me what it is.'

She sat down obediently but remained silent, unsure how to begin. Would he rebuff her, or, worse, be very angry with George? Peter sat beside her, watching the play of emotion on her face. Yet again he cursed himself for setting her at a distance. If only she were not so reserved with him, he thought. Almost without realising what he was doing he took her hand in both of his and held it lightly, one thumb caressing the soft palm. She felt again the strange yearning that swept over her whenever he touched her. Why did she feel this way? He didn't really care about her, did he?

'Come, Penny, it can't be that bad, surely! Did George overturn the curricle?' The gentle note in his voice almost made her cry. Why couldn't he always be like this?

She smiled tremulously. 'No, Peter. George drives as well as you do.'

'I'm glad to hear it, since they were my horses he was driving! Tell me what it is. I promise I won't be angry with you!'

'Or with George?'

The question startled Peter. What on earth did she mean? Surely George had not made advances to her. He stared at her. So that was why she was upset! He released her hand abruptly and stood up, scarcely able to trust his voice. 'Go on, you had better tell me.'

Penelope heard the suppressed anger and said bravely, 'You must not blame George. It was not his fault, Peter.'

'That I can well believe. I said you were being too friendly.' Penelope blinked in surprise, unable to follow his meaning at first. Then, as the reason for his anger dawned, she blushed. Peter noted this cynically but made no comment.

Penelope fought down the impulse to retreat, leave the room without telling him. Only the realisation that if he went to George in this mood it could destroy their friendship held her.

'George told me about your cousin, the threats he has made and the money he has borrowed. Is it true that he is trying to kill you, Peter?'

Peter was stunned. 'What? George must be insane to tell you about that! It's little more than conjecture at this stage.'

'He didn't have much choice, Peter. Someone shot at us while we were out driving. Look!' She held out her ruined bonnet. It was removed from her grasp by hands that seemed to tremble. 'Peter, I'm sorry to interfere with your private affairs, but this involves me too.'

He didn't answer at once. He didn't trust his voice and simply stared at the bonnet, realising just how close the shot had come to killing Penelope. Then he dropped the bonnet, taking Penelope into his arms to hold her tightly. 'Oh, my God!' he whispered in a strangled voice. He did not try to analyse his feelings. All he knew was that the thought of Penelope lying dead due to his stupidity filled him with shame and horror.

Penelope gave an odd little sigh of relief as she rested her cheek on his shoulder. She could feel the strength of his arms and knew herself to be safe. They were silent for a moment before Peter spoke. 'I'm sorry, Penny, this is my fault. I should have warned you last night but all I did was insult you. I'm not a very good husband in any sense of the word.'

Her reply startled him. 'Don't be an idiot, Peter! George knew, but he still took me driving. He didn't think there would be any trouble if we stayed on the estate, and if I'd known I would have agreed. How could it possibly be your fault?'

Peter felt doubly shamed by her generosity and said bitterly, 'If I had taken the least thought for you as my wife I would have told you, forbidden you to leave the house and gardens until this mess was cleared up! Instead I lost my temper because I was jealous!'

Penelope gasped in amazement and struggled out of his embrace. 'Jealous? How can you possibly be *jealous* when you don't even like me! You made it quite clear after that first day. You avoided me, and every time I tried to talk to you at all you snubbed me! Then at other times you were friendly and…and kind. Peter, I don't know what to think!'

Peter was silent. What could he say? He had only himself to blame if she was confused about his attitude towards her. Eventually he spoke. 'Neither do I, Penny.'

'I'm sorry, Peter, but I'm not Melissa! Just because one woman betrayed you doesn't mean I will. I don't expect you to love me, but couldn't you at least trust me, even if I do disgust you?' Penelope was crying now. She fumbled for her handkerchief as Peter's arms closed around her again, gently rocking her back and forth.

Peter wondered if anyone else had ever made such a mess of a marriage as he had managed to make of his.

'How could you disgust me, Penny, you idiot? If anything I would have thought that my behaviour must have disgusted *you*.'

Her answer was barely audible through her tears. 'You k-kissed me that first day, and after that we went back to the house and you were different. You wouldn't talk to me, so I thought I must have done something you didn't like. All I could think of was that you didn't like it when I kissed you back. And the other time you kissed me, you…you pushed me away, so I thought I must be doing something wrong.'

He felt ashamed of himself. 'You didn't disgust me, Penny, I promise you, and I *did* like it when you kissed me. It was my fault for being so suspicious of you as a woman, but also I didn't want to force you into my bed, despite what I said initially.'

'But you said that you wanted an heir…and…that…you wanted me…' She stopped, embarrassed, then continued bravely, 'I do not want to be your wife in name only, but in...in truth, and I thought that was what you wanted.'

Peter took her face between the palms of his hands and kissed her gently on the mouth. 'It is what I want, Penny, and not just because I want an heir, but because I want you. That is what scared me so much and made me behave so stupidly. I'm sorry Penny, will you forgive me?'

Penelope nodded, unable to speak, with the tears still on her cheeks. Peter took the handkerchief and dried her eyes. 'Come along, Penny, bed for you. We'll discuss all this tomorrow. Sleep this afternoon. I'll bring your dinner to you on a tray and sit with you this evening. You've had a terrible shock and must rest. George can tell me exactly what happened. He must be in quite a state!' Then, as the possibility occurred to him, 'My God, he's not hurt, is he?'

'No, I should have told you at once!' said Penelope rather indignantly. 'He saved my life, I think,' she continued. 'He must have seen the man, because he shouted and pushed me off the seat.'

'Thank God for George!' said Peter, and gathered her into his arms.

Late that night Peter woke with the odd feeling that someone had cried out. He sat up in the moonlight to listen but at first he could hear nothing. He was about to lie down again when it occurred to him that Penelope might have cried out in her sleep. She had slept all afternoon and he had had his dinner with her in her bed-chamber. Knowing that she was still shaken by the attack, he had ignored her avowal that she was well enough to get up for dinner.

'Just remember that you promised to obey me and stop arguing!'

'But what about George? You can't leave him to fend for himself! He's a guest!'

'He's not a guest! He's my best friend, and I shudder to think what he'd say if I left you alone this evening, especially since you wouldn't let me send for Ellen! Besides, he's not fending for himself! The entire staff, and Meadows in particular, is treating him as a hero!'

Penelope had given up, and Peter was fairly sure she'd been grateful for his company. He had read to her until she fell asleep again. Then he had quietly blown out the lamp and retired to his own room, leaving the door open.

After a moment's hesitation he got out of bed and pulled on his dressing gown, a luxurious affair of deep red brocade. He moved softly to the connecting door and looked through. The moon was shining directly into the room. He could see that Penelope's bedclothes were tumbled and that she was very restless. As he stepped into the room she murmured his name in a distressed tone. Hesitantly he went to the bed to place a gentle hand upon her brow, wondering if she were ill. The cool skin assured him that she was not feverish, merely dreaming, and he attempted to straighten the covers for her.

As he did so, she cried out in fright at her dream. 'Peter, help me! Lost—can't see…where are you?' The note of anguish in her voice touched Peter's heart to the core. He wanted to comfort her but was reluctant to wake her.

Making up his mind quickly, he slipped into the bed

and took her in his arms, whispering, 'It's all right Penny, it's just a dream, you're safe, shh.'

Waking, she turned in his arms murmuring, 'Peter?'

'Yes, little one. It's all right, go back to sleep.' With a relieved sigh she relaxed against him. He smiled to himself as he rested his cheek upon her hair, enjoying the faint smell of lavender that hung about it and the feel of her body pressed to him. Gently he caressed the curve of her hip and felt her quiver responsively.

Gazing down at her loveliness in the moonlight, he wondered if he dared stay. He was agonisingly aware of his own desire and knew he would not be able to control himself for long. Reluctantly he gathered himself to go.

Penelope felt the withdrawal and, gathering all her courage, put her arms around him.

'Peter?'

'Yes.'

'Must you go? Won't you stay with me?'

He hesitated, then said quietly, 'Penny, you are a very lovely woman and I am only a man, not a saint. If I stay any longer I will make love to you. Do you want that?'

'That's why I want you to stay. Please, Peter, I...I want to be your wife...if...if you want me...'

He stared down at her. Her face was turned up to his pleadingly. Unable to deny himself any longer, he kissed her tenderly. His lips dwelt briefly on hers before travelling sensuously down the column of her throat, burning a trail of fire on the soft skin. He heard her gasp with pleasure at the sensation and began to undo the buttons on the front of her nightgown.

When he had dealt with them all he sat up, pulling Penelope with him. Restraining his urge to tear the filmy gown from her body, he slipped it off her shoulders, revealing the perfection of her creamy, rose-tipped breasts. Cupping one in his hand, he caressed it lightly before taking her mouth again. He felt her tremble as he kissed her and her mouth yielded under his. Dizzy with passion, he slid his tongue between her parted lips to explore the honeyed sweetness of her mouth. His hands moved possessively over her slim body, touching her with growing intimacy.

The nightgown was definitely in the way, he decided, and he felt himself to be distinctly overdressed for the occasion. He moved back from her to remove these impediments more easily, but she clung to him and begged, 'Don't stop. Please, don't leave me now!'

'I couldn't if I tried, Penny,' he said, his voice rough with desire. 'But I'm not going to make love to you in my dressing gown! Will you help me take it off?' He guided her hand to the cord which tied the garment. Her inexperienced fingers fumbled with the knot, finally releasing it. Free of the dressing gown, Peter removed Penelope's nightdress completely and pressed her back against the pillows.

She lay acquiescent in the moonlight and he drew a shaky breath at the sight of her loveliness. He lowered himself beside her to take her in his arms, pulling her against his aroused body. She was still shaking, and it occurred to him that she might well be frightened by his passion. He held her tenderly, stroking the dark red curls back from her flushed face. 'Don't be scared of me. I swear I'll be gentle. Trust me, Penny.'

For an answer she slipped her arms about him and pressed herself closer, lifting her mouth to his. Peter responded to the mute invitation, his lips moving demandingly on hers and then down her throat. His hands teased and caressed, drifting over the delicate curve of her waist, her stomach and on to her slender thigh.

At first she simply clung to him, trembling in ecstasy, still unsure of herself. Then her desire to give him as much pleasure as he was giving her took over. Instinctively she copied his actions, tentatively exploring his body. Her hands discovered the powerful muscles of his shoulders and chest, the flat plane of his stomach.

Her light caresses stirred Peter's senses nearly to madness. Gently he grasped her hand to lead it still lower, until she touched him intimately. The heated evidence of his desire was almost frightening.

'Peter?' She was a little scared, uncertain of what he wanted.

He heard the nervousness in her voice and was swift to reassure her. 'Like this, sweetheart. Don't be scared,' he murmured, and showed her.

Delighted with the results of her exploration, Penelope became bolder in her efforts to please him. His pleasure in her shy advances was intense. It was all he could do to keep himself under control and not take her immediately. He did not want to rush her. Instinctively he knew that she was still unsure of herself, knew that it would be only too easy to frighten her if he lost command of himself.

Groaning in pleasure, he lowered his mouth to her breast, circling and tantalising the rosy peak until she cried out in longing. Then, and only then, he slid his hand between her silken thighs to the very centre of her passion. He could barely restrain himself from possessing her at once when he discovered the tender flower of her virginity, already damp with the dew of desire. Not yet! He prayed for control. Dear God, don't let me hurt her or frighten her! He caressed her gently and took her mouth again, feeling it tremble as he acquainted himself with her sweetness.

Penelope moaned in total surrender as he stroked her intimately. She could not think, only feel, as he roused her senses to madness with his touch. His lips claimed hers again, passionate and demanding as he continued his exquisite assault on her body. Her delicate breasts were crushed against his muscular torso as she writhed against him in wordless ecstasy, her hips lifting instinctively.

Peter felt her hips move and knew that she was ready for him. Gently he pressed her legs further apart and slid one hard, muscled thigh between them. He moved his manhood suggestively against her, still fondling the sensitive core of her femininity as his tongue thrust deeply into her mouth in erotic anticipation. Releasing her lips momentarily, he gazed down at her face, flushed with passion, and whispered hoarsely, 'Shall I take you, little virgin? Do you want me?'

The answer was little more than a helpless sob of longing. He hovered over her, balanced on his elbows, stroking her face, and again asked softly, 'Do you want me, Penny?'

Wordlessly she nodded, her arms reaching for him urgently.

'Say it, little one,' he insisted, watching her face.

'You know I do!' she whispered. Her face was bathed in tears.

'I want you, little one, all of you!' he whispered passionately.

Unable to wait any longer, Peter parted her thighs and swung his other leg over so that he lay intimately cradled by her body. With gentle patience he pressed himself against her, throbbing with barely controlled desire as he moved back and forth, teasing her with the promise of his masculinity, his own senses reeling in expectation. Then, as her hips lifted in innocent invitation, he took her. He felt the resistance of the fragile barrier and steadied for a split second before broaching her maidenhead with infinite tenderness.

He felt her stiffen, heard her soft cry of pain mingled with pleasure as he possessed her, and stopped immediately, whispering endearments and encouragement, giving her time to get used to him. Feeling her relax, he withdrew slightly to thrust again.

This time she cried out. 'Oh, Peter, don't stop! Please don't stop!'

They were the last words she spoke for a very long time. She felt his lips come down on hers in absolute mastery, his tongue ravishing her mouth in an erotic counterpoint to the gentle rhythm of his loins. It seemed to Penelope that the darkness swirled around her and exploded as Peter increased the tempo, his thrusts lifting her to wild heights of joy.

Sensing that she was close to the edge, Peter slowed down and pulled back slightly, then, as she cried out in protest, he took her all over again. To Penelope it was as though the world shattered as he surged back into her, taking possession of her very soul.

Peter lay dozing in the early-morning light, listening to a song thrush with Penelope still cradled in his arms, just as she had fallen asleep after their love-making. He looked down at her peaceful face and smiled tenderly as he thought back on their belated bridal night.

She had been so responsive to him, but so endearingly innocent in her passion! It occurred to Peter with a jolt that he had never enjoyed a woman so much in all his experience. Furthermore, he knew that he had never cared so much about a woman's pleasure. It was oddly important for her sake, not just as a feather in his cap.

He caressed her shoulder through the silky auburn curls which spread in wild abandon over her and spilled onto his chest. So soft, so sweet! He couldn't believe that he had been stupid enough to distrust her innocence! His hand moved to stroke her cheek, the corner of her tender mouth which had melted in complete surrender to his desire. He longed to make love to her again, but told himself that to awaken her would be selfish.

At this point the thrush, perhaps aware of his feudal master's need, alighted on the casement, singing vigorously. The speckled breast swelled with ecstatic song, expressing Peter's mood perfectly. Penelope opened her eyes with a contented sigh. She wondered for a moment why she was lying in such an odd, yet comfortable position.

Then memory came flooding back as she realised that she was nestled very snugly in her husband's arms and that he was fondling her cheek. A blush stained her face as she recalled exactly why Peter was in her bed. Had she disappointed him? Or, worse still, disgusted him with her enjoyment?

'Peter?' It was little more than a whisper, but he heard the nervousness in her voice and, watching the emotions play across her face, had a very fair idea of its cause. He had to reassure her. It hurt him strangely that she should have any doubt of his delight in their union.

'Yes, little one, are you all right?'

She wondered at the concern in his voice. 'Yes, why do you ask?'

He gathered her still more closely in his arms and went on, 'You were so lovely, and I wanted you so much, that I thought I might have hurt you.'

The sincerity in his voice and the fact that one hand had found its way to her breast, where it was making it very hard for her to think straight, let alone speak, convinced her that he had not been *too* badly disappointed. Surely, too, he had not minded that she had enjoyed it if he was persisting in an action he knew she would respond to!

She was unsure how to answer him, finally opting for the truth. 'It only hurt a little, just at first, then...' She stopped, shyly.

'Then?' he prompted teasingly, enjoying her embarrassment.

'Then...it was w-w-wonderful!' Then, gaining confidence, 'And you, did you...? I mean, was it...? I didn't know what to do...'

'Are you asking if I enjoyed making love to you?' interrupted Peter. 'I must be a very bad lover if I could leave you in any doubt that you were beautiful in every way. And if you had any thought that I had finished with you, Madam Wife, get rid of it right now. I've wasted nearly two months of our marriage and I intend to make up for lost time!'

He then proceeded to demonstrate quite incontrovertibly how much he had enjoyed himself. His reassurances were wholly convincing to Penelope, who responded in a manner which left her husband in no doubt that his bride had no regrets about the belated wedding night.

When George entered the breakfast parlour he found Peter polishing off the remains of what had obviously been a hearty meal. Peter looked up as his friend appeared. 'Good morning, George.'

'Morning, Peter. How did you find Penny this morning?'

Now what the deuce was there in that, wondered George, to make Peter blush? He blinked in surprise as Peter disappeared behind the newspaper.

'She's very well, but I've managed to persuade her to breakfast in bed,' answered Peter. 'George, I don't think I really thanked you for what you did yesterday. There…there are no words. Penny told me that you saved her life…'

'Don't be an idiot, Peter, you would have done the same! So would anyone!' said George, flushing. 'I'm just glad that she's still alive and unhurt.' He noted with delight that Peter had dropped the rather formal use of his wife's full name. Without being precisely glad about the attempt to murder Penelope, he realised that it had permanently shaken Peter out of his mood of distrust.

The entrance of Meadows saved George from further embarrassment. The butler had been very much upset the previous day and it was obvious that he was still shaken. He poured a cup of tea for Peter and handed it to him, saying, 'I've sent Gelert up to Miss Penny, Master Peter, and her breakfast. Are you sure she's quite all right?'

'She's fine, Meadows. I'm going up to her after Mr Carstares and I discuss what's to be done. I'll tell her you were asking.' By avoiding George's eye Peter somehow managed to keep a straight face until his butler had left the room.

'Told you so!' said George smugly, '"Miss Penny"! D'you think he even noticed what he said?'

'Probably not!' said Peter with a grin.

Conversation revolved largely around how to deal with the previous day's attack. George was of the opinion that Peter should return to town with Penelope to let Bow Street deal with the affair, and Peter was inclined to agree.

'If it were just myself I'd stay here, but Penny will be safer in town. Here she would have to be confined to the house at all times. Obviously now we have to assume that the bridge was *not* an accident. At least in town it will be far more risky for anyone to make an attempt upon either of us.'

George nodded and said, 'But you can't deal with it alone, Peter. Even if only for Penny's sake, you must let the Runners know.' It was apparent to George that the attempt on Penelope's life had shocked Peter into a realisation of how foolish he had been. There was a note of tenderness in his voice when he spoke of her, making it plain to see that his determination to protect her did not stem merely from a sense of duty, but from affection.

Peter was silent for a moment. 'The last thing I want is publicity, but I think you're right. I'll send a message to Penny's sister and brother-in-law. They might be able to come up to town as well. Penny isn't very fond of town, and if we go it will mean attending some functions, or there will be gossip. She'll find it easier with family there.'

'Will you trust a letter like that to the post?' asked George.

'No, I won't. You're going to take it! Richard Winton's a decent chap, very fond of Penny, we can count on him in a corner. Besides that I suppose Carrington will be eager to assist, after Jack tried to elope with his sister?'

George shook his head. 'No doubt he would, but he and his mother have taken a house in Bath for several months. They have taken Amelia out of school and are introducing her quietly into society to take her mind off the whole business. Carrington feels it's best for him to stay close. Encourage the chit to confide in him a bit so he can guide her more easily.'

'Oh.' Peter thought about that. 'He's probably right. Well, I can't ask him to drop his own responsibilities to solve my problems! We'll manage with you and Winton to stand buff!' He got up and paced around the room. 'Blast Jack! If I get my hands on him he'll rue the day he was born!'

'No proof, old man. He'd deny everything even if we could get him arrested.'

'I wasn't thinking of getting him arrested! I had something far more personal in mind! And I wish to God Carrington *had* called him out! He'd have blown a hole in him and saved us all a lot of trouble!'

Chapter Thirteen

Three days later Lord and Lady Darleston, accompanied by Gelert, left Darleston Court for London. Penelope had been horrified by the thought of London society, but once the entire situation had been made plain to her she had been forced to admit the sense of going to London. The prospect of being with Phoebe had gone a long way towards reconciling her to the necessity, so she set out happily enough.

They arrived in London on a cold, wet evening. Dusk was falling and the cobbled streets shone wet in the lamplight. 'Nearly there, Penny. Are you tired?' asked Peter, concerned at her white face.

'A little,' she confessed, thinking to herself that it was worth being tired to hear the caring note in his voice. Since the night after the attack Peter had not slept with her, but his manner towards her had been consistently affectionate and protective. He had insisted that she recover completely from her shock and be properly rested before the long trip to London, and Penelope was instinctively aware that he needed time to adjust to the new intimacy of their relationship. Yet the door between their rooms had remained open, and when she was restless at night or bad dreams disturbed her sleep Peter always seemed to be there.

Shyly Penelope felt for Peter's hand and leaned against his shoulder. It was all so different from their last journey together in a chaise, she thought. Then she had been terrified of her unseen, unknown husband. This time she knew that even if he never loved her, at least he was her friend. Peter looked down at her and gently disengaged his hand, but only to slip his arm around her shoulders. She turned to him, smiling as she felt his hand under her chin, lifting it gently. Then his lips were on hers in a brief, tender kiss.

The chaise drew up before the Darleston townhouse in Grosvenor Square. Peter looked out at it through the pouring rain, noting the lights shining from it. Meadows had come up earlier in the day with the rest of the staff to open the house. A footman ran down the stairs from the front door to open the door of the chaise and let down the steps. 'Here we are, Penny. Let me help you out,' said Peter. He lifted her out and set her carefully on the pavement. Gelert frisked around them, delighted to be out of the confines of the chaise.

Meadows greeted them at the door. 'Good evening, my lord and lady. Refreshments are laid out in the library. I trust that your journey was not too tiring?'

'Thank you, Meadows. You're very formal all of a sudden,' said Peter.

'Mr and Mrs Winton, Mr Carstares and Miss Sarah Ffolliot are awaiting you in the library,' said Meadows with dignity.

An undignified shriek came from halfway down the hall accompanied by the sound of running feet. *'Penny!'*

Penny swung around and held out her arms to catch her little sister. 'Sarah! Whatever are you doing here?'

'Mama has gone to stay with Mrs Lacy in Bath because she's ill and begged Mama to come, so the house is shut up and I am staying with Phoebe and Richard. They weren't going to bring me to London but I told them I'd come on the stagecoach if they left me behind or sent me to Bath!' explained Sarah breathlessly. 'Oh, I *am* glad to see you!'

'Good evening, Darleston. I do apologise for springing this hoyden on you without warning.'

Peter turned to see Richard Winton and Phoebe watching the reunion in amusement.

'Richard!' gasped Penelope. 'Where's Phoebe?'

'I'm here, dearest,' said Phoebe, running to her.

The meeting was on the whole a noisy one. The three girls all talked at once, while Gelert signified his delight in having them all together by barking frantically as he leapt from one to another in a manner highly prejudicial to the safety of several chairs.

'Thank you for coming, Winton,' said Peter over the din, holding out his hand.

Richard took it in a friendly grip and said, 'No thanks are needed, Darleston. Penny is as dear to me as my own sister. Carstares explained everything.'

'Good. Will you stay for dinner? Where are you putting up?' asked Peter.

'We are at my sister's house, and we should be delighted to stay for dinner. Carstares has already informed your staff that we would be doing so,' said Richard with a grin.

'Good for him! By the way, where is he?' asked Peter.

'In the library, poring over your chessboard. Sarah has him very neatly trapped!'

'Good Lord, George is quite a dab at chess!' said Peter in amazement.

'Not as good as Sarah, I'm afraid!' laughed Richard. 'John Ffolliot was an expert and he taught all the girls. I avoid playing with Sarah. She's nearly as good as Penny. Phoebe I can at least beat three times out of five, but I suspect she gives me the odd game to salve my dignity. Sarah and Penny have no such delicacy, as you will doubtless find out!'

'Shall we rescue him, then? Meadows, when will dinner be ready?' asked Peter.

'In twenty minutes, my lord.'

'Excellent! Thank you Meadows.'

'You're not going to interrupt the game, are you?' asked Sarah indignantly, catching this conversation. 'Mr Carstares and I have been having such a good time. He has offered to teach me piquet after dinner.'

'At least that may give poor George a chance to salvage his pride after a game of chess with you!' said Penelope. 'Leave the chessboard set up, dearest. You can always finish the game later.'

At the end of dinner the ladies very correctly withdrew, leaving the gentlemen to the enjoyment of their port and brandy. The presence of the servants at dinner had precluded any discussion of the problem at hand, so the men did not linger but joined the ladies in the drawing room almost immediately. A fire had been lit and several lamps cast a warm glow over the room. It was a large apartment, furnished luxuriously but without ostentation. Most of the furniture was of an antique date, and dark wood gleamed with beeswax. Penelope and Phoebe were ensconced on a Queen Anne sofa, while Sarah sat on a rug before the fire with Gelert.

The three girls looked up as the gentlemen entered, and Gelert thumped his tail in greeting. It occurred to Peter that he had not seen this room appear so home-like since his mother's death. Somehow, he thought, Penny made it different. Phoebe had vacated her seat beside Penelope and gone to sit with Richard, so Peter, rather self-consciously, sat beside his wife.

She turned to him at once. 'Peter—Phoebe, Sarah and I have been talking, and we think it will be a good idea if Sarah stays here with us. That will give me a constant companion who will arouse no gossip. What do you think?'

Peter was taken aback. 'What do you think your mother would say? It is a good idea, but Mrs Ffolliot might conceivably object to me endangering two of her daughters. Besides, I was planning to look after you myself!'

'If Penny's in it then so am I!' said Sarah.

Peter smiled at her and said, 'We're all in it, thanks to my unspeakable cousin. Your mother, however, might prefer you to be kept out of the firing line. I've little doubt Winton would prefer Phoebe out of danger!'

'I would, of course,' said Richard. 'But if we try to handle this without involving them we'll never know what they're up to. Much better to work with them, in my opinion. I sent a message to Mrs Ffolliot, telling her the situation. Her reply reached us at my sister's house. She can't come herself as her friend is ill and needs her. She wrote that if Sarah was a problem we were to send her to Bath but that she would be more useful in London. If she sends for Sarah I'll be very much surprised; this was probably the sort of thing she had in mind.'

'Very well, Sarah stays here. Penny can lend you what you need tonight. We'll send over for the rest tomorrow, Sarah,' said Peter. He was rewarded with a beaming smile from his young sister-in-law and a hug from his wife. 'What about George?'

'I can stay in my lodgings or here, whichever you think best,' said George.

'I think we need to consider our strategy,' said Richard thoughtfully. 'We can tackle this in two ways, as I see it. One, we can make it perfectly obvious that we are surrounding Penny and Darleston. You know, make Frobisher realise that we are on to him. Scare him off. Or, two, we can be a little more subtle, let him think we don't know and—'

'Try to smoke him out!' interrupted Sarah. 'Good idea, Richard!'

'Naturally if it were Sarah he wanted to relieve us of,' continued Richard, 'the second plan would be best. Since, however, we want to avoid any further danger to Penny, my first suggestion might be more appropriate.'

'Definitely!' said Peter with feeling. 'Sorry to seem disobliging, Sarah, but I have no intention of giving my cousin the slightest chance of harming Penny! It might be third time lucky for him! George, you're staying here, if you really don't mind.'

George nodded cheerfully. 'Much more comfortable than my lodgings!'

'Never mind, Sarah,' said Penelope consolingly. 'I dare say we can have a lot of fun scaring Mr Frobisher!'

Phoebe smiled. 'You will be able to play lots of chess, Mr Carstares!'

'Much obliged to you, ma'am!' said George dryly.

'What about Carrington?' asked Richard. 'He's a good friend of yours, Darleston. Where is he at the moment?'

'In Bath, unfortunately,' responded Peter. 'He's tied up with some family matters. I can't ask his assistance at the moment. Mainly because he would feel obliged to give it and I don't think he should!'

'Well, that's a pity, but obviously it can't be helped,' said Richard thoughtfully. 'Meanwhile, how do we start our scare campaign?'

Peter thought for a moment and then said, 'I think, if Penny can stand it, that we launch ourselves into the autumn Little Season. We are bound to meet Jack, which will give us the chance to hint him off. Also George told me that Jack has been spreading unsavoury rumours about our marriage, so we'll take the opportunity to squash those as well!'

Sarah looked thoughtful. 'Of course I don't wish Penny to be hurt, but I don't think it will work. How are we going to know if he has been really scared off? He might just lie low for a while and then try later. You can't spend the rest of your lives wondering if your cousin is trying to kill you!'

The others were silent. Sarah had unerringly put her finger on the weakness in their strategy. Finally Peter answered. 'What concerns me is the threat to your sister. If Jack thinks that he can't get to her he will try for me...'

'*No!*' interrupted Penelope, 'You are not going to go around offering yourself as a target! I won't have it!'

The fear in her voice surprised everyone. Peter stared at her in wonder. Did she care for him that much? He knew she was fond of him, responded to him physically, but love? The thought made him uncomfortable, ashamed that he did not love her—whatever his heart might, on occasion, tell him to the contrary.

'Penny...' he began.

Penelope heard the constraint in his voice and knew she had betrayed herself. She tried to lighten the atmosphere. 'I'm too young to be a widow!' There was a general laugh at this.

'Very well,' said Richard. 'Let's start by seeing if we can scare him off. I think we'll know if he's really scared or just lying low.'

Penelope nodded. 'That's a much better idea. I definitely do not fancy having any more pot-shots taken at me!'

Later, in the privacy of her bed-chamber, Penelope mentally kicked herself for being so foolish as to give Peter a clue to her feelings. Little fool! she thought. The last thing he wants is love! Sighing, she lay back against her pillows.

'At least he has come to care for me a little,' she whispered. His kindness and tenderness towards her were unfailing.

Her thoughts drifted back to the night he had spent in her bed. Never had she imagined that making love could possibly be so wonderful. Trembling at the memory of the fire he had ignited in her body, she wondered when he would come to her again. Briefly she considered going to him, but recoiled from the thought in fear of betraying herself any further. It was not just a matter of pride. She knew that to declare her love would make Peter uncomfortable, it might even cause him to withdraw from her again. He had never spoken of love and she was not naive enough to think that because he had bedded her with such tender skill he must needs love her.

A gentle knock at the door from Peter's room startled her from her thoughts.

'Come in,' she called, pushing back the covers to sit up.

Peter walked in, holding a candle. Shadows flickered on the walls from its dancing light. He gazed at Penelope, sitting almost lost in the shadows of her bed-hangings.

'Peter? Is that you?' she asked shyly, as his footsteps brought him close to the bed.

'Yes, I just wanted to make sure you were comfortable,' he said, looking down at her. He wondered if she had the slightest notion that Ellen always chose the most revealing nightdresses imaginable. Desire burned in his veins as his eyes rested on her, but he told himself firmly that she must be tired. Surely he could wait just one more night!

She smiled at him, saying, 'I'm very comfortable, thank you.' She held out her hand. Every fibre in her body cried out for him to stay, but somehow she said simply, 'Goodnight.'

He took her hand, kissed it, and then looked into her face. His heart lurched at what he saw there: love, desire, trust. Instead of releasing her hand he sat down on the bed, put the candle on a bedside table and took her in his arms.

'This is likely to be a very long "Goodnight", little one,' he whispered.

His mouth was on hers, wooing her tenderly, then more fiercely as he felt her ardent response. Her kisses inflamed him and he pushed away the covers to slide into the bed. Releasing her momentarily, he tore off his dressing gown, then lay down beside her, pulling her back into his arms. She yielded to him completely, her soft curves moulding to his hard, muscled contours. He groaned in excitement as he felt her mouth open under his like a flower. Never in all his life had he wanted a woman as he did now.

Much later, lying clasped in Peter's arms, Penelope found to her distress that she was crying silently. She did her best to hide it, but Peter felt the tension in her body. Startled, he lifted a hand to her cheek and found it wet. 'Why, Penny, you're crying!' he said in horror. 'Sweetheart, I didn't hurt you?'

She shook her head, tears still trickling down her cheeks, 'No, you didn't hurt me at all! It was wonderful! I...I'm fine...just a bit shaken.' How could she explain to him that she was crying because she loved him, because she knew he did not love her? How to tell him that every time he touched her, or spoke to her, her love increased? That when he made love to her it was an agony not to be able to say that she loved him?

Suddenly he understood. He had suspected that she loved him; her passionate response to his lovemaking told him a great deal. Now he realised just how difficult the whole relationship had become for her. No matter what he said or did he was going to hurt her unbearably. Tenderly he used the sheet to dry her cheeks, knowing that there was nothing he could possibly say to comfort her. To do so would be an intolerable wound to her pride, which would not allow her to accept pity. All he could do was hold her until she drifted off to sleep.

Chapter Fourteen

It seemed to Peter as he escorted his wife into the glittering, crowded ballroom that most of the Ton was present at Lady Edenhope's Ball. Two weeks had been spent in intensive shopping to outfit Penelope for the social whirl and this was their first appearance. He exchanged a glance with Richard Winton and said softly, 'This is going to cause quite a sensation!'

Penelope's hand trembled on his arm. The buzz of chatter in the room told her just how large the gathering was. She felt isolated, lost.

Peter looked down at her, understanding her nervousness. 'Don't be scared, little one. I will be with you all the time. Trust me!'

Penelope smiled up at him, reassured. The room was so ablaze with light that she could easily make out his tall figure beside her. 'I know. You wouldn't want me to trip over someone important and destroy your credit!' she teased.

'Nothing of the sort! *My* credit could withstand a dozen such scandals!' he replied with considerable aplomb. 'It is merely that I pride myself on being able to do just as good a job as Gelert. Think how mortifying for me if I had to admit publicly that your dog is more capable than I am!'

'Yes, I suppose we should keep that fact in the family!' answered Penelope with a laugh.

Phoebe, observing the look of shining confidence replace fear on her sister's face, murmured to Richard, 'Something tells me that this match is working very well. Not even Papa could have got Penny to a function like this!' She knew, without being told, just how much Penelope had come to care for Peter and trust him. Suddenly she was sure that Peter had come to care for Penelope. How else could he have understood, let alone banished her fear?

A footman announced them. 'Lord and Lady Darleston, Mr and Mrs Richard Winton.'

The hum of conversation ceased abruptly as the élite of society turned to inspect the unknown girl who had caught one of the richest prizes on the Marriage Mart. The marriage of Miss Phoebe Ffolliot to Richard Winton had surprised few. The marriage of Darleston to a girl whose very existence had been unsuspected was another matter.

Jack Frobisher had hinted at some sort of scandal, and despite his unpopularity the whiff of gossip had aroused curiosity. Most people knew of the row at Lady Bellingham's ball and they speculated on the probability that there was more to the situation than the bland announcement in the *Gazette* had told them.

The split second of silence was broken by a collective gasp of astonishment as society took stock of the twins. A babble of conversation broke out. Darleston and Richard were, as ever, immaculately turned out, but it was the staggering resemblance between the two women which was the topic of discussion. Penelope and Phoebe had taken a mischievous pleasure in dressing their hair alike and wearing very similar gowns of soft green silk, cut revealingly across the shoulders.

Odd scraps reached their ears.

'Good God! Peas in the pod ain't in it…'

'Which one did we meet?'

'Hope Winton and Darleston can tell 'em apart!'

Peter and Richard exchanged grins as this last remark drifted to their ears. Neither one had the slightest trouble distinguishing his wife, and the suggestion that they might struck them as ridiculous in the extreme.

Lady Edenhope came to greet them, 'Dear Peter, thank you so much for coming to me first! You have ensured that my party will be gossiped about for days! And Mr Winton, congratulations! Mrs Winton, I wish you happy!' She turned to Penelope, 'My dear, allow an old friend of Peter's to wish you very happy. I knew this wretch in his cradle. His mama and I came out together. We were the best of friends always.'

Penelope smiled and said shyly, 'Thank you, ma'am. I am so pleased to meet you. Peter has told me all about you.'

'Well, you must come with me to meet the sharks. I am sure they are all just dying to be presented to you! They all met your sister last year, but we had no idea there were two of you!' said Lady Edenhope merrily.

'For heaven's sake, Aunt Louisa, you'll be heard!' said Peter in amusement. 'I'll come with you, if I may. You may not have realised, Aunt Louisa, but Penelope is blind, so I have got used to warning her about steps and obstacles.' He knew as he said this that at least half a dozen people had heard him. The shock on their faces was mirrored in Lady Edenhope's eyes.

She made a gallant recovery. 'Oh, you poor girl! Fancy being married to this handsome creature and unable to appreciate him fully!'

Penelope chuckled, 'Indeed, ma'am. I have been feeling most frustrated ever since my sister described him to me.'

'Never mind, my dear, he will have to be content with one less admirer. Very likely it will do him good! Come along!'

It was evident to Peter that his mother's closest friend, having taken a liking to Penelope, meant to make sure she was accepted by the Ton. It was also evident that Lady Edenhope's sympathetic response, tinged as it was with humour, had gone a long way towards setting Penelope at ease.

However, as she escorted them around the room the whispers sprang up in their wake. Amazement was the most common reaction. Everyone knew the story of the first Lady Darleston, and there were plenty of snide murmurs that Darleston had now picked a girl who would be totally dependent on him. Others, more shrewd, noticed the very obvious affection between the couple and discounted the idea. Some, like Lady Edenhope, who had known Peter well before his disastrous first marriage, were delighted to see him so relaxed and happy.

One of these was Lady Jersey, acknowledged Queen of the Ton. She came up to Peter with words of welcome. 'Darleston! How delightful to see you! And your bride! Please do introduce us!'

'Of course. Penelope, this is Lady Jersey, another old friend.' Peter stood back to watch his wife deal with the voluble peeress, who was living up to her nickname with a vengeance. She rattled on cheerfully but her inconsequent tongue did not prevent her from taking stock of the situation. Penelope responded to her chatter shyly, but with a humour that won approval from that notoriously high stickler.

'So difficult for you, Lady Darleston, not being able to see this den of lions you are flung into!' said Lady Jersey at last. 'I admire your courage. I vow I should not dare!'

'I did not dare last year,' admitted Penelope. 'But Lord Darleston has convinced me that you are not all ogres and that I must keep him company, at least some of the time.'

'Excellent! But do you know, Lady Darleston, at one time I feared that Darleston was becoming an ogre himself, and a bit of a recluse? I do think you must take some credit for halting the process. He is such a decorative addition to London!'

'So I have been told, Lady Jersey. But Lady Edenhope assures me it will do him good to have one admirer the less!'

A charming ripple of laughter greeted this answer, 'I'm sure it will! Lady Darleston, it has been delightful to meet you. I shall call on you in the near future and bring you vouchers for the, er…shark-pool, I think Lady Edenhope would call it!'

She moved away graciously to spread the word that Lady Darleston was quite delightful. A pity she was blind, of course, but if she and Darleston were happy there was an end to the matter. And, really, anything must be better than his marrying Caroline Daventry! Oh, good heavens! One would have had to receive her!

As Peter watched her go he said softly to Penelope, 'Well done! She means to give you vouchers for Almack's.'

'Was that what she meant?' asked Penelope. 'Goodness, I shall have to practise my dancing!'

'What an excellent idea!' said Peter. 'I shall be delighted to assist you!' Then, seeing George Carstares making his way through the crush towards them, 'Good God, here's George. What made you so late? We gave up and left without you!'

'My cravat. Matter of extreme importance! Hello, Penny. Enjoying yourself? Devilish squeeze, ain't it? Your cousin's here, Peter.'

'Jack? How charming!' Peter looked keenly around the room, and immediately spotted his cousin near the refreshment tables.

Jack Frobisher was looking straight at him. His face was mask-like as his eyes met Peter's icy glare and swung back to his companion. Peter recognised her at once. Lady Caroline Daventry! The voluptuous blonde turned to gaze across at him. He returned the look coldly, observing the scornful half-smile on her lips as her eyes raked Penelope. Deliberately he stepped in front of Penelope, presenting his back to his erstwhile mistress.

'Can't say I care for his choice of companion,' commented George in a thoughtful tone of voice, missing none of this by-play. He cocked a mobile eyebrow at Peter.

'Neither do I,' was the quiet answer. Peter was thinking furiously. Jack was one thing. He could probably be frightened off. But Lady Caroline was another matter. She had enough intelligence to be extremely dangerous. She had steered clear of open scandal but it was well known that she had been his mistress. Was Jack cultivating her assistance?

Peter could well imagine how angry she must have

been that her plot to entrap him had failed. Her rage at his swift marriage must have been beyond belief, he thought sardonically.

'Who is it?' asked Penelope curiously. She could hear the edge in Peter's voice and feel the tension in his body.

He said lightly, 'No one that you would know, my dear.' Not to save his life could he have brought himself to mention his ex-mistress to Penelope. Penelope turned to him and he saw that she was wearing what he thought of as her 'second-sight look'.

He knew quite well that she was not fooled when she forbore to ask any further questions, merely saying, 'Oh, well, I suppose we can start our campaign to scare the skirter!'

'We can,' said Peter with a reluctant grin. 'But for heaven's sake don't use that sort of language in company! People will think George and I taught it to you!'

'More likely to blame my father, if they were at all acquainted with him!' said Penelope with a laugh.

Richard and Phoebe came up at that moment. 'Have you seen who's here?' asked Richard, jerking his head in the direction of the unsavoury pair.

'Of course,' answered Peter. 'George was just saying that the combination is not a pleasant one.' He looked at Richard evenly. Richard, of course, was perfectly aware of the earlier connection between Darleston and the lovely Lady Caroline. He knew something, too, of the lady's reputation for harbouring grudges, but correctly deduced that Peter would prefer to leave her out of the discussion at present.

Phoebe, being quite unaware of all this, said innocently, 'I don't think I know the lady with him.' She stared through a break in the eddying crowd, just as

Lady Caroline turned towards them again. 'Oh! Yes, I do! It's Lady Caroline Daventry. Well, she's very beautiful but I don't like her much. She was rather horrid to me in a polite way after you danced with me at Almack's, Peter.'

'Which reminds me,' said Peter smoothly, 'that I have never danced with my wife, and I observe that the orchestra is beginning a waltz. May I have the honour, Lady Darleston? You did say that you wished to practise didn't you?'

'I didn't mean in public!' she protested. 'Are you sure you wish to, Peter?'

'Of course. We shall stay near the edge. Anyway, by this time the gossip that you are blind has been around the room half a dozen times. Trust Sally Jersey for that!'

He led her to the dance floor and swung her into the dance. At first Penelope was nervous, but Peter was very good at steering her away from possible trouble. Gradually, as she relaxed, she began to enjoy the dance.

Peter felt the change and said in a bantering tone, 'See! I am not such a bad dancer after all. It might interest you to know that lots of people are staring at us in the rudest way. You'd think they had never seen me dance with a beautiful woman before!'

'I'm sure you have danced with many, my lord,' answered Penelope, smiling up at him affectionately.

'Of course, it adds to my consequence!' said Peter laughing. They continued to chat easily throughout the dance, and Peter kept Penelope in a ripple of laughter with his at times caustic comments on the people they passed.

Richard watched the pair and said softly to George,

'I was against this marriage, you know. But it looks as if I was wrong. I haven't seen Penny this happy in company for years. And she is happy, isn't she, Phoebe?' He turned to his wife.

'Oh, yes!' said Phoebe. 'She could not appear so relaxed if she did not like and trust him.'

'I think it has been good for Peter too,' agreed George. 'Did my level best to talk him out of it, but it's the best thing he could have done. Oh, good evening, Lady Castlereagh.' He greeted one of the patronesses of Almack's.

'Good evening, Mr Carstares, Mr Winton, Mrs Winton,' said that stately lady. 'I have just been remarking to Lady Jersey how happy Lord Darleston appears. It must be a great pleasure to all his friends to see him look so much like his old self. Mrs Winton, allow me to wish you happy. I believe I have not seen you since your marriage.'

Phoebe blushed, smiling. Lady Castlereagh had always been very kind. 'I believe that you and Lady Darleston are twins! I do hope your mother and husbands can tell you apart, for I am sure that I should not be able to!'

'It is very easy, Lady Castlereagh,' said Richard. 'My sister-in-law, as you must have heard, is blind. She is generally accompanied everywhere by a very large dog who guides her every move!'

'But not at a ball!' said Lady Castlereagh with a twinkle.

'No, ma'am. Here she must rely on Darleston and her family,' agreed Richard gravely.

'Quite so. Ah, here they come. Darleston, I congratulate you! And Lady Darleston, I wish you very happy indeed. I have just been saying to your sister that I should find it impossible to tell the pair of you apart. But Mr Winton informs me that your dog attends you everywhere, so when in doubt I must depend upon that! Allow me to assure you that he will always be welcome in my drawing room if you are so kind as to call!'

Penelope stammered a confused thank-you. The thought of making morning calls without Gelert had been a source of worry to her. If Lady Castlereagh accepted him in her home every other lady of fashion would follow her lead.

She tried to convey her gratitude to Lady Castlereagh, who said, smiling, 'My dear, don't mention it. I should find it so very vexing to be blind myself that I shall be happy to assist you. Sally Jersey tells me she has promised you vouchers for Almack's. We shall all be pleased to see you there.' She made her farewells and moved away to greet other friends and comment on the charming bride Darleston had chosen.

At the other side of the ballroom were two people who viewed the social success of Darleston's bride with savage anger. Jack Frobisher felt cheated. He had counted his cousin's title and wealth as his own. To be supplanted by a second marriage was insupportable.

'Damn Peter!' he burst out.

Lady Caroline looked at him and said softly, 'Control yourself, my friend. You are not the only one who wants to scuttle this marriage. From now on we work together! If all goes well we can both enjoy the money and the title. Remember the price of my silence is marriage!'

Frobisher shrugged and nodded. 'You drive a hard

bargain, Caroline, but if you can help me it will be worth it to get my revenge on the pair of them.'

Lady Caroline said curiously, 'You're not in this just because of the money and title, Frobisher. What else are you after?'

Frobisher gave an ugly laugh and said, 'I would dearly like the chance of a little chat with Lady Darleston, uninterrupted by her dog!' There was no mistaking his meaning.

Lady Caroline smiled evilly, saying, 'Done! She's all yours! Pay me a morning call in the next day or so to discuss ways and means. We had better not be seen too much together. Why don't you see if you can find out whether your cousin has any suspicion of your involvement in the shooting? For now, I'm off home. Louisa Edenhope's parties are such insipid affairs!'

'What you mean is that you can't bear to watch the prize you lost flaunting another woman under your nose,' said Frobisher.

Lady Caroline's colour rose at this taunt. It had already occurred to her that this was Lady Edenhope's sole reason for inviting her. She turned on her heel and left him.

Well satisfied with the progress he had made, Jack Frobisher helped himself to a glass of champagne from a passing footman. He drank a silent toast to his revenge on Penelope and Darleston. A pity his cousin had had the wench first, but doubtless he could think of any number of things Darleston would be far too gentlemanly to subject his wife to! An unpleasant smile came to his lips as he contemplated the future.

He moved off through the crush of people, nodding to various acquaintances, many of whom commented on his cousin's bride.

Frobisher merely smiled and said, 'Ah, yes, poor Ffolliot!' At this his listeners smirked knowingly. Frobisher observed the success of his efforts to stir up gossip. Already he saw himself as Earl of Darleston. Wrapped in this pleasant dream, he sauntered through the crowd towards the card room. A chance glimpse of Lord and Lady Darleston brought Lady Caroline's suggestion back into his mind. He stood irresolute, wondering if he dared greet his cousin.

The decision was taken out of his hands. Peter had already seen him. 'Here comes Jack,' he said softly to his companions.

Richard said fiercely, 'Good, let's give him a fright! Show him we know!'

'Good idea if it were just Jack involved, but the situation may be different now,' was the rejoinder. 'Better to draw him in, lull any fears he may have. That way we may be able to trap him. What do you think, Penny? Can you bear to meet him again after what has happened?' It sickened him to think of Frobisher being anywhere near her, and Penelope could sense his distaste for the whole situation.

'If it will help you, Peter,' said Penelope. Darleston could hear the constraint in her voice. Her fingers resting on his arm trembled. He laid his hand on hers and pressed it reassuringly.

'Here goes, then,' said Darleston, beckoning to his cousin with a friendly smile.

Jack approached in some trepidation. Surely Peter had glared at him earlier. Perhaps the glare had been for Lady Caroline. There was no trace of unfriendliness now, however.

'Good evening, Jack,' said Peter. 'You are already acquainted with my wife and her sister, Mrs Winton, but may I present Mr Winton? Winton—my cousin, Mr Jack Frobisher.'

'Good evening, Mr Frobisher,' said Richard politely. 'I don't believe we met when you visited the Ffolliots last spring.'

'Er…Good evening, Mr Winton,' said Frobisher uncomfortably.

He turned to Penelope. 'I heard you had been unwell. Took a toss from a horse, did you not? I hope my cousin is looking after you properly!'

'My lord has been very kind,' she replied steadily, wondering just how he had heard about that 'accident.' He continued heartily, 'Must be difficult, being blind and all, having to find your way around that damned great barrack in Grosvenor Square. You just tell me if you need any help!' That, he thought, might be the ticket to get into the house and lull any suspicions.

'How kind of you, Mr Frobisher,' said Penelope. 'Lord Darleston has been so kind as to show me around already. But if you call I shall remember to have my dog under control.'

Darleston was startled to discover that he was torn between the urge to laugh at the infuriated expression on his cousin's face and the desire to plant him a facer on the mere suspicion that he had laid a finger on Penelope.

Somehow Frobisher managed to control himself, 'Ah, yes. Your dog has such an uncertain temper, fair Cousin!'

'Do you find him so?' asked Darleston in feigned surprise. 'Why, I find his behaviour quite predictable and logical!'

'No doubt he mellows on longer acquaintance,' said Frobisher.

Penelope listened carefully. He sounded nervous, ill at ease, and no wonder considering the turn the conversation had taken. The voice was over-eager to ingratiate but he seemed to gain confidence as Peter continued to be civil. Richard, however, sounded as though he were having difficulty containing himself at some of Frobisher's rather distasteful comments.

'Believe you live near the Ffolliots, Winton. Must have been a hard choice for you, choosing a wife. Could have just tossed a coin, eh?'

'I have never had the slightest difficulty distinguishing between my wife and her sister, even when they tried to fool us as children,' replied Richard in tones of utter boredom. 'Excuse me, please. I can see a friend I wish to speak to. Come, Mrs Winton.' He cast Peter a look of apology as he retreated.

'High and mighty, ain't he?' said Jack. 'Well, I must be going, Cousins. I shall pop in to see how you are going along. Evening, Carstares.' He moved away in the direction of the card room, confident that his formidable cousin had no idea of the plot against him.

His departure was much to the relief of Peter. Frobisher's blatant sizing up of Penelope had been almost too much for his self-control. 'What's your verdict, George?'

'Nervous, at least at first. Penny?'

She hesitated before saying, 'I agree. And he seemed over-hearty towards the end. A little over-confident.

'I've had enough of this business for one night,' said Darleston. 'I suggest we find Richard and Phoebe and repair to the supper room. Then we can dance some more before going home!'

* * *

The rest of the evening passed pleasantly, and Lord and Lady Darleston arrived home at about three in the morning. When Meadows opened the door accompanied by Gelert Peter stared in amazement. 'What the devil are you doing up, Meadows? I said you were not to, didn't I?'

'Begging your pardon, my lord, but with all this nasty business going on I preferred to know you were safe home. I did go to bed but I couldn't sleep,' replied the butler with dignity.

Peter stared at him helplessly and then turned to Penelope, saying, 'See what sort of a demoralising effect you are having. Even Meadows doesn't trust me to look after you. Up to bed with you, my lady, while I deal with this insubordination.'

Penelope laughed. 'Goodnight, Meadows! Thank you. I shall give you a little bottle of laudanum next time we are out late!'

She went upstairs to find Ellen waiting for her, also contrary to instructions. 'Why, Ellen, you and Meadows are as bad as each other!'

'His lordship's valet, Fordham, is up too,' said Ellen, grinning at her mistress unrepentantly. 'Now stop fussing, milady. I had a little nap on the day-bed. See how pleased Gelert is to see you safe!'

'Oh, Ellen! What could possibly happen to me at a ball?' asked Penelope, petting Gelert, who was jumping around her like a puppy.

'I'd have said nothing could happen down at Darleston, but I'd have been wrong!' was Ellen's grim rejoinder. 'We did make Miss Sarah go to bed. She went off to sleep like a baby!'

'Thank goodness someone did!' said Penelope, as she submitted to being undressed and arrayed in a very pretty nightgown. When Ellen sat her down at the dressing table and produced the hairbrush, however, she rebelled, sending her off to bed with dire threats of being sent back to the country.

No sooner had Ellen left than Peter walked through the connecting door in his dressing gown, saying expressively, 'Our servants! Did you know Fordham was up? I haven't let him stay up for me in years!'

Penelope chuckled as she continued to brush her hair. 'Never mind. At least they care about us!'

Peter watched her for a moment before walking over to remove the brush from her grasp. 'May I, Penny?'

'If you wish,' she answered shyly.

He brushed her hair in silence, enjoying the feel of the silken curls, gazing at her in the mirror. Firmly he told himself that she was probably tired, that he should leave her alone, that his lovemaking only increased the pain of the relationship for her. He told himself this every evening when he came to her room, ostensibly to bid her goodnight. And every night he found himself unable to return to his own bed. She never asked him to stay, he understood that her pride would not permit it, but always she responded to his advances passionately.

Now his eyes kept straying from her face to the delectable curves so temptingly revealed by the nightgown. Those soft curves which fitted so miraculously to his own body. His gaze lingered on her lips, such a sweet mouth which yielded to his demands in total surrender.

Unable to help himself, he put the hairbrush down, grasped her shoulders and pulled her up to stand against him. One arm slipped around her waist as he bent his head to kiss her neck. She could feel the heat of his mouth and turned in his arms, pressing herself against him. Her breath came unevenly. She wondered just how long her legs would be able to support her.

'I want you, Penny, you're so lovely!' said Peter shakily. She simply lifted her mouth to his and kissed him. Then his hands were at her breast, undoing the buttons of her gown. Gently he pushed it off her shoulders. As it slid to the ground with a silken whisper he stepped back to feast his eyes on her loveliness. Swiftly he removed his robe and took her in his arms again, his mouth tender and seductive. His hands ranged over her trembling body, delighting in her response.

Penelope could feel the hard strength of his body and then felt him lift her into his arms, his mouth still locked to hers. She nestled in his arms as he crossed the room to deposit her gently on the bed.

He stood looking down at her for a moment and then joined her. 'Penny, sweet little Penny,' he whispered, before his mouth came down on hers.

Chapter Fifteen

Two days after Lady Edenhope's ball Penelope sat alone in the cushioned luxury of her drawing room wondering just how many members of the Ton were going to pay bride visits. Admittedly some of them were friends of Peter's, but many, she was well aware, had come out of sheer curiosity. Lady Castlereagh and Lady Jersey had been among the earliest visitors. They had called together, bringing the promised vouchers for Almack's. Their visit had been extremely pleasant.

The presence of Gelert had not bothered them in the slightest. Lady Jersey had everyone so far as to say that all women of consequence should have one to discourage unwanted callers, 'Just think how useful! Lady Darleston, you will be setting a fashion. I don't suppose you would consider lending him to me?'

'Nonsense, Sally! Lady Darleston will have enough unwanted callers in the next few days to keep him busy. As for you, if your butler does not know by now whom to admit you should replace him!' Lady Castlereagh had replied, and continued kindly, 'I dare say you will receive a great many callers, Lady Darleston. Most of them will only call once, out of curiosity to see Darleston's bride. We had all quite given up hope that he would marry again, you see!'

Penelope was turning this tactful warning over in her mind when Sarah came in and said, 'Can I go to Hatchard's to buy a book? Ellen will go with me if you say yes.'

Penelope stood up and stretched. 'Give me twenty minutes to change into a walking dress and I'll come too. Peter won't be back for some time and I haven't been out all day. I'm tired of visitors. We'll take a walk in the park afterwards. Gelert needs one.'

Half an hour later they set out with a footman in attendance to carry the parcels, for, as Sarah said, 'It's no good going to a bookshop and expecting to only buy one book! Besides, Roger will probably enjoy the walk because he likes Ellen so much!'

Sarah was full of energy and skipped along, laughing at Ellen's remonstrances which were the more forceful due to her embarrassment at Sarah's wholly accurate observation of the regard in which Roger held her.

'It's no good, Ellen!' said Penelope in amusement. 'We're not used to London and having to be so terribly well-behaved. I'm not sure who is in more need of exercise, Sarah or Gelert!'

'Well, there's no doubt who's the better behaved!' said Ellen bluntly. 'Give over, Miss Sarah! You'll never get a husband if you're not more ladylike!'

'Pooh! Who wants a husband? I'm not going to get married until I meet someone who can give me a good game of chess! Why, Phoebe says she actually *lets* Richard win occasionally just so that he can feel superior. I won't do that!' said Sarah in disgust.

'I'm sure you won't!' said Penelope. 'What is the book you want to buy?'

'Peter told me about it. It is called *Northanger Abbey*, he thinks I would enjoy it. What are you laughing at, Penny?'

'Nothing, Sarah!' said Penelope unconvincingly. 'It is nice to see you have enough respect for Peter to take his advice on the choice of a book!'

'Oh, well, he plays chess properly, even better than George, and he said he'd pay for the book if I didn't like it,' said Sarah ingenuously. 'But I think I shall because it is by the same person as *Pride and Prejudice*, and we liked that excessively. Actually, he offered to buy me the book as a present, but I didn't think I should let him. I wouldn't like him to think I was *sponging* off him. Even if he was like Montoni in *The Mysteries of Udolpho*, which doesn't seem very likely.' This last in tones of infinite regret.

'Did you tell him that?' enquired Penelope with a grin.

'Yes. He said he could see my point but that he ought to be prepared to back his advice, and that was why he said he'd buy the book if I didn't like it.'

Amusement at Peter's tactics made it difficult for Penelope to maintain her gravity. Obviously he was determined to win over her suspicious young sister! Equally obviously Sarah's vivid imagination was having a hard task in the face of Peter's kindness and good nature. What she would say when she started to read this book Peter had recommended was anybody's guess. No doubt, thought Penelope, it would be distinguished by a certain directness of expression!

They continued along South Audley Street, discussing books and music happily. The conversation was not limited to Penelope and Sarah only. Ellen's opinion was frequently sought, since she often read aloud to her mistress, and she swelled with pride to think that her thoughts and ideas were valued. Even Roger, a young man who knew his place to a nicety, was dragged into the discussion of music.

'It's no good saying, "I don't know, I'm sure, miss!" You hear us playing all the time and you must know which bits you like, Roger!' said Penelope firmly. Roger gave in and admitted that although he quite enjoyed Mozart, Beethoven held more appeal for him. More stirring, if they took his meaning.

'Hmm. I can see we're brewing a revolution below stairs, Sarah!' said Penelope in amusement. 'No more Beethoven when Roger is about. A straight diet of Haydn and Mozart with perhaps a little Handel should curb these dangerous tendencies!'

Roger blushed and disclaimed any revolutionary tendencies, saying that Ellen and Mr Meadows would bear him out. In this fashion they beguiled the walk to Hatchard's in Piccadilly. The sheer noise of the traffic in this thoroughfare smote on their country-bred ears with stunning effect. Penelope was hard put to it to make any sort of sense out of the jumble of sounds and maintained a firm grip on Gelert's collar.

On her other side Sarah pressed close, sensing her sister's confusion. Upon reaching the shop they stood outside for a moment while Sarah gazed through the bow windows at all the latest publications.

'It is nice,' she said, 'to be able to walk here as a matter of course, change books at Hookham's and so on, but I think on the whole I prefer the country. Town is so dreadfully noisy!'

With this comment she led the way into the shop.

This was Penelope's first visit to Hatchard's, and an assistant at once rushed forward to protest at the entrance of a large dog. However, his outrage was transformed into fawning obsequiousness when he realised that his new patroness was none other than the Countess of Darleston, whose dog was already an accepted presence in Tonnish circles.

He assisted them to find the book they sought and diffidently suggested that they might also enjoy the latest works by the author of *Guy Mannering*, if these had not previously come their way. Penelope was entranced at the suggestion. Papa had read *Guy Mannering* to them all with great success, so she unhesitatingly invested in *Rob Roy* and *The Heart of Midlothian*, commenting that Peter would probably be reading aloud for a year!

Sarah was struck speechless at this extravagance, especially when Penelope told her to choose an extra book for herself. 'And if you dare to say a word about *sponging*, Sarah, I'll slap you!'

By the time they left the shop Roger was laden with parcels, for Penelope had been struck by the happy thought of buying a present to send off to Mrs Ffolliot in Bath, as well as Southey's *Life of Nelson* for Peter.

It also struck her that Roger might not relish a walk in the park thus burdened. 'Roger, if you would prefer to take the parcels straight home rather than walk in the park you may do so,' she said with a smile.

Roger, however, had no intention of being sent home, and stated his complete willingness to carry twice as much before he would even consider deserting his mistress.

Accordingly the entire party set off towards Hyde Park Corner. It was drawing close to the hour of the fashionable promenade and many members of the Ton were converging on the park. A great number of people greeted Penelope with pleasure, among them Lady Edenhope and her friend Lady Wickham, who promised Penelope a card for her ball the following week.

'Such a pleasure that Darleston is back in such good spirits, Lady Darleston. We are all delighted! And this must surely be a younger sister. Charming, quite charming!'

Penelope laughed and said, 'Indeed, this is my sister Sarah. She is staying with us at the moment while my mother is nursing a sick friend. I hope you will visit us soon, Lady Wickham.' They parted merrily, with Lady Wickham promising to visit and bring the invitation card personally the very next day.

A waft of powerful scent announced another presence, and a cooing voice said, 'Dear Lady Darleston, you must forgive me for presenting myself in such an informal way! I am Lady Caroline Daventry. I saw you at Lady Edenhope's the other night. Such a squeeze, was it not? But you and dear Peter were surrounded. I vow there was no getting near you! Permit me to wish you happy! What a conquest you have made! We all thought Peter would remain single.'

Penelope's mind worked swiftly. The name was familiar. Surely this was the woman who had been with Jack Frobisher the other evening! Peter had changed the subject as soon as her name was mentioned. He and George had both seemed somewhat embarrassed.

Lady Caroline managed to insinuate herself between Sarah and Penelope. For days she had walked in the park, hoping for just such a chance as this to get into the Countess of Darleston's good graces. Well did she know that she stood not the slightest chance of being admitted to the house, but she was counting on Darleston's fastidious nature to have recoiled from warning his bride against her.

Lady Caroline seethed with suppressed fury as she stared at the slender girl who held the position she had counted as hers for the taking. She could not for the life of her understand what Peter saw in the chit. Red hair, for heaven's sake, although the generous might call it auburn. A bit on the thin side, and blind, if you please! Yet she could have screamed in vexation as she recalled the way Darleston had gazed at his bride, the pride in his bearing as he presented her to high society. Damn the wench! She had stolen Darleston!

'How kind of you, Lady Caroline. You are an old friend of my lord's?' asked Penelope politely. Her hand gripped Gelert's collar warningly as she heard the faintest of growls from him.

'Very old friends, Lady Darleston. Indeed, I am quite wounded that I was not invited to the wedding. But I understand your father and brother...so sad! No doubt Darleston could not bear to wait to carry you off! Quite a romance, is it not?'

All this was said in tones of great good humour, but Penelope was quick to detect the smirk in her voice as she claimed long friendship with Peter. Also she was aware of enmity behind the dulcet accents and wondered at it. What reason could the woman possibly have for allying herself with Jack Frobisher? And why was Peter so reluctant to discuss her? Then Phoebe's remark about Lady Caroline's behaviour to her flashed into her mind and everything fell into place.

The conviction that she was conversing publicly with her husband's mistress—well, ex-mistress, she hoped—did not have quite the effect on Penelope that one might have expected from a delicately bred girl. Sensible enough to realise that her husband's past amours were no concern of hers, she found the situation extremely funny, and it was only with great difficulty that she managed to control her features as she listened to Lady Caroline. It occurred to her that in this case the whole situation must be of the greatest interest to all of society, and that a public set-down would only exacerbate the situation. Besides, she might be quite wrong in all her suspicions!

'Dare I hope, Lady Darleston, that you might join me for a drive in the park tomorrow afternoon? I should be delighted to present you to my friends.'

'How very kind of you, Lady Caroline, but I have already accepted an invitation to drive with Mr Carstares,' said Penelope, resolving to inform George of his kind invitation the minute she reached home.

'No matter. Another day, perhaps!' replied her ladyship carelessly. To be sure it would have been too good to be true if the chit had accepted her invitation! Anyway, it would be far safer for all of them if she were to vanish without any tangible evidence of complicity on the part of Lady Caroline Daventry.

'Lady Caroline, may I make my youngest sister, Sarah, known to you? She is staying with us at the moment.'

'Goodness, is this another sister? No doubt we may look to see her make her début and catch a husband!' The thinly veiled sneer suggested that there was something rather curious about the swift marriages of Penelope and Phoebe.

Penelope merely smiled and said, 'At the moment the only use my sister has for an eligible bachelor is to learn to drive and beat him at chess. She is not quite fourteen.'

'Ah, well, time enough, then!' said Lady Caroline, with a patronising glance at Sarah. She blinked slightly as she met that damsel's steady regard.

Sarah had swiftly come to the conclusion that she did not like Lady Caroline at all. Furthermore she had shamelessly overheard a conversation between George and Peter which suggested that there was some connection between Jack Frobisher and Lady Caroline. It was also plain even to her inexperienced gaze that the conversation between Lady Caroline and her sister was, for an unknown reason, occasioning some shocked looks from various quarters. Obviously Penelope could not extricate herself without an embarrassing scene.

Unobtrusively she dropped back to walk with Ellen and Roger. 'Ellen, is it just my imagination or should we do something about this?'

Ellen nodded vigorously. 'That we should! But what? The gossip that it will cause if the mistress openly snubs her ladyship! Though why she should be called "lady" is beyond me!'

Sarah, however, had already made a plan. 'Roger, his lordship is probably still at White's with Mr Carstares. You must go at once and tell him to meet us here. If necessary we'll pretend you have taken the books home. Take this money for a cab and run!'

Roger grinned at her, said to Ellen, 'She's got a head on her shoulders, for all she's gentry!' and obeyed.

Lady Caroline, quite unsuspecting, continued to chat sociably, and Penelope responded in a friendly but dignified fashion, stifling the urge to bury her nose in her handkerchief. Listening carefully, she decided that Lady Caroline was under some stress. Something was making her nervous.

Finally, a seemingly innocent question gave her the answer. 'I suppose you see little of Darleston during the day? In his club, no doubt? Will he be joining you here?'

'I shouldn't think so,' said Penelope, wishing to herself that Peter *would* appear. No sooner had she thought this than her quick ears heard a carriage draw up beside them.

Gelert uttered a blood-curdling snarl and Penelope could feel the fur on his neck rise up, bristling. She could only think of one person likely to bring that response from the dog. She knew a moment's fear, but fought it down and said calmly, 'How do you do, Mr Frobisher? I believe you are acquainted with Lady Caroline and my sister.'

Jack Frobisher was stunned. How the devil had she known? He could see from the look of shock on Caroline Daventry's face that she had not told Lady Darleston who was approaching.

Sarah mentally applauded this stroke. Gelert's reaction had not been lost on her, and she could see that Penelope's confident identification of Frobisher before he had even spoken had momentarily shaken the man. Determined to make her presence felt, she moved up beside her sister and said, 'Good afternoon, Mr Frobisher! I see that your arm is better.'

Jack Frobisher stared at her in acute dislike but said politely, 'It is indeed, Miss Sarah. I hope you are enjoying the sights of London.'

'Oh, yes. Of course one sees so many odd things, and people!' said Sarah sweetly.

Jack's eyes narrowed. 'Your sister has not altered by a hair's breadth, Lady Darleston. But you! Allow me to inform you that I have never seen you looking so well. Your new station in life seems to agree with you!'

'Such a welcome addition to your family, is she not, Frobisher?' said Lady Caroline.

'Indeed she is! And will you not honour me by taking a turn around the park in my curricle dear Cousin? I am sure Lady Caroline will be only too happy to chaperon Miss Sarah.'

Penelope's stomach turned over. Common sense told her that he could not possibly kidnap her in full view of the Ton, but a carriage accident…? Besides, the thought of being alone with Frobisher under any circumstances terrified her. How to get out of this politely and avoid scandal! She wondered desperately just how many people were listening. What would happen if she let Gelert go?

'How kind of you, Mr Frobisher, but I must decline. It is time that my sister and I were returning home.' She hoped that would do the trick.

'But, Cousin, I should be only too happy to drive you to Grosvenor Square!' said Frobisher suavely.

'Oh! I would not dream of expecting Sarah to walk while I am driven home!' said Penelope firmly, breathing a mental sigh of relief. Surely this excuse was unexceptional!

Frobisher pressed on. 'But Miss Sarah could not be so churlish as to deny me the pleasure of your company!'

'Of course not!' said Sarah with alacrity. 'Especially as here come Darleston and Mr Carstares, who will doubtless escort me home!' For there *were* Peter and

George, a hundred yards away, striding towards them purposefully.

Penelope, whose breath had practically stopped at Sarah's first words, recovered her self-possession and said innocently, 'No doubt Darleston has come to escort us home. Perhaps another day, Mr Frobisher!'

Frobisher bit off an exclamation of annoyance, changing it to a sneeze. Lady Caroline was far more successful in concealing her disgust.

'How delightful!' she exclaimed. 'I declare I've not seen Darleston for an age.' Her mind worked fast. Curse the man! How like him to appear just when one would wish him not to! Had he been tipped off? Or was he merely doting on his insipid bride!

Peter approached the little group swiftly, mentally schooling himself to hold his temper in check. Fury that his ex-mistress should have had the effrontery to approach his wife almost choked him. Leaving aside his suspicions of Lady Caroline's motives, the thought of Penelope having anything to do with the woman was unbearable.

And Penelope, how much had she guessed? He knew how quickly her mind worked, how sensitive she was to people's moods and thoughts. She frequently read his thoughts with unnerving accuracy. Could she possibly have divined the situation? Even at this distance he could see that Penelope was frightened: something in the way she was gripping Gelert's collar and holding herself. At this point he saw who was in the curricle beside the three ladies.

George spotted Frobisher a split second later and spluttered, 'Good heavens! D'you see who's with them? Thank God for Sarah!'

'As you say, George. What an impossible situation

for Penny! She can't administer a snub to either of them in public without causing a scandal. Hurry up, George, before she's tempted to let the dog go! For some reason apart from this business she is scared of Jack!'

He saw the party turn towards him and raised his hand in greeting with a polite smile firmly affixed to his face. A strong odour of scent assailed him; it was with difficulty that he bit back an exclamation of disgust. One look at his wife's face informed him that she shared his distaste.

She was turned towards him, a welcoming smile mingled with heartfelt relief. 'My lord, and Mr Carstares, how lovely! I was just telling Lady Caroline that you would not be joining us here! And here you are, making a liar out of me. You are acquainted with Lady Caroline, I believe? And your cousin, of course. He was so kind as to offer to drive me home, but now you are here he need not trouble himself.'

Peter nearly exploded! No wonder she had looked so upset! Well did he know the gossip that would have ensued had Penelope allowed the Ton to see her distaste and fear.

'Of course. Lady Caroline, what a surprise to see you.' He bowed as he spoke. 'Cousin. I trust you are well?'

'Never better, Darleston. Believe me, conveying my new cousin home would have been an undiluted pleasure!'

Lady Caroline responded archly, 'Why, Darleston, you cannot have supposed that I would be the least backward in any attention to your wife!' Her tone was sweet but there was an edge to it which warned Darleston that the woman was up to something.

'Not at all, Lady Caroline. I am sure if I had given the matter a moment's thought I should have expected to see you!' The implicit suggestion that he had *not* considered her worth a moment's thought was wasted on neither lady. Penelope, however, was far more successful at concealing her reaction.

Lady Caroline's eyes blazed suddenly but she managed to respond with an artificial titter. 'My dear Darleston, I do not expect to be remembered among so many! And now I really must go. Mr Frobisher, you may escort me home.'

'With the greatest pleasure, dear Lady Caroline!'

Lady Caroline left with her escort and Peter turned to face his wife. Before he could say a word, she asked, 'Does Lady Caroline always wear that much scent, Peter?'

'Frequently. Perhaps we had better discuss this at home.' Penelope could hear the suppressed anger in his voice and decided to drop the subject. Sarah, who had intended to ask her brother-in-law to explain everything, took one look at his face and came to the conclusion that she could just as well ask George later on.

George looked solemn, but not nearly as grim as Peter. She peeped at him from under her bonnet and caught his eye.

Involuntarily his expression lightened, and he flicked her nose with a careless forefinger. 'Well done, brat!' he said softly.

Sarah's heart rose at the knowledge that she had done the right thing.

They walked home without much conversation. Penelope was very subdued to think that Peter was angry, although she could not think what she could have done to have avoided the situation. She was also curious as to how Peter had known what was afoot. That Sarah had something to do with it she was certain.

Upon reaching the house, Peter said, 'Come to the study, please, Penny. I need to speak to you privately.' Then, turning to his sister-in-law, 'Thank you, Sarah! I'm buying that book, so let me hear no more rubbish about *sponging*! See you at dinner, George.'

They went into the study together and Penelope immediately asked, 'How on earth did you know, Peter? I've never been so glad as I was when Sarah said you were there! What did she do?'

'She sent Roger around to White's,' he replied shortly.

She waited patiently for Peter to speak again. He was silent for a moment, and then said, 'I would prefer you to take steps to avoid any further conversation with Lady Caroline. If she approaches you again, refuse to acknowledge her.' His voice sounded flustered.

Penelope considered her reply. 'Won't that cause gossip?'

'Not as much as if you recognise her,' said Peter shortly. He felt uncomfortable, even hypocritical.

Penelope's next question took him totally by surprise. 'Why, Peter? Because she was your mistress?'

Outraged that she would dare to question him, he turned to her, saying coldly, 'You forget yourself, Lady Darleston. It is no concern of yours if she was, or is still, my mistress!'

Penelope was fully aware that she had gone too far. She did not resent his past involvements, or his remonstrance, but the suggestion that he might still be involved with Lady Caroline made her feel physically sick with jealousy. Close to tears, she did not trust her voice for a moment.

Then she said carefully, 'I beg your pardon my lord, please excuse me. I...I... have something to attend to.' She rose to her feet, knowing that she was going to cry, preferring, in her pride, to conceal her pain.

Accompanied by Gelert, she left the room for the privacy of her bed-chamber. Even there she tried very hard to hold back her tears. 'Watering pot!' she said angrily. 'I won't cry! I won't!' But the sudden thought of Peter making love to Lady Caroline as he did to her was too much for her precarious self-control. She sank onto the day-bed, buried her face in her hands and wept despairingly.

When Peter walked quietly through the open connecting door ten minutes later she was still crying. Gelert was snuffling at her desperately, pawing at her gown, whimpering in sympathy. Peter was already feeling the lash of his conscience, and had come to apologise, but the sight of Penelope weeping so bitterly shocked him. He hesitated in the doorway, wondering if he should go away. Then he remembered the terrible night before the attempt on her life down at Darleston. He had left her to cry herself to sleep then, after hurting her. He couldn't do that to her again.

Gently he spoke her name. 'Penny?' She started up in shock. The pain he saw in her face told him just how great was his power to wound her.

'Go away!' she said furiously. He ignored that. Three quick strides took him across the room and he was beside her, holding her tightly.

'Sweetheart, you mustn't cry! I'm not worth it! All I seem to do is hurt you. I'm sorry, Penny, you had every right to ask that question. Caroline Daventry *was* my mistress. She is not now. I swear it.' He could feel her shaking in his arms and cursed himself for the cruel thing he had said. He knew that Penelope felt more for him than mere affection. He also knew that she would cut out her tongue before admitting to anyone that she loved him. Tenderly he stroked her hair, holding her until her tears at last abated.

'Better now, Penny?' She nodded, still not trusting her voice. He continued with difficulty. 'You had better know the whole story. Lady Caroline considered herself as a likely candidate for the role of Countess of Darleston. She tried to have an advertisement of our engagement inserted in the *Gazette*. Fortunately the editor had the sense to check it with me first. It was that coupled with the proximity of Jack to the title which prompted me to marriage.'

'Why didn't you wish to marry Lady Caroline?' The question was little more than a whisper and Peter took his time in answering it.

Finally he said, 'Because, even if I didn't know it, I wanted my wife to be like you. Not a second Melissa. Caroline only wanted to marry me for my money and title. She does not care for me in the slightest, nor I for her.'

'But you married me without love,' said Penelope.

Peter was silent. What could he say? He knew she loved him, but would never say so. His own feelings were still confused. He was fond of her, she roused him physically as no other woman ever had. But did he love her?

At last he said, 'There has never been any pretence between us. Lots of misunderstandings, but no pretence or lies, and we have come to care for each other. I doubt that you could lie to anyone, and I know that

I could never lie to you. Penny, I am glad I married you. You have made me feel whole again.' He wished he could say more, but he knew she would not believe a declaration of love even if he could bring himself to lie to her.

'Now, tell me all about it. Did you get any hint that she might wish you harm?' he asked.

Penelope described the whole incident while Peter listened carefully.

'Do you think she is really in league with your cousin?' finished Penelope. 'She wanted me to drive with her tomorrow but I said I was driving out with George.'

'Good, I doubt she would dare try anything when you were known to be in her company, but it would certainly raise some eyebrows if you were to be seen with her again. She may well be in league with Jack. Certainly I have given her reason to hold a grudge, and if she is working with him then Jack is no longer in complete control. That makes the situation far more dangerous. Caroline is much smarter than my cousin. Besides which we could probably make Jack alone back off. I don't think his desire for money would make him risk his neck.'

'What about Lady Caroline?' asked Penelope.

'I'm not sure of her involvement,' answered Peter slowly. 'She has a tendency to hold grudges and I have known her to go to extreme lengths to pay one off. Jack by himself would be more likely just to demand money from me, as he has done in the past. He has no real quarrel with me apart from the fact that we dislike each other!'

'He has a quarrel with me,' confessed Penelope. 'Remember I told you that Gelert bit him? It…it was because he…he tried to kiss me once and I hit him in the face. It was awful. When he wouldn't stop I screamed, so Gelert came in and attacked him.' Peter could feel her distress. She was shuddering at the memory as she continued, 'He told me then that he wasn't finished with me, so maybe he would help her to get back at me.'

She felt Peter's arms tighten around her. When he spoke there was icy rage in his voice. 'If Frobisher dares to touch you again, Penny, I swear I'll kill him.' The murderous fury in his heart was a total surprise to him. It was not mere jealousy. The thought of Penelope frightened and helpless in the power of a man like Frobisher aroused a protective instinct in him.

Penelope touched his face gently, tracing the strong line of his jaw. He relaxed suddenly and kissed her. 'Never mind, Penny. We'll sort it out somehow!'

Greatly daring, she said, 'Perhaps we should simply have lots of babies. Then they might think there were too many of us to get rid of!'

Peter chuckled. 'Well, I'm doing the best I can, Penny, but I think it might take too long! Not that I object to trying, of course!' The vision of Penelope nursing his children was immensely satisfying, somehow. Not merely a son, but daughters as well, preferably just like Penelope.

Lady Caroline Daventry was in a dangerous humour when she returned home. The encounter with Darleston's bride had infuriated her. Insipid wench! she thought furiously. The prospect of turning her over to Jack Frobisher appealed to her greatly. But how to achieve it? Had Darleston's appearance been a coincidence or had he been somehow tipped off?

Not for a moment did she suspect Sarah! That a child could have taken action was beyond her comprehension. All she could think was that someone in the park had consequently met Darleston and mentioned seeing his wife.

As she entered the house with Frobisher she caught sight of her butler and said, 'Bring suitable refreshment to the drawing room when I ring. Otherwise do not disturb us! I am not at home to anyone!' She went upstairs with Jack Frobisher and shut the drawing room door behind them with a bang.

Frobisher flung himself into a chair and asked abruptly, 'Was that coincidence?'

'God knows! Possibly someone who saw us subsequently met him and tipped him off. He was not pleased to see either of us, I fancy.'

'He most certainly was not!' agreed Frobisher. 'Do you think he suspects us, or did he merely take exception to his ex-mistress having the effrontery to approach his bride?'

'I should think the latter. I doubt not that his appearance was chance. How could he have known? Nevertheless, this is going to require some careful thought, my friend. Her ladyship was scared for some reason…'

There was a faintly questioning note in her voice, but Frobisher merely smiled enigmatically. He said thoughtfully, 'It all hinges upon us getting the girl, of course. That will bring Darleston after her and we can trap him easily enough.'

'You fool! The last thing we want is Darleston right on our heels!' exclaimed Lady Caroline. 'He'll be ripe for murder! No. We lay a false trail to give us time to prepare for him.'

Frobisher considered this carefully.

Lady Caroline added, 'That will give you more time for whatever you have planned for the bride, of course.'

Frobisher's eyes narrowed. 'Very true, Caroline. I wouldn't want to go to all this effort for nothing, after all. But where do we take the wench?'

'France. I have an old friend there who will help us readily enough. We will be able to conceal the girl in his château near Dieppe. The place is shut up, with no one there at all, so we can take her there with no one the wiser. My friend the Marquis will deny all knowledge, suitably bribed. He prefers Paris and never goes near the château. Listen. We still have to work out how to take her. That's the hard part. Once you have her it's easy. I have the house in Scotland, so I'll set off in my chaise the same night. They are bound to try to find out where we are so we'll make it easy for them. Make it look as though we've both taken her to Scotland. By the time they catch up with my chaise, it will be too late to catch you.'

'I'm impressed, Caroline. Then do I let Darleston know somehow?' asked Frobisher.

'You let the girl get a message to him. One of the villagers can be duped somehow into revealing her whereabouts but not who has her,' said Lady Caroline. 'That will fetch him, but he'll have no proof of who holds her. Furthermore, fear of scandal will prevent him making the affair public! He and the girl can simply disappear.'

'Hmm. It might just work, you know. It will have

to. As you say, Darleston will be ripe for murder, and I don't fancy being in his way.'

'I don't advise it,' said Lady Caroline grimly. 'After a reasonable period, you can reappear. There will be no proof except my knowledge, and once we are married you are safe!'

Frobisher looked amused, 'Charming,' he murmured. 'Absolutely charming! I can't imagine why we mere males persist in thinking of your sex as weaker! Now, do you have a scheme for actually kidnapping the girl?'

Her ladyship was silent for a moment, then she smiled and said, 'I think I've hit on something.'

'Excellent. Caroline, I make you my compliments,' said Frobisher. 'Why don't you ring for something with which to toast our success!'

Chapter Sixteen

Lady Wickham's ball was destined to be recalled in the mind of the Ton as the most startling social event of the year. The excellence of the refreshments and the attendance by all of consequence did not suffice to make it memorable. It was the scandal occasioned by the mysterious disappearance of the Countess of Darleston and the language used by her husband which ensured that it would live in the minds of all as an entertainment of no mean order.

The evening started in the most unexceptionable way possible. Lord and Lady Darleston arrived slightly late, with the Honourable George Carstares and her ladyship's sister and brother-in-law. They were observed to be in the cheeriest of moods. A number of people who had openly suggested that Darleston had remarried for convenience and an heir were obliged to reverse their opinion.

The look of adoration on the Earl's face as he waltzed with his lovely wife left no one in any doubt that he was head over heels in love with the chit. Nor could anyone in their right mind, observing the Countess of Darleston, possibly believe her to have been coerced into marriage to clear her brother's debts! The idea was ludicrous! It was patently obvious that she adored her husband! More likely the engagement had been the reason for Darleston's forbearance with the young fool!

Peter himself was no longer in any doubt. For the past week the realisation that he had fallen very deeply in love had been borne in on him. Finally, that very evening, as Penelope had come into the drawing room arrayed in a silver gauze ballgown, he had admitted to himself that he loved her. But the presence of Sarah and George had made any declaration impossible.

Sarah, however, had seen the look of adoration on her brother-in-law's face and had wondered. She knew, of course, that Penelope was very deeply in love. The fact that she said nothing about it told Sarah that she did not wish anyone to know. Sarah understood why, her love for Penelope providing an understanding beyond her years. She had grieved for Penelope's problem, and seeing Peter gaze at her sister with undisguised love in his eyes had given her hope.

When Peter and Penelope had been leaving for the ball with George, Sarah had done something she had never done before. As a matter of course she had hugged Penelope, but had also given Peter an impulsive hug, then stepped back, blushing.

Peter had been a bit startled, but he had flicked her cheek with one finger, saying with a grin, 'Don't stay up too late, brat!'

Nothing happened to mar the evening until the arrival of Lady Caroline Daventry. A few whispers ran around the ballroom when Lady Caroline was observed dancing very close to Lord and Lady Darleston. Naturally the intelligence that she had actually approached the young bride and been acknowledged had got about. Darleston's outraged intervention had lost nothing in the telling. There had been some chuckles at this, but many were shocked that the woman had dared.

Those who were charitably inclined and too far away to see said afterwards that Lady Caroline must have been extraordinarily clumsy. Others who were closer swore that she stepped on Lady Darleston's gown on purpose. Peter led his wife from the floor immediately, totally ignoring Lady Caroline's fulsome attempt to apologise.

'Is it ruined, Peter?' asked Penelope.

'I think it might require more than mere pinning up,' he replied.

Their hostess came bustling up. 'Dear Lady Darleston, come with me at once. You can't possibly pin that up. I shall take you upstairs where my maid shall mend it for you. Such clumsiness, *most* unsubtle! We shall not be long, Darleston.'

Lady Wickham swept Penelope upstairs to her boudoir and summoned her maid. 'Clara, please find a needle and thread to mend Lady Darleston's gown. When you have mended it you may escort her ladyship back to the ballroom. She cannot see, so you must be very careful. Tell her about steps and so on. Do you understand?'

'Yes, milady,' answered Clara.

Lady Wickham said, 'I must return to the ballroom, Lady Darleston. Do not, I beg of you, refine too much upon this little episode. Caroline Daventry has gone entirely too far!'

Jack Frobisher had observed the episode from a sheltered alcove. Silently he applauded his accomplice's ploy. He watched Lady Wickham take Penelope upstairs and smiled fiendishly when she returned alone. 'Well done, Caroline.' He produced a small phial from his pocket, emptied the contents into a glass of champagne and unobtrusively made his way upstairs.

Clara had not got very far with her repair job when a voice at the door said, 'Your mistress wants you immediately, Clara.'

'She asked me to do this,' protested Clara.

'Well, she wants you downstairs for a moment. In the library. You'd better hurry.'

'Oh, very well. Excuse me, milady. I'll be as quick as I can.'

'No matter,' said Penelope cheerfully.

The maid left. A moment later the door opened. Penelope swung round. She could make out a figure moving towards her. 'Clara?' she asked. There was no answer. Suddenly frightened, she opened her mouth to scream for help, but it was too late. She was taken in a powerful grasp, a glass forced to her mouth, the contents tipped ruthlessly down her throat. Then a hand was clamped over her mouth as she tried to scream again. Her frantic struggles grew weaker as consciousness slipped away.

Frobisher dropped her and ran to the door. He looked out but saw no one. Swiftly he went back to pick up his senseless victim. A footstep at the door startled him.

Lady Caroline said, 'Hurry, Frobisher, the chaise will be waiting and you don't want to miss the tide at Newhaven. That drug may not last long either. It works fast, but sometimes it wears off easily. I must leave now and head for Scotland. Enjoy yourself! The maid is locked in the library.' She was gone on the instant.

Frobisher made his way to the back stairs. A curious footman accepted the explanation that the lady had taken too much champagne and was being taken home to avoid scandal. He also accepted the coins pressed into his hand with the injunction to keep his mouth shut.

Clara waited ten minutes in the library and then discovered that the door was locked. It took her another twenty minutes to attract the attention of a footman. When she reached Lady Wickham's boudoir she was shocked. An overturned chair and broken champagne glass told her that she had been duped. Terrified, she raced downstairs to the ballroom. Swiftly she pushed her way through the startled guests, with little regard for their consequence, until she found her mistress.

'Milady,' she gasped into a startled silence, 'Lady Darleston's gone. A man came and said you wanted me in the library, so I left her. When I went back she was gone, a chair turned over and a champagne glass broken!'

'What?' shrieked Lady Wickham. 'Foolish girl! I sent no message!' She shook the hapless Clara, who was nearly in tears.

Peter, standing nearby with Phoebe, Richard and George, wondered if his heart had stopped, for it gave such a sickening lurch. He never remembered much about the next few moments, except for grabbing the maid and racing upstairs with her. George assured him later that the language with which he cursed Caroline Daventry and Jack Frobisher would have shaken an infantryman, and that a number of ladies had actually fainted.

He regained some measure of control as he surveyed the evidence of Penelope's struggle. He sniffed the champagne glass, wrinkling his nose at the sickly odour.

Richard, George and Phoebe had followed him upstairs with Lord and Lady Wickham. The latter was weeping and wringing her hands.

Lord Wickham said, 'I'll try to find out which way they went.' He left the room.

'Drugged?' asked George tersely.

Peter nodded. Phoebe gave a cry of horror and clung to Richard.

'I'll kill them,' said Peter softly. 'I swear I'll kill them.' He swung around and his gaze fell on the sobbing Clara. Even in his own agony, his heart went out to the girl. 'Don't blame the maid, Lady Wickham. I should have stayed with Penny. It's my fault. We knew there was danger, but Caroline and my cousin were too clever for us.'

'The question now,' said Richard, 'is where the devil are they going? They haven't much of a start. We may be able to find out by questioning their servants.'

'Caroline has a place in Scotland,' said Peter. 'They might take her there, but it's a long way. They must know I'll be on their heels.'

'That's what they want,' said Phoebe suddenly. 'Don't you see? By taking Penny, they can trap you.'

'But if we're too close behind the whole thing could backfire on them,' said George. 'If I were them, I'd want a good lead so that I could prepare a decent trap. Caroline Daventry may be a bitch, but she's smart enough to think of that.'

Lord Wickham returned. 'Caroline Daventry left

alone by the front door, but a man carrying a woman left via the back of the house. One of the footmen saw him, but he was cloaked and hooded and the back stairs are so ill-lit that he wouldn't recognise the fellow, so we have no proof of who was involved. Charles said he heard a carriage of some sort in the mews.'

A puzzled little voice from the doorway asked, 'Is something wrong, Mama?' They turned around to see Miss Amabel Hartleigh, the six-year-old daughter of the house, clutching a doll.

'No, sweetheart, go back to bed,' said Lady Wickham.

'Was the lady very sick?'

The grown-ups stood as though they had been turned to stone.

Peter went to the child, dropped to one knee and asked, very gently, 'What lady was that, my pet?'

'The red-haired lady. The man carried her out and there was another lady.'

'Was there? Did you hear anything they said?'

'Yes. I was going to come down the stairs a bit, to watch the dancing, but I heard their voices so I hid behind a door.'

'What did they say?'

'The red-haired lady didn't say anything. I think she was asleep. The other lady said something about a chaise.'

'Anything else?'

'Yes. Something about the tide at Newhaven and going to Scotland. Oh, and she called him Frobisher.'

Peter hugged her. 'Good girl! What do you want most in the world?'

'A pony.'

'Well, you shall have one. I'll keep you mounted for the rest of my life!' He turned to the others. 'We've got them! Obviously we were meant to think of Scotland—probably if we went to Caroline's house we would discover that she *has* left for Scotland. Frobisher won't be expecting us this close behind, so we've an advantage. We go back to Darleston House and collect horses, as well as my chaise to bring her back. Phoebe, will you come with us in the chaise?'

'Just try to leave me behind!' was the answer.

The reaction at Darleston House when they arrived was one of horror. All the servants loved their mistress, and the white agony of the master's face was pitiful to behold.

Sarah was still up. She dragged a warm cloak from her wardrobe and along with Gelert presented herself to George and Phoebe in the hall. 'I'm coming too.'

'The devil you are. It's too dangerous!' snapped George.

'Shut up, George! If you try to leave me behind I'll saddle a horse myself and follow you anyway! If Phoebe's going, so am I!' was the uncompromising answer.

Phoebe nodded and said firmly, 'Of course she's coming!'

Richard came in. 'The chaise and horses will be round directly. What are you doing Sarah?'

'Coming with you! Don't bother to argue about it!'

'Where's Peter? He may have something to say about this!' said Richard.

'Fetching his pistols,' answered George. 'Dammit, Sarah! You can't come. Your mother would be furious

with us for taking you! I warn you, people are likely
to be killed tonight! Peter is out of his mind!'

'Good!' said Sarah. 'Maybe now he'll stop being
scared to admit that he loves her!'

Peter arrived in the hall with his pistols just in time
to hear this outburst.

Sarah met his eyes defiantly and said, 'Don't you
start, Peter. I'm coming with you and that's all there
is to it!'

He looked at her gravely. 'If we left you I suppose
you'd come after us, wouldn't you?'

'Of course.'

He simply nodded and said, 'I've ordered my racing
curricle as well. We have to take Gelert, and he can't
possibly run the whole way. Fortunately I have cattle
stabled on the Newhaven Road. We can change as
often as necessary.'

Meadows ran in. He thrust a greatcoat at Peter.
'Brandy flask in the pocket, Master Peter. For God's
sake, bring her back!'

Peter gripped the old retainer's shoulders. 'Trust
me, Meadows, we'll catch them!'

A clatter of hooves announced the arrival of the
curricle, chaise and horses.

'Who is on the chaise?' asked Peter.

'Your coachman,' said Richard. 'He insisted.
George and I are riding with you. That way if we have
to leave the main road to follow them one of us can
wait to give the chaise directions.'

'Let's go, then. They're an hour ahead of us. Tide's
not till nine, but I want to catch them before they can
reach Newhaven!' He met George's eyes, unable to
voice his fears for Penelope's safety in Frobisher's
hands.

Sarah and Phoebe were handed unceremoniously into the waiting carriage. 'Newhaven, John,' said Peter. 'Spring them and change horses as often as necessary. All that matters is speed. Check at all the usual posting inns for instructions; we'll leave messages.'

The coachman nodded and cracked his whip. The restless team sprang into motion, thundering over the cobbles.

'Let's ride, gentlemen! Come on, Gelert!' Peter swung himself into his curricle, followed by the dog, and smiled grimly at his companions. Without another word they galloped after the chaise, swiftly passing it. Sarah was looking out to watch them go by. George saw her and raised his whip in salute, then they were gone.

Penelope regained consciousness slowly. She had a splitting headache, no memory of what had occurred, and the rocking of the chaise confused her. Waves of nausea threatened to overcome her, made worse by the motion of the carriage. Gradually, as the after-effects of the drug wore off, she realised that she was lying along a seat in a carriage. Instinct warned her to keep quiet and listen. Gradually she became certain that she was not alone. A faint sound of breathing and small movements told her there was someone on the opposite seat. Who was it?

The carriage slowed slightly, and immediately her unknown companion moved to the window, leaned out and yelled, 'Put 'em along! I can't risk missing the tide at Newhaven! We'll change teams at the next posting station!'

Penelope recognised Frobisher's voice instantly, and with increasing terror she slowly pieced together what had happened. The tearing of her dress had been a clever ploy to separate her from Peter, and they had fallen for it! Now she was on her way to Newhaven and Peter had no way of knowing where they were going. She shuddered at the implications of what she had just heard. Stay calm! she ordered herself, but it took every bit of self-control she possessed not to give in to her fear. It occurred to her that if she continued to feign unconsciousness she might be able to take him by surprise at the posting inn and call for help.

Desperately she clung to that faint chance, schooling herself to remain as limp as possible, even when a hand grasped her chin and forced it up. 'Still out cold, are you?' came Frobisher's voice. He released her chin, but his fingers slid down over her throat briefly. 'By God, I'm looking forward to this!'

It was all Penelope could do not to recoil, screaming, from his touch and the brutal note of lust in his voice. She lay still for what seemed an eternity, trying to convince herself that Peter would somehow be able to follow her or that she would be able to escape when they changed horses.

A sudden slowing down of the galloping horses warned her that they were nearly at the posting station. Wait to see if he gets out, she thought. All chance of escape vanished, though, when she felt those dreadful hands grasp her again. Casting all pretence and caution to the winds, Penelope struggled in futile desperation. She was flung to the floor of the carriage and held there. One powerful arm gripped her, holding her helpless, while a hand smothered her nose and mouth in a cloth. Unable to breathe, Penelope lapsed into unconsciousness.

She came to her senses with her hands tied behind

her back. The horses were again thundering on at a steady gallop. Weakly she tried to sit up, but was instantly grasped and dragged back.

'We are quite alone, Lady Darleston. And this time we won't be interrupted by your dog.'

Frantically Penelope fought to free herself from that cruel hold, but gradually she was forced down by his superior weight and strength. She could feel Frobisher's hands tearing at the bodice of her gown, feel his hot breath on her face. Terrified, she tried to evade his mouth, but one hand came up to grip her throat while the other fumbled at her exposed breast. Then, as she screamed in terror, his lips were on hers, choking her screams as he forced his tongue into her mouth. Finally, in absolute desperation, she bit him.

She had a brief moment of satisfaction as he jerked back from her and swore. Quickly she tried to roll away, but he grabbed her again, saying savagely, 'You'll regret that Lady Darleston. Scream as much as you like. Nothing can help you now!'

Peter and his companions thundered along the Newhaven road, leaving a trail of dust in the moonlight. George was beginning to wonder if they would ever catch up when they came to the last posting station and heard that the chaise was only fifteen minutes ahead of them. They galloped out of the village with fresh horses. Peter's mouth was set in a grim line. His fears for Penelope had grown with every mile, until he was nearly insane with them. The chance comment let fall by the hostler about Frobisher's dishevelled appearance horrified him. He had prayed desperately that Frobisher would at least keep his hands off Penelope until the chaise reached Newhaven.

Finally, half a mile ahead, they saw the lights of a carriage just before it disappeared around a bend in the road.

'There it is!' called Peter. 'Slow down a bit. We have to plan this.'

'How do we tackle them?' asked Richard.

'You take them from the front!' was the answer. 'The road winds a lot just here. Take to the fields at the side of the road, get around ahead of them, behind that hill to cut off the last bend, and then charge. With a bit of luck their horses will panic. You and George take the nearside and deal with the postilions. I'll hold back until I can see you, then Gelert and I can come up on the other side and tackle anyone on the box. Then we can deal with whoever's inside.'

'All right, let's do it!' said Richard.

'Look! There's a gap in the hedge!' called George, and angled his mount towards it. He sailed over, closely followed by Richard. Together they raced across the fields, swinging up over the shoulder of the hill. As they tore down to rejoin the road they could see that they were going to be well ahead of the chaise. The bends in the road had slowed it down considerably.

They reached the road while the coach was still out of sight and pulled up. The horses' flanks were heaving. George cast a glance at Richard and said, 'If any harm has come to Penny, I don't fancy Frobisher's chances. I've never seen Peter like this!'

Richard shook his head. 'It won't just be Peter he has to deal with, George!' he said, then, listening sharply, 'Here it comes!' They could hear the thunder of the horses. The chaise swung into view around the last bend and suddenly, mingled with the noise of the hooves, came an agonised scream.

In the curricle, fifty yards behind the chaise, Peter went berserk. Gone was his plan to check that George and Richard were in position. A cold fury took possession of him and his team felt the lash of the whip as he dropped his hands and sprang them into a full gallop. Then, beyond the chaise, he could see two horses charging down the road at a breakneck pace. Gelert stood on the seat, barking at the voice of his mistress. Peter could not spare a glance for the dog, but he said, 'Penny. We're going to find Penny!' Gelert redoubled his barking.

The chaise horses were terrified at the approach of George and Richard. Desperately the post-boys tried to control the team and avoid the attackers, but the nearside wheels slid into the ditch, violently tipping the chaise at a drunken angle. One wheeler was down and the other horses plunging and rearing.

The horsemen were upon them! The servant on the box, thinking he had to deal with highwaymen, raised a pistol, but it was struck out of his hand by Carstares's whip and the shot went wild. He dodged, and then heard the thunder of the curricle on their offside. He turned in terror as Gelert launched himself from Peter's side onto the box. His weight hurled the hapless guard to the ground, knocking him unconscious, just as Richard dragged the lead post-boy from his seat. Gelert managed to roll clear of the frantic horses. He staggered to his feet and leapt, barking madly, at the door of the chaise. Peter, his team well in hand, brought them to a plunging stop and jumped from the vehicle. George flung himself from his horse, grabbing a pistol from the saddle holster. Peter joined him, pistol in hand, and together they tore open the door to the chaise.

'Stand back if you want her alive, Darleston!' snapped Frobisher. He sat in the corner of the carriage, one arm gripping the unconscious Penelope and a knife in his other hand. Peter grabbed Gelert's collar and hauled him back.

'Put your pistols down and get back, but stay in sight of the door! And keep that dog under control!'

Peter and George obeyed, watching helplessly as Penelope was dragged from the chaise. Her ripped gown and bound hands horrified them. She hung so limply at Frobisher's side that for one dreadful moment Peter thought she was dead. A faint moan, as Frobisher shifted his hold, reassured him, and he tightened his grip on Gelert's collar as the dog struggled to get loose, snarling fiercely.

'Right back, Darleston. You! Winton! Bring a horse around!'

'Do it, Richard,' said Peter between clenched teeth.

Richard brought his horse forward wordlessly.

'Fine. Now join Darleston and Carstares!' Frobisher hoisted Penelope up across the horse's withers and turned to the others. 'If you try to follow me you'll regret it. I'll leave her for you a few miles down the road. I'm sure the horse will be much faster with a lighter load. But if I so much as suspect pursuit, she dies. I've nothing to lose, so don't risk it.'

He bent down to pick up one of the pistols. As he did so Peter released Gelert. The dog attacked with a bloodcurdling roar of fury, and went straight for the throat. The pistol went off as man and dog rolled together under the belly of the startled horse. Peter leapt forward, catching Penelope's limp body as she was flung from the rearing animal.

'Gelert! Back!' yelled Richard as the horse descended, screaming in fright. The dog saw the danger and twisted clear, but Frobisher's shriek of terror ended abruptly as the steel-shod hooves crashed down. Sickened at the sight, George and Richard turned away.

Peter was kneeling in the road, cradling Penelope in his arms. Desperately he fumbled at her throat for a pulse, unable to breathe until he felt it, steady under his fingers. Tears of relief slid down his cheeks. Next he untied the cord binding her hands, cursing softly when he saw the scoring on her wrists. Whimpering in pain, Gelert limped over. He snuffled at Penelope, and licked Peter's face. Blood dripped from a long shallow wound on his shoulder.

'Put this around her,' said Richard, removing his greatcoat. 'We've got to keep her warm until the girls arrive. We'll go on to Newhaven and find a doctor there.' Carefully they wrapped her in the garment, checking at the same time to see if anything was broken. All they could find was a great bruise on her left temple. She moaned softly when Peter gently probed the bruise, but he could feel no evidence of a crack.

George came over, looking rather sick. 'Frobisher is dead. The horse smashed his head in.'

'What about the servants?' asked Peter.

'One with a broken leg. They claimed not to know what was afoot, but I tied them up anyway. What do we do with them? Not to mention Caroline Daventry! What about her?'

'Leave them here with one of you on guard. I gave Meadows a note for the Bow Street Runners. They can collect them and sort it out. As for Caroline, with Jack dead we can't prove her involvement to the satisfaction of a court. But you can take it from me that she's finished in society!'

'Is Penny all right?' George asked anxiously.

'I don't know,' said Peter unsteadily. George looked at his white face. Never had he seen Peter so totally devastated. Not knowing what to say, he gripped Peter's shoulder hard and they waited silently for the arrival of the other chaise.

Chapter Seventeen

Somewhere, a long way off, there was an appalling headache. It seemed to be away at the end of a long dark tunnel, a tunnel which swung sickeningly about her. Someone was moaning. Dimly Penelope realised it was herself. Then she could feel a hand holding hers. A very familiar voice was saying something terribly important. Desperately she tried to hear, despite the fact that the effort brought her closer to that headache.

'Penny, sweetheart! Oh, Penny, my darling, it's all right. You're safe now! Little love!'

The long wait had been agonising for Peter. Despite the doctor's assurances that she would recover, he had just spent the longest day of his life. Now, as Penelope finally stirred, he could no longer hold back the words of love he had been longing to speak. He had no idea whether or not she could hear him, but he had to speak. All day he had sat with her, his eyes fixed on her white face. Phoebe and Sarah had sat with him in turns, their faces almost as pale as Penelope's. Shortly after midnight he had insisted they both go to bed, promising to call them if there were any change.

With a huge effort Penelope opened her eyes. The

dimly lit room was completely new to her. All the light was coming from a fireplace on the opposite side of the room. Puzzled, Penelope concentrated on the strange man leaning over her. Anguish stared from his dark brown eyes, a normally olive complexion was drained of all colour and his dark curly hair was dishevelled. I'm dead, thought Penelope in total confusion. Who is this man?

'Penny? It's me, Peter. It's all right, you're safe.' It was Peter's voice, tender and beloved. Was this what he looked like?

'I'm dreaming,' she said weakly.

He stroked her cheek tenderly. 'No, dearest, you're awake. I'm really here.' The strange look on her face frightened him. 'Penny, darling, what's wrong?'

'Don't wake me, Peter. It's such a wonderful dream. I can see you in it…and you said you loved me.' Her voice trailed off and her eyes closed as she drifted back to sleep.

Stunned, Peter stared at his sleeping wife. She could see him! Could the blow to the head have restored her vision? It must have done! Swiftly he made sure that she was comfortable and went to the door. He opened it and looked out into the corridor. A gleam of light shone from under the door of Sarah and Phoebe's room. He ran to it and knocked softly.

'Come in.' He opened the door. Both girls were sitting up in the same bed. Phoebe had her arms around Sarah, who had obviously been crying. They blinked at Peter's wild eyes.

'Peter, is something wrong? Why have you left Penny?' cried Phoebe, throwing back the bedclothes.

'She woke up,' said Peter in a choked whisper, 'and

she could see me! She thought it was a dream, but it wasn't!'

The two girls stared at him, unable to believe their ears. 'She…she could see you?' stammered Sarah. 'Are you sure?'

'She said she was dreaming, because she could see me, then she went back to sleep,' said Peter.

Phoebe said in tones of wonder, 'That bruise, it's exactly where the bruise was when she fell off her horse and lost her sight. At the time the doctor could find nothing wrong with her eyes. He said there must be some damage, interfering with the messages going to her brain. The blow on the head must have reversed the damage! Oh, Peter, how wonderful!' She jumped out of bed and snatched up a dressing gown. 'Go back to her, Peter. I'm going to wake Richard! Come on Sarah!' She rushed from the room.

'I'll get George,' said Sarah excitedly. 'I can't believe it's true! Can we see her?'

'When she is a little stronger, Sarah. I think she still has a dreadful headache. She is asleep again now. I'd better go back.' He suddenly found himself being enthusiastically hugged by Sarah. He returned the embrace and said, 'Go on, hoyden! You'd better tell George!'

He went back to Penelope's room. She was still sound asleep. Very quietly he crossed the room to her and settled himself beside her on the bed. A deep contentment had come over him. All the confusion he had felt was gone. This was his wife and he loved her more than life itself. It was as simple as that. Nothing else really mattered any more. Completely relaxed, he leaned back against the bed-head, dreaming of all the things he and Penelope would do together. Children, he thought. That would be wonderful!

Towards dawn he felt Penelope move beside him, then her eyes opened. She looked dazed.

'Better now, love?' he asked softly.

Penelope stared at him in disbelief. What had happened to her? Suddenly she remembered the chaise, the brutal strength of her abductor. Had it all been a nightmare? Despite the pain in her head she tried to sit up, but was gently restrained.

'No, dearest. Just lie down and rest. I won't leave you, I promise.'

'Peter?' She was shocked at how weak her voice sounded. 'Is this a dream? Is that really you?'

'Yes, it's really me. Go back to sleep. I'll be here.'

'My head hurts, but I can see you!'

'I know, darling. You must have hit your head when the chaise overturned. The doctor will be back again later this morning. He said that you'd have a headache when you woke up. It's nothing to worry about, especially if you can see again.'

'The chaise? Then it wasn't a nightmare? Oh, Peter, I was so scared!' She began to weep uncontrollably. 'He w-wouldn't stop…tried to stop him, but my hands were tied…kept tearing at my gown…oh, God! His hands! He said…scream…no one to hear! He must have… Oh, Peter, I couldn't stop him!'

Convulsive sobs racked her slender body. Tenderly Peter lifted her and cradled her in his arms. He realised in horror that she thought she had been raped.

He said urgently, 'Penny, stop it! We did hear you, darling. We were close enough to the chaise then, just about to stop it. It ended up in the ditch. Frobisher is dead, Penny. He'll never hurt you again.'

'Then he didn't…? I thought…you'd hate me!'

'Stop thinking it, Penny. We heard you screaming just as we attacked the chaise.' His cheek rested on top of her head. Lovingly he put one finger under her chin and brought her face up to his. 'Penny, even if Frobisher had done that to you, it would not have made the slightest difference to the way I feel about you.'

'The…the way you feel about me?' she faltered, hardly daring to hope.

He looked deeply into her wide grey eyes, bright with tears. 'I love you, Penny. I've known it for a long time, but I was too scared to say it. I knew it the day you told me Frobisher had attacked you and I didn't feel jealous, simply protective and murderous! The thought of you being in his power sickened me! A man who would take advantage of a blind girl! But even before that—the first night I made love to you…and you gave yourself to me so sweetly… Penny, I loved you then. I was just too stupid to realise it.'

Her face was transfixed with joy as she gazed at him. She couldn't believe what she was hearing, what she could see in his eyes. 'You l-l-love me?' she asked in amazement. 'You don't just mean you're fond of me?'

His arms tightened around her. 'Oh, Penny, darling Penny, I couldn't even begin to tell you how much. You're mine. I'll never let you go! When we caught up to the chaise and heard you screaming, I was ready to commit murder! And George and Richard weren't much better!'

Tears of happiness slid down her cheeks. 'You really love me? Oh, Peter, I've loved you so much! I tried not to let you see. I thought you wouldn't want that and I didn't want to bother you!'

'I did know, Penny,' he admitted. 'Remember I told you once that you wouldn't know how to lie? Everything about you told me, but I also knew why you said nothing.'

'You knew that I loved you? How?'

He smiled. 'You told me with your body every time I made love to you!'

'Oh!' She blushed furiously as she met his gaze.

'Dare I hope, dearest Penny, that you will continue to tell me that you love me?' he asked teasingly.

Shyly she nodded, unable to speak. Her eyes told him all he needed to know. Later there would be a time to tell her that the others were here, that they had all come after her. Later they could plan the rest of their life together, a life of love and joy which he knew could only increase with the coming years.

*   *   *   *   *

If you enjoyed what you just read,
then we've got an offer you can't resist!

Take 2 bestselling
love stories FREE!
Plus get a FREE surprise gift!